FROM THIS MOMENT ON

by

PJ Trebelhorn

2010

FROM THIS MOMENT ON
© 2010 By PJ Trebelhorn. All Rights Reserved.

ISBN 10: 1-60282-154-2
ISBN 13: 978-1-60282-154-5

This Trade Paperback Original Is Published By
Bold Strokes Books, Inc.
P.O. Box 249
Valley Falls, NY 12185

First Edition: June 2010

THIS IS A WORK OF FICTION. NAMES, CHARACTERS, PLACES, AND
INCIDENTS ARE THE PRODUCT OF THE AUTHOR'S IMAGINATION OR
ARE USED FICTITIOUSLY. ANY RESEMBLANCE TO ACTUAL PERSONS,
LIVING OR DEAD, BUSINESS ESTABLISHMENTS, EVENTS, OR LOCALES
IS ENTIRELY COINCIDENTAL.

THIS BOOK, OR PARTS THEREOF, MAY NOT BE REPRODUCED IN ANY
FORM WITHOUT PERMISSION.

Credits
Editor: Victoria Oldham
Production Design: Stacia Seaman
Cover Design By Sheri (graphicartist2020@hotmail.com)

Acknowledgments

First of all, I want to thank Radclyffe and Bold Strokes Books for believing in my writing enough to give me the opportunity to be published. This is a dream come true for me, and to be associated with BSB is just icing on the cake. This is a wonderful company with a great group of people, and I am truly honored to be a part of it.

I have to also thank my editor, Victoria Oldham. You made a dreaded process enjoyable, for the most part, and I look forward to working with you again. Your guidance has served to make this a better finished product. Stacia Seaman—thank you for your insight and direction. Your expertise is greatly appreciated.

And Sheri, you've given me a truly awesome cover for this book, and I thank you. You remain the best cover artist there is, in my opinion.

I want to thank my mother, who has always been there for me, even when I wasn't always there. Mom, you'll never know how much your support has meant to me.

And to my father—I wish that you could have lived to see this. I still miss you every day.

Dedication

For Cheryl
My life, my love

CHAPTER ONE

"S hit," Devon Conway murmured in frustration as she sat up from the dream that had plagued her for the first two years after Jo's death. She roughly wiped away her tears as she tried to forget the panic that had coursed through her when she'd realized Jo wasn't in bed with her the morning the hospital had called. She ran an unsteady hand through her sweat-soaked hair while trying to slow her breathing. The terrible ache in her chest she'd first experienced that horrific night was back again, and her heart felt as if it were making a very real attempt to burst right out of her chest. She was shaking, and she knew better than to attempt to stand up just yet. Experience had taught her that it was best to wait for her pulse to slow.

It had all been so damn real this time. Usually she only dreamed it in fragments here and there—in spits and spurts, as her godmother liked to say. This time, though, it had been a complete replay of that awful night that had changed Dev's life forever. She wanted nothing more than to curl up in a ball and cry, just as she had done after hanging up the phone that morning three years earlier.

But that wouldn't change anything, so after allowing herself a few minutes to fully wake up, and for her pulse to fall back to an almost normal rate, she swung her legs over the edge of the bed and finally attempted to stand. On unsteady legs, she made her way to the bathroom. She had tried so damned hard over the past three years to forget about that night and to simply focus on the good times she and Jo had shared. Up until now, she thought that she had succeeded in that endeavor. The past year had been virtually nightmare free.

"It was a mistake to come back here," she said to the mirror as she leaned on the bathroom counter. She looked haunted; her skin was pale and her once bright blue eyes had lost their spark. For so long, she had felt like she was just going through the motions. She'd felt dead inside. Dev had hoped that coming back here to Easton—the city where she and Jo had made their lives together—might help her to heal. The few friends they had made together were still there, and Dev had alienated herself from everyone when she'd left. *It would serve me right if no one even speaks to me,* she thought cynically. As soon as the funeral was over, Dev had simply disappeared, without so much as a single word to anyone. Not only that, but she'd never even attempted to get in touch with anyone, other than Sheila. Dev had made sure that her godmother had known where she was and had a way to get in touch with her if she needed to. In the beginning, she had convinced herself that it was just to have someone in town to help her with the life insurance settlement. She soon realized, though, that she would never be able to completely sever her ties to this place, and now there she was, living with Sheila again. Staying in the house where she'd grown up had not been her first choice, but it had been the most logical choice at the time.

It had been Dev's intention never to come back to Easton, but when Sheila had called her to let her know that her old boss was selling his garage, Dev began to seriously rethink the plans for her future. Despite what had happened to Jo, this was where Dev had always been the happiest, and at thirty-nine years old, she finally decided that it was time to at least try to get some of that happiness back again.

Jo was never coming back, and there wasn't anything Dev

could do to change that. It had taken her three very long and lonely years to come to that realization.

Devon showered and dressed before grabbing a slice of leftover pizza from the fridge on her way out the door. She'd ended up falling asleep after checking in on the guys remodeling the garage, and she thought now that maybe a few hours in a bar—or in someone else's bed—could drive these memories from her mind. Dev was glad that Sheila had gone to dinner with her daughter Rhonda, because she was in no mood to answer the inevitable questions about where she was going and when she'd be back. After taking a moment to make sure that her helmet was securely in place, she kick-started her Harley and pulled out of her godmother's garage.

❖

I swear to God that I am never going out for drinks with her again.

It was a mantra that Katherine Hunter repeated in her mind, and she promised herself that this time it would hold true. She was coming to the realization that she had been left alone to find her own way home, as usual. Obviously Laura must have met a woman between where she had left Kat sitting at the bar, and the bathroom. Kat glanced around one last time before pulling out a ten-dollar bill and depositing it on the bar in front of her. As she stood to leave, she was met by a rather attractive woman who was eyeing her as though she were the nightly special.

"You aren't leaving yet, are you, honey?" the woman asked as she extended an arm past Kat to rest her hand on the bar. "Why don't you come and dance with me?"

"Thanks, but I'm not interested," Kat said with a smile and a shake of her head. She tried to move past the woman, but it only made the stranger move closer. *Attractive, yes, but she knows it. She is just way too full of herself.*

"If you aren't interested, then why are you here?" she asked, her mouth just a little too close to Kat's ear for her liking. Kat flinched and pulled away when the woman put a hand on her hip, but there wasn't enough room to move to dislodge the hand. She caught a whiff of perfume and felt her heart clench at the realization that it was the same scent that Paula had favored. She needed to get away.

"I'm waiting for someone," she said without thinking. Kat mentally kicked herself for that little lie, but it had been the first thing that entered her mind. *I swear to God I'm going to kill Laura one of these days.*

"Then I'll buy you a drink while you wait." The hand on Kat's hip began to move around to her ass, and she grabbed the wrist to pull it away.

"Keep your hands off me." Kat tried to sound threatening but only managed to sound incredibly irritated. *Jesus, why can't she just take no for an answer?*

Kat looked around the immediate area, trying not to appear as if she were a deer caught in the headlights. She saw someone approaching the bar alone and took a deep breath. *Maybe she'll rescue me,* was Kat's first thought. She reached out and grabbed the unsuspecting woman by the arm before she had the chance to think about what she was doing.

"There you are," Kat said and tried her best to sound convincing. The newcomer looked at her as if she had two heads. "You're late. I was about to give up on you."

"I'm sorry," she said with a shrug and a smile, and Kat felt herself relax slightly at the realization that she was actually going to play along. Kat watched as she looked back and forth between her and her would-be suitor. She quickly put an arm around Kat's shoulder and leaned in for a brief kiss on the lips. Kat's first instinct was to push her away, but she reminded herself that she *had* invited this. "I tried to call you, but only got your voicemail. Who's your friend here?"

"Marie," she said. The disappointment was clear on her face, but she stuck her hand out anyway.

"Devon," Kat's rescuer said. She moved her arm to encircle Kat's waist in a possessive gesture. She took Marie's hand briefly before leaning back against the bar. "Thanks for keeping her company, but I think I can handle things from here."

"No doubt," Marie said with a knowing smile.

Kat watched as Marie walked away, and was well aware of the fact that Devon had not yet released the hold she had on her waist. *Jesus, what if I've traded one letch for someone worse?*

At that disconcerting thought, Kat really looked at Devon. Was it possible that this one was even more striking than Marie had been? Kat got the distinct feeling that Devon wasn't as aware of her appeal. She tried to pull away from the body pressed against hers, but Devon only tightened her hold.

"Dance with me," Devon said. It wasn't a request, but a demand, and that arrogance irritated Kat. But she didn't feel threatened like she had with Marie, and that irked her even more.

"I have to leave," Kat said, trying once again to pull away.

"Come on, I just did you a favor," Devon pointed out with a smile. "Although I have to say that you could do a lot worse than Marie. What was the problem?"

"I'm not interested," Kat said. "Maybe *you* could hook up with her."

"Maybe," Devon said with indifference. She finally removed her arm from Kat's waist as she turned to face her, one elbow leaning on the bar. "The least you could do is tell me your name."

"Katherine." Kat picked up her purse and took a deep breath as she met Devon's gaze. Kat faltered momentarily as she tried to find her voice once again, sensing that those lust-filled eyes were undressing her. "Thank you for your help, but I really need to be going."

"Let me ask you something," Devon said. "If you aren't interested, then why are you here?"

"That's original," Kat said as she finally forced herself to look away from Devon. "Marie tried to use that same line on me."

"Maybe because it's a valid question, and not just *a line*," Devon said with a shrug. "Most of the women who aren't here with someone are looking for someone to take home. Why should I think you're any different than the rest of them?"

"Because I am. I came in here with a friend just to get a drink."

"Then where is your *friend* now?" Devon asked with a slow smile. Kat watched as she gave the bartender the money for the beer that was set in front of her. Devon chuckled quietly when Kat didn't answer her. "Maybe you should have had your friend rescue you."

"She left with someone," Kat said, cringing at the realization that she had just helped to prove Devon's point that everyone was here looking for a hookup. "This may be a tremendous blow to your ego, but I truly am not interested. Thank you for helping me out with my little problem, and I really wish I could say that it was a pleasure meeting you."

Kat turned to leave, and she could feel the weight of Devon's stare as she walked out the front door. She wasn't about to be a one-night stand, and it infuriated her to think that not one, but *two* women had assumed that she would be willing to be just that. Laura had tried to tell her that she needed to loosen up, but Kat had never had a one-night stand, and she wasn't about to start just before her fortieth birthday. How could anyone possibly find satisfaction with a stranger for a few hours? The entire concept made absolutely no sense to her. She pulled out of the parking lot, sexually aroused and angry that she had no one at home to take the edge off for her.

❖

"Ouch." Dev watched Katherine walk out of the bar. She was definitely attractive, but the chilly personality left a lot to be desired. Still, she had to admit that she was more than a little intrigued at Katherine's indifference toward her. It was refreshing to know that there were some women who wouldn't make it too easy for her. Dev turned away from the door before Katherine disappeared through it, because she was afraid that if she watched that ass for any longer, she would have no choice but to follow her.

Dev shook her head as she braced her forearms against the bar. She had a feeling that Katherine could have taken her mind off her nightmare quite nicely, at least for a few hours. Ironically, many women just *assumed* that she wanted to go to bed with them, when in reality, this was the first time she'd been in a bar in over a year. Just because she'd been fast and loose before Jo didn't mean she had reverted to that lifestyle since her death. It would be so easy to fall back into those habits, though. Katherine's rejection made her realize that a quick conquest might not be as simple as it once had been. The bottle was almost to her lips when she felt a hand on the small of her back. She turned her head slightly to see Marie standing next to her, a sly smile on her lips.

"Looks like she shot us both down, my friend," she said dryly. "Maybe it's for the best."

"How do you figure that?" Dev asked. She'd played this game too often to not know what Marie was getting at, but she decided to go along for the ride. No time like the present to get back into the swing of things.

"Well," Marie said as she moved her hand slowly down and inside the back of Dev's jeans. When Dev didn't pull away, she moved closer, so that her body pressed against Dev. "It frees us up to enjoy each other's company."

"And what makes you think that I want company?" Dev asked, thinking how incredibly predictable the whole charade was. *Yeah, this could definitely be fun. No ties, no expectations.*

No emotions. She turned to face Marie, making no attempt to stop her hand in its downward motion.

"Are you trying to tell me that you don't?" she asked as she leaned in to place her lips on the sensitive spot right below Dev's ear.

Devon tried to stop the swift intake of breath that the other woman's touch spawned, but it was obvious that Marie had heard it by the way she pulled Dev closer. *So what if it isn't as satisfying as it used to be? At least it will take my mind off Jo for a few hours.*

"I think I have my answer," Marie whispered into Dev's ear. She groaned in anticipation when Dev's hands cupped her ass, and she complied with the pressure of Dev's thigh as it insinuated its way between her legs. "Come home with me, Devon."

"You need to know that one night is all that I can offer," Dev said. She felt herself growing hard as Marie began rocking back and forth against her thigh.

"Emotionally unavailable?"

"Something like that."

"I don't recall asking for any more than that." Marie leaned back and kissed Dev's jawline. "I think you need to get me out of here now, though."

Dev pulled away from her as she reached out to grab her hand, and then led her silently toward the door.

❖

Dev smiled when she saw Jo hovering above her. She reached out and pulled Jo down on top of her as they kissed passionately.

"God, you feel so good, Dev," Jo said when Dev rolled them both over and ran her hand slowly up the inside of Jo's thigh. "Nine years with you, and I still feel like we're on our honeymoon. Shouldn't that feeling wear off at some point?"

"Not if we're lucky," Dev said to her as she slid her fingers

slowly inside Jo while simultaneously leaning down to take a nipple in her mouth. As Jo surged against her, Devon knew that she would be perfectly content like this forever. Jo was beautiful, funny, and completely devoted to Devon. They were perfect together, and unbelievably happy.

Dev tensed when Jo's fingers dug into her shoulders, and then Jo's mouth was at her ear.

"Fuck me, Dev," she said. "Jesus, I need you to fuck me."

Dev sat up quickly and shook her head to get rid of the disconcerting vision. She glanced around at her unfamiliar surroundings, her heart still hammering wildly in her chest. *Damn it, I haven't had a sex dream about Jo in months. Why now?*

"Baby, are you all right?" A gravelly voice came from beside her.

Dev flinched at the touch of a hand on her bare back, and she immediately stood up and began looking for her clothes as she ran her fingers through her short black hair. Her nerves were on edge, and she suddenly had the feeling that she had to get out of there.

"What are you doing?" Marie asked. She got out of the bed and walked over to Dev. "Come back to bed."

"I have to go."

"No, you don't."

"Yes, I do," Dev said with a humorless laugh. *Christ, what does it say about me that I have a sex dream about my dead lover while I'm in another woman's bed?*

"When can I see you again?" Marie tried to put her arms around Dev, who deftly sidestepped the attempt. She winced slightly at the soreness in her thighs. She hadn't had a workout like the one Marie put her through in quite some time.

"I told you last night that this was all there could be," Dev said, quickly shoving the hem of her shirt inside her jeans and zipping them up. It never ceased to amaze her that women would agree to anything to get you into bed, but then the next morning they thought they could change your mind. Things certainly hadn't changed much in the past twelve years. "Did you think I was kidding?"

"We had fun, didn't we?" Marie became defensive. "We could have a lot more fun if you'd give me a chance."

"No doubt," Dev said as she raked her fingers through her hair before fishing the keys to her bike out of her pocket. She hesitated when she saw the look of disappointment on Marie's face. *Shit.* "Look, I truly am emotionally unavailable. I'm not interested in dating. It's got nothing to do with you personally, Marie. I tried to tell you all of this last night, and you said it wasn't a problem for you."

"I didn't think you were serious. Nobody ever really means that, do they?"

"I meant it," Dev said. "I'm fucked up, okay? I don't do the relationship thing."

"Fine, then just get the hell out." Marie turned and disappeared into the bathroom, slamming the door behind her.

Devon stood there staring at the bathroom door and wondered for a moment if she should try and talk to her. She shook her head after a second and headed for the front door.

CHAPTER TWO

D evon started a pot of coffee before making her way upstairs to shower and get dressed for the day.

"Thanks for the coffee," Dev's godmother said as she joined her at the table. "You were out all night, weren't you?"

"Please don't start with me," Dev said quietly.

"I'm worried about you, Devon."

"I need to find a place of my own," Dev said.

"I thought we agreed that you'd stay here with me until the garage opened," Sheila said. "That's another few days away, right?"

"I've imposed on you for long enough, Sheila." She leaned back in her chair and stared at her godmother. At sixty-seven years old, Sheila Franklin still cut an imposing figure. Dev couldn't believe that it had been almost thirty years since she had taken in the scared little girl Devon had once been. "Have you told Rhonda that I'm here?"

"No, honey," Sheila said. "You asked me not to. I would never betray your trust like that. Even to my daughter."

"You mean like I betrayed hers?" Dev let out a humorless laugh as she stood and walked to the china cabinet that took up the entire length of one wall in the dining room. One shelf held nothing but photographs, and Dev looked at the one that had been taken the Christmas before Jo had died.

You wouldn't be so damned happy if you'd known what was waiting for you six months down the road, she thought as she looked at the laughing image of herself. She was wrapped in Jo's arms, and they'd just told Sheila that Jo was six weeks pregnant. They'd had their whole lives to look forward to when that picture was taken. At least that was what she had thought at the time.

"You know damn well that's not what I meant, Devon," Sheila said with undisguised admonishment.

"Why?" Dev turned back around to face her, and Sheila flinched slightly at Devon's obvious pain. She was clearly trying to keep her tears from falling. "Jesus, Sheila, Rhonda's your daughter. Why have you stood behind me all these years?"

"Because you're my daughter too," Sheila said.

Dev, however, had always been hardheaded, and never did know when to let things go.

"No, I'm not," she said. She rubbed a hand briskly over her face and shook her head in exasperation. This wasn't the first time they'd had this argument, and Dev was fairly certain it wouldn't be the last. "I was just some kid whose mother offed herself. You didn't want me—I was just an obligation you had."

Dev withered under Sheila's gaze. She was the only person Devon had ever met who could actually make her back down from a fight, and it irked her no end to learn that Sheila could still accomplish that.

"That's not true, and you damn well know it," Sheila said vehemently. She stood and stormed into the kitchen.

"Damn it," Dev said under her breath. She pushed her fingers through her hair again as she contemplated following Sheila, but decided it would probably be best to just leave her alone for a moment or two. She returned to her seat at the dining room table and finished her coffee while she waited.

She continued to look at the photo of her and Jo. Other than the setback in the form of a dream the previous afternoon, Devon was aware of the fact that she was finally to the point where it didn't hurt quite so much to think about Jo anymore. She had to admit that nightmare had really thrown her for a loop. For the first two years after the accident, Dev had dealt with that dull ache in her chest, and now it was back, all because of that dream.

"Are you ready to have a civil conversation with me?" Sheila asked as she reentered the dining room and resumed her seat.

"I'm sorry," Dev said.

"I never gave you any reason to believe that you weren't wanted here." Sheila raised a hand and shook her head when Dev opened her mouth to say something. "We always did everything we could to make you feel wanted and loved, Devon."

"I know that, and I said I was sorry," Dev said. "What more do you want from me?"

"I want you to stop and think before you run your mouth once in a while. For the life of me, I don't know how you've managed to survive as long as you have with that character flaw."

Dev laughed. She couldn't help it. Sheila had always been able to make her laugh when things got tough. She wished she had given Sheila the opportunity to work her magic when Jo died, instead of running away the way she had.

"I think maybe it's time that Rhonda knows what happened," Dev said quietly. She glanced away from Sheila's intense stare, because she knew exactly what was coming next.

"Why? Because you feel guilty and need to clear your conscience?" Sheila asked, the levity she'd tried to inject earlier gone more quickly than it had come. "I certainly know you well enough to realize that when all is said and done, you're going to do what you want to do. But Devon, I really think you should take into consideration the reasons *why* you want to do it. Mark my words—nothing good can come from telling her."

"You don't think this is one of those things that will someday come back to haunt everyone involved?" Dev asked.

"No, I don't. Because there are only three people in the world who know about it, and I'm fairly certain that none of us want to see Rhonda hurt. She's never done anything other than take you under her wing, Devon. I really don't think she could love you any more if you really were her sister."

"You think I don't know that, Sheila?" Dev asked a bit more sharply than she had intended. She leaned back and let out an exasperated sigh.

"I know you know it, but I think sometimes you choose to forget it."

"Jesus, I fucked up. I admit that. Now I just want to own up to what I did."

"I think perhaps your chivalry is misplaced. You didn't do what you did alone, and she'll be just as pissed off at me as she will be at you," Sheila said with another shake of her head. "But we aren't who she'll be mad at the most, and you know that as well as I do. Maybe it would have been different had you decided to tell her then, but what's the point in doing it now?"

Dev knew she was right. Sheila was always right. Sometimes Dev didn't know why she even bothered to argue with her about anything. In this instance, it really was all about Dev wanting to clear her conscience, just like Sheila had said.

"Fine, I won't say anything," Dev said.

"Thank you. You'll see, honey—it will be so much better this way."

"I should go," Dev said as she got to her feet. "There's a garage apartment over in Palmer that I want to take a look at."

"You know you can stay here, honey." Sheila walked her to the door. "It's really not a problem."

"I know. I just think I need to get my own place. I'm thirty-nine years old. How cool does that make me when I tell women I can't bring them home because I live with my mother?"

"You are so bad," Sheila said and gave her a playful shove.

"I might stop by and see Rhonda too. I think it's time I let her know I'm back in town."

❖

Dev pulled into the driveway of an old farmhouse and looked around as she shut the engine off. The house had obviously been redone in recent years, and the farm itself was no longer in existence, but the original charm had been preserved. There was a wraparound porch that went all the way around the house, as far as she could tell. It would be a nice place to spend summer evenings, but it was hard to imagine that during mid-October in eastern Pennsylvania, even if they were enjoying unusually warm weather.

The backyard had been fenced in, obviously to allow the beagle residing there room to run and explore. He was at the fence now, barking wildly at Dev, who had parked her bike in front of the garage just a few feet away.

Dev removed her helmet and set it carefully on the seat. The dog watched her warily as she took a few steps toward him, but he had stopped barking and was eyeing her suspiciously. When she reached the chain link fence, she crouched down and held her hand out to him, allowing him to smell her and to make up his own mind as to whether she was friend or foe.

"You're a handsome boy," she said quietly, and as he glanced up at her his tail wagged hesitantly. "What's your name?"

After another moment he licked her fingers, and then pushed his wet nose into her palm. She laughed as he began to jump around happily, showing off for his new friend.

"His name is Buddy," she heard from behind her. She stood and turned to face the man who had approached. He held his hand out in greeting. "Rick Hunter."

"Devon Conway." She glanced at the apartment that was set on top of the garage, and then back at Rick. "I stopped by to inquire about the living space for rent."

"Did you call first?" he asked.

"No. I know I should have, but I'm kind of in a hurry to find a place. I hoped it would be all right if I just came by."

Dev stood watching him as he glanced at his watch, and then

down the driveway toward the road. The confusion on her face must have been apparent when he turned back to face her.

"I'm sorry. My sister actually owns the house, and she isn't here. I'm sure she won't mind if I show the place to you. Hell, maybe she'll even give me a commission if I end up renting it while she's out. I'll be right back with the key."

Dev nodded and took a moment to look around the yard while he headed back to the house for the key. There was a big oak tree in the front yard that looked as if it had to be more than a hundred years old. The maple in the back provided great shade from the afternoon sun over the garage. The lawn was perfectly manicured, and there wasn't a weed in sight. *This guy's sister must spend a lot of time on the yard.* Personally, Dev hated yard work—mostly because Sheila had always used it as a punishment whenever Dev had done something wrong.

"All right, let's go take a look," Rick said as he emerged from the house once again and walked to the steps that went up to the apartment. Dev followed, and was pleasantly surprised by what she saw.

There were two skylights above the main living area, and there was plenty of natural light even with the massive maple tree. It was furnished, which was definitely a plus in Dev's current situation. The kitchen was just a small galley area, but would suffice, since Dev generally ate take-out anyway.

"The bedroom is a bit small, but what do you really use it for other than sleeping?" Rick asked as he led her through a door.

There was a queen-size bed, and really not any room for much else. Another door off the bedroom led to a bathroom, which was just big enough for the toilet, sink, and a stand-up shower. *It's perfect,* Dev thought as she looked around the place again. The only thing she really needed the apartment for was sleeping and showering. It was precisely what she was looking for.

"How much is the rent?" she asked, trying not to sound too anxious.

"Four hundred a month, with first and last as a deposit. I think she's looking for a six-month lease, but she might be willing to go month-to-month."

"No, six months is good for me. What about garage space? Do you think that might be something your sister would be willing to discuss?"

"I don't see why not." Rick shrugged as they walked back down the steps, and he motioned for her to follow him back to the house. "She only has one car, and the garage will hold three. She might want a little more money for that, though."

"Fine."

"So, you're interested?" he asked, pulling a chair out from the dining room table for her.

"Very," she said as she took the seat. After unzipping her jacket, she leaned back and ran a hand through her hair. Dev glanced around her surroundings, but there was very little to give any clues as to who the owner was. The lack of pictures—or any personal items—was sorely evident. "When would I be able to move in?"

"Now." He set an application down in front of her and gave her a pen before sitting across from her. "It's ready to be lived in. She wanted to get someone in there before the winter really hits full-force. This is mostly just for references, and to verify that you are gainfully employed."

"I own my own business," Dev said, realizing she liked the way that sounded. "I bought a garage a couple of weeks ago, and it should be ready to go in about another week."

"Mechanic?" he asked with a smile. He seemed to really look at her for the first time, and it made Dev uncomfortable. She shifted a bit in her seat before concentrating on filling out the application. "Hey, I think that's great. As a matter of fact, my car's been making a funny noise. You think maybe you could take a look at it?"

"Sure," she said, motioning to the paper she was filling out. "The address is on here. Bring it by after we officially open."

He was silent while she finished writing, much to Dev's relief. When she was done, she flipped it around and slid it across to him. She began tapping her foot nervously while he looked it over. When he got to the references, he glanced up at her with a smile.

"You know Rhonda Franklin?"

"I hope that isn't a problem," Dev said jokingly.

"Not at all," Rick said. He leaned back in his chair and regarded her across the table. "My sister knows Rhonda and Chris. I'm thinking she'll actually be happy to know that I rented the apartment to a friend of theirs."

"I take it I'm approved, then?" Dev said.

"You can move in today," he answered as they stood and shook hands. Dev wrote him a check and she took possession of the keys before leaving.

Now came the hard part. It was time to tell Rhonda that she was back.

FROM THIS MOMENT ON

CHAPTER THREE

Dev sat on her bike outside of the art gallery for a moment, wondering if it was a good idea. She'd been back in town for a full week and had managed to avoid any contact with Rhonda, which had not been easy considering she was living at Sheila's. She knew Rhonda would be happy to see her. It was Christine Riley she was worried about.

She was definitely not looking forward to seeing Chris again.

With a deep breath, Dev dismounted and took her helmet off, taking the time to secure it to the hook under the seat before finally turning, squaring her shoulders, and walking through the front door. There was a bell that signaled her entrance, but upon first glance, there didn't seem to be anyone around.

"I'll be right there," a voice called from the rear of the gallery.

"No problem," Dev said as she walked slowly through the space. She was instantly drawn to a painting hung on the right side, and she felt as though her breath had been forced from her lungs. It was the painting that Jo had been working on when she died. Dev approached with trepidation and had to fight the urge to reach out and touch it. Jo had talked her into posing for the piece, and the memory of that first day she had lain on the bed naked for it caused a sad smile to tug at the corners of Dev's mouth.

"That's a beautiful piece, isn't it?"

Dev tensed slightly but didn't turn around. She contemplated her chances of escaping without Rhonda actually seeing her face. She had lost weight, and with her hair cut shorter, she was pretty sure Rhonda wouldn't recognize her from behind.

"Yes, it certainly is," Dev said softly. "Who is the artist?"

"Her name was Joanne Riley," Rhonda said. Dev flinched at the casual use of the past tense, even though she had expected it. "Her sister Christine owns half of this gallery, and she finished this piece after Jo passed away three years ago."

"How much are you asking for it?" Dev asked, suddenly feeling as though she needed to have something of Jo's hanging in her new apartment. *Or maybe I just don't want some stranger having a naked painting of me in their living room.*

"Four thousand," Rhonda said, and Dev finally turned to face her.

"Then I guess it's true what they say about an artist's work being worth more after they die, huh?" Dev asked, and then she waited for an instant while she watched the confusion on her old friend's face transform into recognition.

"My God, Devon," she said, her surprise evident. Suddenly, Rhonda threw her arms around Dev's neck and kissed her cheek as she squeezed her tightly. Dev had always been amazed at the strength Rhonda possessed. She was about five inches shorter than Dev, and she couldn't have weighed more than one-twenty, but Rhonda had the physical power of someone twice her size. "I'd just about given up hope that we'd ever see you again. Where the hell have you been?"

"Everywhere but here," Dev said as she picked Rhonda up off her feet and returned the fierce hug.

"Come in the back." She grabbed Dev's hand and pulled her toward the office. "I have coffee made."

Dev halted abruptly, causing Rhonda to almost stumble when Dev removed her hand from her grip.

"Is Chris here?" she asked warily. Suddenly she wasn't sure she was ready to face Chris just yet.

"No." Rhonda glanced at her watch and then back at Dev. "She's out running a few errands. She'll be gone for about half an hour. Come sit down and talk with me for a few minutes."

"How pissed is she at me?" Dev asked when they'd taken a seat on the couch, and each had a cup of coffee in their hands.

"I won't lie to you, Devon. For a few months there, I thought she might have killed you if you'd shown up. I think she's since realized why you did what you did, though."

"Really?" She took a drink of the java and closed her eyes with a contented smile as the hot liquid slid down her throat. *God, I've missed Rhonda's coffee.*

"Jo was her sister, Dev," Rhonda said. "Chris knew you were hurting, and when you wouldn't talk to her after that night in the hospital, she was deeply wounded. She needed you to lean on, and she thought that you would have needed her too."

"She wasn't *just* her sister, Rhonda." Dev winced at the tightness in her chest. *Damn it, I thought I was over the worst of this. It was that damn dream that brought it all back.* "She was her *twin* sister. I honestly don't think I could have done what I needed to do that night without Chris there to help me through it. But when it was over, and Jo was gone—I couldn't look at Chris without seeing Jo. And that hurt more than you can ever imagine."

"Oh, honey," Rhonda said. She stood and motioned for Dev to do the same, and then she hugged her tightly. They stood like that for a moment, and then the bell out front rang, signaling a new arrival to the gallery. Dev stiffened, but Rhonda refused to loosen her hold. "Don't worry, it's still too soon for it to be her. I really wish you would have talked to me about this back then, Devon."

"Oops," said a female voice from behind Dev. "Rhonda, does Chris know that you're entertaining women in the office while she's not here?"

"Chris knows I would never cheat on her," Rhonda said with a smile. She finally released Dev and turned her to face the woman who had joined them in the office. "Katherine Hunter, this is Devon Conway. Dev is an old friend of mine. More like a sister, really."

"Who the hell are you calling old?" Dev asked in feigned indignation. She dutifully extended a hand as she finally looked at the newcomer for the first time. Katherine was probably a couple of inches shorter than Dev's five foot ten, and her wavy brown hair fell to her shoulders. Dev tried to hide her surprise but found that she was unable to stop the smile that tugged at the corners of her mouth. She looked into Katherine's incredibly gorgeous green eyes and registered the shock that she saw there. *Obviously she thought we'd never run into each other again.* "It's truly a pleasure to meet you."

"You're Devon Conway?" she asked as she extricated her hand from Dev's grasp. "You're the one who posed for Joanne Riley's painting that's hanging out there?"

"Kat," Rhonda said as she shook her head. Dev said nothing in response as she watched Kat's expression change from shock to confusion. "You said you were going to be here an hour ago. What happened?" Rhonda asked.

"My car broke down on the way from the veterinary clinic," Kat said, pouring herself a cup of coffee. She could feel Devon watching her, and her hands began to shake slightly. Kat found herself wondering if that look of lust from the previous evening was still in Devon's eyes, but she refused to look.

"Well, you're in luck, then," Rhonda said as she touched Dev's arm. "Devon is an auto mechanic. You do still do that, don't you, Dev?"

"Do you really think I would have changed careers this late in my life?" Dev asked, but her mind was still on Kat's question about her posing for the painting. Dev was surprised the inquiry hadn't been accompanied by the stab of pain she had grown so used to. She gave herself a mental shake and managed a smile at Rhonda. "Motorcycles too."

"Oh my God, is that your bike out front?" Kat turned to face Dev. "It's a beautiful ride."

"Thanks," Dev said. It didn't escape her attention that Kat seemed to be avoiding mentioning that they had met the night before. She wondered if there was some reason Kat didn't want Rhonda to know about it.

"What the hell are you doing riding a motorcycle, Devon?" Rhonda asked. "Those things are so damn dangerous."

"And driving a car isn't?" Dev asked acerbically. She regretted saying it as soon as the words left her mouth, but she refused to apologize.

"Shit, I'm so sorry," Rhonda said quietly. She suddenly looked as though she wanted nothing more than to find a rock to crawl under.

Kat looked between the two women and stepped back, seemingly to move out of firing range.

"I wear a helmet, and I don't drive like an idiot," Dev said. "I'm as safe as I can be, Rhonda." Dev flinched when she heard the bell ring out front again. Dev knew that it had to be Chris this time. Her luck had finally run out. She was definitely not ready for this.

"Rhonda, where are you?" Chris called.

"The office," she called back. Dev saw the look of concern on Rhonda's face just as Rhonda motioned Kat to go out front.

"Good morning, Chris," Kat said as she exited the office.

Dev felt her heart begin to race, and her throat suddenly went dry.

"Hey, Kat." A moment later, Chris walked into the office. She stopped in her tracks when she saw who was in the room. "Devon."

The chill in the air was palpable, and Dev resisted the urge to look away from Chris's intense gaze. Chris certainly did not sound like she had let go of the anger Rhonda said she had felt. What really surprised Dev, though, was the fact that she did *not* see Jo in Chris's face. Yes, they were identical, and yes, her muddled brain had those few days between Jo's death and her funeral where she saw Jo every time she looked at Chris. But just as she had always been able to tell them apart while Jo was alive, she found that she still could. That realization made Devon relax, because her greatest fear had been that she would be reminded of Jo every time she looked at Chris.

"Hi, Chris," she said after a moment. "You look good."

"I think I'm just going to go out front and see if I can help Kat," Rhonda said as she slipped out of the office, closing the door behind her.

"What are you doing here, Devon?" Chris asked when they were finally alone. She hadn't yet moved from her spot just inside the door. Dev really couldn't think of a single reason not to tell Chris the truth. Dev had been with Jo for nine years, and they were practically family.

"I think I resorted back to adolescence on a certain day about three years ago," Dev said. She resumed her seat on the couch as she watched Chris finally move from her spot. Dev waited until she was seated behind the desk to continue. "I'm guessing that it's about time for me to finally grow up."

"Why are you here now?" she asked. "I needed you *then,* Devon. Christ, I loved you like a sister. Where the hell have you been?"

Dev shook her head slightly, fighting the impulse to laugh at that statement. Chris had never loved her like a sister, and she was kidding herself if she believed that was true. Dev decided to take the high road and ignore the remark.

"When I saw you at the funeral, all I really saw was Jo," Dev said. "It was killing me, Chris. You two always looked so much alike. I was so afraid that if I stayed here, I might have done something really stupid, like telling Rhonda about what happened."

"Jesus, Dev, if you would have stuck around, we could have helped each other to get through it all. Where did you go?"

"I've spent the last three years running from a situation that I've finally realized I can't change," Dev said with a tremulous smile. "I never stayed in one place for very long. I think I've been in just about every state in the union."

"Are you seeing anyone?"

"I don't see how that's really any of your concern." It didn't surprise her that this would be one of the first things Chris would want to know. Chris had always been just a little too concerned about Dev's private life.

"I have no ulterior motive, Dev," she said, sounding sincere.

Dev sighed before answering. "No, I'm not. I haven't really been interested in that."

"There hasn't been anyone? God, you didn't go straight on us, did you? Because there would be a lot of heartbroken women if you did."

Dev laughed in spite of the way her heart still hurt. "No worries on that front," Dev said with a sly smile and a quick shake of her head. "There just hasn't been anyone that's intrigued me enough."

"No sex?"

"I didn't say that," Dev said, and Chris finally laughed. God, it felt good to be back here talking with her again. It was almost as though she could forget about all the bullshit that had happened between them. "I'm just not interested in dating."

"Don't you think it's about time?"

"For what? Love? I don't know if it will ever be time," Dev said with a sad smile. "Jo was everything to me, Chris—you know that." Dev hesitated before continuing, because thinking about this always choked her up. "It wasn't just Jo's life that I had to make a decision about that night—she was carrying our baby."

"Sweetie, she wouldn't want you to be torturing yourself this way—you know that, don't you?" Chris asked. "You really need to get on with your life. Don't go on living it alone because you're afraid of getting hurt. I want you to be happy, and so would Jo. And, Dev, if you don't mind my being frank, you sure as hell don't look like you're happy."

"I'm happy enough." Dev shrugged, but she knew deep down that she wasn't—not really. The past three years she'd felt as if she'd been wandering aimlessly, and she knew she needed to reestablish her roots. Hopefully this new business venture would at least help her to get her professional life back on track.

"Why did you leave without so much as a word to me?"

Dev had wondered when Chris would get around to this subject. *So much for forgetting all the bullshit.*

"There wasn't anything to say, Chris. I needed to get away and forget about what happened between us."

"So it meant nothing to you?"

"You took advantage of me in a stressful time. I wasn't thinking clearly." Dev had never felt so much guilt as she had the morning after Jo died. She tried to keep the anger in check as she gripped her knees and met Chris's gaze. Dev had known that this first meeting with Jo's twin sister would be awkward, but she had hoped Chris would be mature enough to let their history sleep.

"I took advantage of you?" Chris laughed, but Dev heard no humor in the sound. "Jesus, Devon, I don't remember you saying no, and maybe you're forgetting that it was a pretty stressful time for me too."

"I'm not going to discuss this with you, Chris. It's over, and there's nothing I can do to take it back." Dev stood and began to pace in front of the desk. "I don't want it brought up again."

"Fine," Chris said, holding up her hands in defeat. Dev knew better than to believe she would just let it drop. Chris would no doubt wait for the perfect time to bring it up again. "So, how long are you planning on sticking around?"

"Benny finally retired, and he sold me his garage," she said. "So I guess I'll be around indefinitely."

"That's great, Dev," Chris said with what looked to be a genuine smile. "So how come you aren't there now?"

"Are you telling me to leave?" Dev asked.

"No, it's just that I seem to remember Jo complaining a lot about you being a workaholic," Chris said with a chuckle. "I really can't see that changing just because you own the place."

"Actually, I'm having some work done to it, and updating a few things." She was having new lifts installed and having the entire garage area redone. She had already hired three mechanics and an office manager, and everything would be ready to go in about ten days. "I'm forcing myself to relax until then."

"Listen, we're having an opening here in the gallery tonight," Chris said. "Why don't you come by? Maybe the three of us could grab a late dinner afterward. It starts at six, and most people are out of here by nine."

"Sure," Dev said without giving it much thought.

If she was going to get back in the swing of things, there was no better time than the present. She made her good-byes to Chris and turned to leave. As she walked out into the gallery, she saw Kat hanging a piece of Jo's art. Dev attempted to calm her breathing and tried to still her shaking hands. Dev took the unguarded moment to really look at Katherine for the first time. Her hair was pulled back in a ponytail, and Dev took note of the strong arms and shoulders when Kat lifted the canvas to place it on the wall.

"I could take a look at your car for you if you want," Dev said, causing Kat to jump slightly.

"If that's some lame excuse of a pick-up line, then you really should work on your technique a bit," Kat said, her attention staying focused on the painting.

"Maybe I should remind you that *you* were the one who made the first move last night," Dev said as she reached around Kat to help steady the artwork. She took a deep breath and caught the scent of Kat's citrus shampoo. She hoped that Kat didn't notice the change in her breathing when she realized she was staring right at Jo's last completed piece of art. It was a painting of the house that they had shared in downtown Easton. Her voice faltered slightly when she spoke. "In fact, you actually latched on to me, if I recall correctly."

"My mistake," Kat said as she finally turned to face her. Kat's pulse quickened as she found herself only inches from Devon's face. She faltered for a split second before regaining control of her senses once again. "I had no idea you were a stalker."

Dev laughed as she took a step back in order to give Kat her space. She thought that she saw just the hint of a smile forming at the corners of Kat's lips, but then Kat's face transformed into an unreadable mask.

"Believe me, I'm no stalker," Dev said, but she knew Kat had absolutely no reason to believe her. "Rhonda and Chris are like family, and I was just trying to be nice by offering to help you out. But if you don't want—"

"Wait," Kat said, interrupting her and briefly touching her arm as Dev turned to walk away from her. How stupid would it be to turn down an offer like this? As far as she knew, Devon really was just trying to help, and Kat had to admit that what had happened the night before had actually been her doing. She shook her head sheepishly. "I'm sorry. I would be happy to accept your offer of help."

"Good," Dev said and relaxed a little. As she glanced at her watch, she did a quick calculation of how long it would take her to get her things from Sheila's, drive over to the new apartment, and get back to the gallery. "I have a few errands to run, but I could be back here to pick you up at about two if that's good for you."

"Perfect," Kat said. She hoped she wasn't making a mistake by letting Dev help her out. If she really was such a good friend of Rhonda's, then maybe she had misjudged Devon the night before. "Thank you."

CHAPTER FOUR

"Y ou did tell her that this is a show of Jo's work, right?" Rhonda asked when Chris mentioned she had invited Dev to the opening.

"No. It must have slipped my mind," Chris said, not bothering to hide her irritation. Rhonda was well aware that this was a lie—how could Chris have forgotten to mention that it was her sister's show? But she also recognized that Chris would never admit to her that she knew Dev wouldn't show up if she had known it was Jo's show.

"This is *so* not a good idea," Rhonda said. She and Kat had just finished hanging the final pieces for the show, and Rhonda had joined Chris in the office. "You should probably at least call her and give her a heads up. Maybe give her the opportunity to cancel."

"She can't hide from it forever, Rhonda," Chris said. "I've been living with this work ever since Jo died. I finished the last piece myself, for God's sake. Dev's done nothing but run away from the things that she said meant so much to her. Maybe she needs a shock to her system."

"I just don't think it's right, that's all," Rhonda said. "I don't know that it's necessary to shove her blindly into it."

"Then *you* call her." Chris stormed out of the office, and

Rhonda watched her as she continued right out the front door of the gallery.

Chris and Jo had been so close throughout their entire lives that Rhonda had been scared to death that she would lose Chris when Jo had died. There had been a few extremely frightening months where Rhonda had worried that Chris wouldn't come home every time she went somewhere without her. Things had finally gotten back to normal about eighteen months earlier, and Rhonda had been able to breathe a bit easier.

But with Devon back in their lives now, Rhonda was worried. She loved Dev with all her heart, but it was clearly opening old wounds for Chris. It was obvious to her that Dev needed them now, and Chris clearly still needed that extra connection to Jo that only Devon could provide. The problem was going to be getting Chris to see that.

"Is everything all right?" Kat asked cautiously as she peered into the office after Chris had stormed out.

"I don't know," Rhonda said. She took a seat as Kat entered and sat across from her.

Rhonda looked at Kat for a moment. She had been helping them with their shows for the past year or so, and she had become a good friend to them both. Chris had adamantly denied it, but Rhonda was convinced that Chris was attracted to Kat. Rhonda didn't worry too much about it since she knew Kat would never betray her trust like that. She tried not to think too much about why she never thought that *Chris* wouldn't betray her trust like that.

Rhonda also did her best not to think about the fact she was thirteen years older than Chris, but it was something that had worried her from the time the two of them had become serious. Jo had only been three years younger than Dev, and they had always seemed so much in love. Rhonda had never heard them argue—certainly nothing like the knock-down, drag-out fights that she and Chris were famous for. Rhonda's biggest fear was that Chris might someday decide to find someone closer to her own age. After all, Rhonda would be turning fifty in just over a week. Why would Chris want to be with someone that old when she could have almost anyone she wanted?

"Chris invited Dev to the opening tonight," she finally said as she leaned back in her chair.

"And that's a problem?" Kat asked.

"The problem is Chris neglected to mention to Dev that it was a show of Jo's body of work," Rhonda said. "We never talked about Devon with you, did we?"

"No. You just mentioned that she posed for that one painting. Maybe this isn't any of my business."

"Maybe not," Rhonda said. "It's Dev's story to tell, but I will tell you this much—she and Jo were lovers, and they were together for nine years. After Jo died, Dev disappeared, and we didn't see or hear from her until a couple of hours ago. I just don't think it's right for Chris not to warn her about the show."

"Wow," Kat said quietly. She had sensed that there was something pretty intense between Rhonda, Chris, and the beautiful newcomer, but she'd never have guessed this in a million years. Maybe it was time to rethink the animosity she felt toward Devon. "Listen, Dev is picking me up around two so she can take a look at my car. I can give her a heads up if you want."

"Damn, you work fast, don't you?" Rhonda said.

"Hardly," Kat said with a grin. Rhonda knew about her past—at least enough of it to know the reasons why Kat had no desire to get involved with anyone. Kat had to admit that she found Devon intriguing, though. *Intriguing? Jesus, you can't even acknowledge when you find another woman incredibly sexy?* That thought startled her a bit, but she managed to recover quite nicely. *No amount of sexy can make up for aggravating.* "You were the one who informed me she was a mechanic, remember? She talked to me before she left and offered to take a look at my car. What was I going to do—say no?"

"Of course not," Rhonda said with a quiet chuckle. She sighed and then turned serious. "You don't need to tell her about the show, though. Have her come inside and I'll tell her about it."

❖

Kat was waiting outside the gallery when Dev pulled up on her bike. Dev smiled at her as she removed her helmet and handed it to her.

"Put this on," she said as she ran a hand through her short hair and steadied the big bike with both of her boot-clad feet planted firmly on the ground.

"What about you?" Kat asked.

"It's not a law anymore in Pennsylvania." Dev shrugged as she motioned for Kat to climb on behind her. "I don't have an extra one, and I'd feel better if you were wearing it."

"Rhonda said she needed to talk to you," Kat said as she secured the helmet with the chinstrap.

"I don't have time right now. I really need to meet with my contractors after I take a look at your car. She can talk to me at the opening tonight. Come on. Let's go."

Kat knew it wasn't a good idea. She considered arguing with Dev, but knew when she kicked the bike into gear and revved the engine that it would do no good. She lowered the tinted visor and swung one leg over the bike.

Dev waited for her to get situated, and when Kat put her arms around her waist, Dev reflexively covered Kat's hands with her own and turned her head slightly to speak over her shoulder.

"Where are we going?" she asked. Kat gave her the directions, and then Dev pulled into traffic. Dev was acutely aware of Kat's body pressed tightly against her back, and for some reason, that fact bothered her. Dev had certainly been with other women since Jo, but none of them had demanded her body's full attention like this.

Kat's hands shifted every so often, causing the muscles in Dev's abdomen to twitch slightly. There was an obvious pulsing between Dev's legs that she tried to attribute to the vibration of the machine beneath her, but the throbbing would intensify every time Kat shifted her hips and tightened her hold on her.

As she finally pulled to a stop next to Kat's car, which had been left on the side of the road, Dev thanked God for getting them there in one piece.

❖

"So, is it serious?" Kat asked when Dev slammed the hood down and stepped away from the car. Dev shook her head as she wiped her greasy hands on the legs of her jeans. When their eyes met, Kat felt something she hadn't experienced in a very long time—desire. Devon really was incredibly sexy, and Kat had the distinct feeling Dev wasn't even aware of it. Kat, however, was a bit disturbed that she herself was *very* aware of it.

"I won't know how bad it really is until I can get it up on the lift, but my preliminary diagnosis is that you need a new engine," Dev said as she leaned casually against the side of the car. She had her arms folded across her chest, and her head was cocked to one side. "I can fix it for you, but it would be at least a week before I could get to it because my business isn't quite ready to go yet. You really should probably have it towed to another garage. But if you want my honest opinion, you might be better off just getting a new car."

"I want you to fix it," Kat said without giving her response any thought. She wasn't sure which of them was more surprised at her words. It wasn't like it would be easy for her to get to work without the damn car, but she suddenly wanted to be sure that she wouldn't lose contact with Devon. The mystery surrounding Dev intrigued her, and she wanted to learn more about her. "I can wait for it."

"Well, if you're sure." Dev sounded skeptical. She pushed off the car and took a step toward Kat, but stopped. Dev wasn't used to the feelings she was experiencing. The sexual attraction was easy to figure out, and it was apparent that Kat was feeling that much by the way she looked at Dev. But Dev got the feeling that Kat wasn't the type for a one-night stand. *It's just because she put me in my place last night. She's piqued my interest is all.*

"I'm sure," Kat answered.

"Look, we didn't really get off on the right foot with each other last night," Dev said awkwardly. "Do you think maybe we could start over?"

"Yeah. That would be nice."

"Hi," Dev said, closing the distance between them. She held her hand out in greeting. "I'm Devon Conway."

"Katherine Hunter." Kat couldn't suppress the smile that pulled at her lips. "You can call me Kat, though." For some reason she couldn't let go of Dev's hand. What came out of her mouth next surprised her. "Can I buy you lunch?"

"I'd like that," Dev said, but didn't pull her hand away. It felt nice, and she loathed the thought that their contact would end. Inevitably though, it did, and Kat finally took a step backward. Dev motioned toward the Honda behind her. "You should get someone to tow that for you. If it sits here much longer, the cops will take care of it for you."

"Where should I have it towed?" Kat asked as she pulled her cell phone out of the pocket of her leather jacket. Dev gave her the address of the garage and then waited against the car while Kat called the motor club. Snapping the phone shut, she said, "How about that lunch?"

"You should probably wait for the tow truck," Dev said. "I'll meet you at the garage. Don't you need to get back to the gallery?"

"No, I only help to hang the shows, and we're done with that. I'll be back there tonight, though. I heard that you were invited to attend."

"Yeah, but I'm not sure that I'll really go. Who is the artist anyway?"

Kat just stared at her for a moment, and then silently cursed

Chris for not having told Dev earlier. This really should not be her responsibility, as Rhonda had pointed out. But Dev had asked, so was it right to not respond to the question?

"Joanne Riley," Kat said carefully as she leaned on the car next to Devon. She felt Dev tense, but her expression never betrayed what she was feeling.

"Is that right?" she said. *Damn you, Chris. Of course, if I'd have given it half a thought, I would have realized it was Jo's show. Why else would they have been hanging her work?*

"Listen, Rhonda told me that Jo was your partner," Kat said after a moment, and Dev quickly averted her gaze. It seemed as though she found something suddenly very interesting by her feet. "You can tell me that it's none of my business, because it probably isn't, but can I ask you how she died?"

"It's none of your business," Dev answered automatically, but she smiled to lessen the harshness of her words as she glanced sideways. Kat laughed and nudged her playfully with her shoulder.

Dev was granted a reprieve when the tow truck pulled up in front of Kat's car. She excused herself and went to speak with the driver.

Kat watched her as she walked away, and was struck by the confident way that Dev carried herself. *So damned attractive. And so very, very sexy.* It had been a long time since anyone had affected her this way, and she couldn't deny what she was feeling. Dev's black hair was just long enough that it was unruly from the motorcycle ride, and that only added to the appeal, making Kat wonder what that hair would feel like in her hands.

FROM THIS MOMENT ON

CHAPTER FIVE

A re you sure you don't want someone else to repair your
car?" Dev asked when they were seated with their
greasy fast food meals in front of them. Not exactly a romantic
setting, but it wasn't exactly a date either, was it? *Jesus, when
was the last time I was even on a date?* She had ridden ahead to
the garage on the Harley and met with her contractors. "I won't
be open until a week from Monday."

"I want you to do it," Kat said, but was at a loss to explain
the reasons why—even to herself. "I only work a couple of miles
from home, and it will be good for me to walk anyway, as long as
the really cold weather holds off for a while longer."

They fell into a comfortable silence, and Dev spent the
time studying Kat's face when she wasn't looking. Her skin was
flawless, and she noticed for the first time how the light green
T-shirt Kat wore hugged her chest. Sometime on the ride to the
garage, Kat had released the ponytail, and her hair rested on her
shoulders.

"Excuse me?" Dev asked, looking up from Kat's full lips
when she realized Kat had been speaking to her.

"I said you're staring at me."

"You're very easy to look at." Dev chuckled at the snort she got
in response. "Most women would take that as a compliment."

"I'm not most women."

"I think I'm beginning to realize that." Dev nodded as she

lifted her milkshake to take a drink. "It doesn't change the fact that you're very attractive."

"Do you ever take a break from picking women up?"

"Why can't you just take a compliment?" Dev leaned back in her chair and stared at Kat. She had never met someone who was so defensive. She raised an eyebrow when Kat stood abruptly.

"We should go," Kat said. "Why don't you just drop me off at my place, then you can go home and get ready for the opening. I need to walk my dog anyway."

"You'll need a ride to the gallery," Dev said with a smile. "Would you allow me to be your escort?"

"Why not?" Kat shrugged. They collected their trash and deposited it in the garbage can by the front door before heading over to the bike.

Dev silently handed the helmet to Kat before swinging a leg over and starting the engine. When Kat didn't immediately get on behind her, she glanced over her shoulder. She grinned when she saw Kat staring at her backside. "You like what you see?"

"Jesus, you are incorrigible." The words were muttered under Kat's breath, but Dev heard, and she chuckled. The muscles in Dev's stomach tensed when Kat got on the bike and immediately put her arms around her. She closed her eyes for a moment and tried to regain her composure before finally pulling out of the parking lot.

❖

When Dev pulled into the driveway and saw the big oak tree in the yard, she realized what she hadn't when Kat had given her the address. This was where she was now living, above the garage. She cut the engine and sat there a moment as Kat dismounted.

"What's wrong?" Kat asked as she handed her the helmet.

"I think we need to talk about something," Dev said quietly. She leaned the bike onto the kickstand and turned to face Kat as she stood. "You have a brother named Rick?"

"How did you know?" she asked.

"I was here earlier." She wasn't entirely sure how this was going to go over. She'd been a little worried about the fact that he had rented the place to her without talking to his sister in the first place. Given the inauspicious start she and Kat had the night before, she was even more bothered by that now. "I came to see about the apartment."

"And you met Rick," Kat said. It wasn't a question, so Dev gave no answer. "What aren't you telling me, Dev?"

"You're my new landlady," she said, shifting her weight from one foot to the other. She tried to gauge Kat's reaction to this news by her expression, but it was nearly impossible. "I used Rhonda as a reference, and he thought that it would be all right with you, since you know her too."

"I see."

"I hope this isn't a problem." Dev set the helmet on the seat of her bike and pulled the apartment keys out of her pocket, holding them out to Kat. "I'll understand if it is. I can always go back to Sheila's. I've been there for a week now anyway."

"Sheila?" Kat asked, but made no move to take the proffered keys. "Sheila Franklin? You've been staying with her, but Rhonda only knew you were back today?"

"It's kind of a long story," Dev said in lieu of an explanation. "Sheila raised me from the time I was ten years old."

"I'm not going to make you move," Kat said, making a promise to herself that she would get the whole story about Dev's relationship to the Franklins some other day. "My brother went with his gut, and it's not usually wrong. We'll give it a month or two, and see where it goes, okay? Give me an hour, so I can take care of Buddy and change my clothes. You're still going to be my escort tonight, aren't you?"

"If you'll let me."

"Then I'll see you in an hour."

❖

"Crap," Kat muttered under her breath as she removed the third outfit she'd tried on. *Why the hell do I care what I look like? She's aggravating and wants nothing more than to get in my pants.*

She let out an annoyed sigh and settled on a simple pair of black slacks and a white blouse. After checking her hair and makeup one last time and spraying on a bit of cologne, she returned to the bedroom and shooed Buddy off the bed. She picked up a framed picture from the nightstand as she took a seat.

"I miss you so much, Paula." Kat wiped a tear away before it could ruin her makeup job and then slowly ran an index finger over the picture of the partner she'd spent fifteen years with. "God, I wish you were still here. The past five years certainly haven't been easy without you. I know you told me to get on with my life, but I can't imagine being with anyone but you."

Buddy began barking the second the doorbell rang, and Kat tried to compose herself quickly. *God, I hope my eyes aren't red. That's all I need is for her to know I was crying.* She put the picture back on the nightstand and hurried down the stairs. A glance in the mirror confirmed her suspicions, so she opened the door and then turned away.

"There's some wine in the kitchen," Kat said as she headed back up the stairs. "Pour me a glass too, will you please? I'll only be a few more minutes."

Dev found her way to the kitchen. The bottle of wine was on the counter, along with a corkscrew and two glasses. Dev was getting the distinct feeling that it was about to turn into a date, whether either of them wanted it to or not. *No, Devon Conway does* not *date.*

Dev took both glasses to the living room and sat on the couch, placing the wine on the coffee table before her. She laughed when Buddy jumped right up next to her and leaned into her side, almost as if he did the same thing every night. She scratched his head, but when she heard Kat coming down the stairs, she sat up straight, wondering if the dog was supposed to be on the furniture. Buddy just moved closer so that he was half on her lap.

"He seems to like you," Kat said from the entry to the living room.

Dev glanced up and her breath caught in her throat.

"You look beautiful." Dev openly appraised the stunning creature before her. Kat was wearing black slacks and a white silk blouse, which was unbuttoned enough to hint at the swell of her breasts beneath. Her brown hair was pulled back away from her face and tied in a ponytail. Dev looked down at the dog when she saw Kat blushing at her scrutiny.

"You clean up pretty well yourself, Ms. Conway," she answered. Dev watched Kat appraise her just as blatantly, but then Kat turned her attention to the dog in an obvious attempt to hide the flush on her cheeks. As Kat took a seat on the other side of Buddy, she picked up her wineglass and motioned with it. "Thank you for this."

"No problem." Dev forced herself to look at Kat. She wondered if the desire she felt tugging at her insides was evident in her eyes.

"We have about forty-five minutes before we have to leave for the gallery, unless you want to be the first ones there," Kat said, glancing at her watch. "Are you sure you want to go to this tonight?"

"Honestly? No, I'm not sure." She took a sip of her wine and leaned back against the couch. "But I *will* go—mostly because I know that Chris will expect me not to show up. Especially when she finds out you told me it's Jo's work."

They sat in silence for a few moments, and Dev struggled with her thoughts.

"I'm confused about something. We're going to this thing together," Dev said nervously, staring into her drink. She glanced over. "Is this a date?"

"I'm not sure. I get the impression that dating you could be dangerous."

"Why do you say that?"

"You made it pretty clear last night what you were looking for, and it wasn't a date," Kat said. "And I'm pretty sure that if I'd said yes, we would have slept together, and we wouldn't be sitting here talking right now." Kat held a hand up when Dev tried to speak. "I think you're the kind of person who uses sex to escape from your own thoughts. To just forget about what you can't force out of your head, and you probably only see those women once. I'm not saying that's necessarily a bad thing, but I've never been the type of person who could do casual sex. So, if that's what you expect from the women you go out with, then I would have to say that this is *not* a date."

"You don't know anything about me," Dev said, a bit nonplussed. She shook her head slightly and leaned away from Kat.

"I'm sorry, I guess that was a little out of line."

"What are you, a shrink?" Dev wondered at the fact that Kat had pinpointed her so accurately. She couldn't deny any of the things that she had said.

"No, not a shrink. I'm just observant."

"You're right—I don't usually *go out* with women," Dev said after a few moments of silence. "So, to tell you the truth, I really wouldn't know what to expect from an honest-to-God date. But I can promise you that I would never push you into something you weren't comfortable with."

"Thank you for that," Kat said. "Tell me how you know Sheila and Rhonda."

"Sheila's my godmother. Actually, she raised me from the time I was ten." Dev was happy to change the subject from dating. "Rhonda is quite a few years older than me, but she lived at home while she went to college, and even for a few years after that. I spent a lot of time giving them both headaches with the trouble I got into. Rhonda always treated me like a little sister, though."

"If you're so close to Rhonda, then why didn't she know you were here, and staying with her mother?"

"Well, the short version is that I left town three years ago without a word to anybody. I knew Rhonda would be pissed at me for that, and I asked Sheila to keep it from her because I wanted to be the one to let her know I was back." Dev took a sip of her wine as she thought back to the day she'd run away. "Sheila always knew where I was, but I didn't want to face Rhonda."

"Why? I mean, you said you were like sisters. I would think you'd have wanted to keep in touch with her."

"That explanation would require the long version of the story. There was an accident, and it changed everything."

"And like the question I asked this afternoon, it's none of my business," Kat concluded with a rueful smile.

"I'm sorry." It was weak, but Dev wasn't sure what else to say.

"Don't be. I understand not wanting to talk about things." Kat smiled, and Dev was taken aback by the sadness she saw in it.

"We should probably get going." Dev stood and took her glass to the kitchen.

"You know, Devon, there's going to be a lot of people there tonight, people I assume that you haven't seen since you left town," Kat said from her seat on the couch. It was obvious to Dev that she was struggling with her words. "I could call Rhonda and tell her I can't make it, and you and I could just go to a movie or something. If you'd rather not go, that is."

"As appealing as that sounds, I really think I need to put in an appearance at this show." Dev stood and held out a hand to assist Kat to her feet. "Aside from the fact that what you suggested is too much like a date to deny it, I'm afraid Chris would never let me hear the end of it if I didn't show up."

"Is there something between you and Chris that I don't know about?" Kat asked, teasing.

Dev simply stared at her, knowing that it was an innocent

question, but she couldn't stop the fear and angst that the inquiry caused. Her heart clenched painfully, and she tried to look away, but Kat caught the dismay in her expression before she could.

"I'm sorry," she said quickly. "I was just trying to lighten the mood."

"No, it's all right," Dev said after a moment. "They were twins. Actually, they were identical twins, and sometimes I think it scares me that someone who looks so much like Jo is still walking around. But to answer your question—the only thing between me and Chris is the death of a loved one."

Chapter Six

D ev set her sights and made her way to the table that was set up in the back of the gallery where they had complimentary wine, soda, and hors d'oeuvres laid out. Kat headed in Rhonda's direction to see if she could help with anything as Dev poured herself a glass of red wine and filled a plate with cheese and crackers before turning to survey the room for the first time.

It was a nice turnout, and she thought to herself that Jo would have been proud. Dev had actually forgotten some of the works that were on display, but her eye kept going back to the one she had seen earlier that morning.

"Devon?" a voice beside her asked tentatively. Dev turned to see Leigh Johnson, a good friend who had also served Dev her first legal drink. "Is it really you? Where the hell have you been, girl?"

"That seems to be the question of the day." Dev set down her plate and glass in order to embrace her. "Leigh, it's really good to see you. I was at the bar last night, but you weren't there."

"It figures you'd go in on the one night I have off," Leigh said as they separated. "I'm there pretty much every night. You should come by again sometime. Let an old friend buy you a drink or two."

"I'll do that." She reached back and picked up her wine

once again, taking a sip as she glanced around the room. She saw Kat, who seemed to be deep in conversation with an extremely attractive and very fit blonde. That they were well acquainted was evident in the way they touched each other on the arm as they spoke. Dev looked back to Leigh, trying not to acknowledge the fluttering in the pit of her stomach at the sight of Kat laughing with someone. *Okay, I'm incredibly attracted to her. So why haven't I made a move yet?*

"Girlfriend?" Leigh asked with a smile. Dev almost spat her wine all over the place as she fought back a snort of laughter.

"Hardly," she said. She refused to look in Kat's direction again. "I rent the apartment above her garage. I only just met her."

"Mm-hmm." Leigh's smile broadened, and she turned to pour herself a glass of wine. "You forget that I've known you since you were seventeen, when you and your young stud friends started coming into my bar. Sometimes I think I know you better than you know yourself, Dev."

"Well, you're wrong about this." Dev shrugged, trying to shake the disappointment that accompanied those words. When she turned to face Leigh again, a napkin was shoved into her hand. "What's this?"

"My number. Sundays and Monday nights during football season are pretty wild since we added a television, and you know how much lesbians love their football. Tuesday and Wednesday nights are pretty dead, though. If you ever want to talk, come see me. Or just give me a call."

"Thanks." Dev watched as Leigh disappeared into the crowd, and was startled when she turned to find Sheila at her side.

"Rhonda told me that Chris invited you here tonight without telling you it was Jo's work," Sheila said. "Sometimes I really don't know what possesses her to do some of the things she does."

"It's all right, Sheila," Dev said, hoping it sounded like

indifference, although what she was feeling toward Chris at the moment was anything *but* indifferent.

"No, it's not," Sheila said. "Are you sure you're ready to move out on your own? Who's going to make sure that you're eating right? You can't afford to lose any more weight."

"I'm fine." She scanned the room again and stopped once again at Kat, who was watching her with a smile on her face. *She is so damn beautiful.* Dev couldn't help but return the smile

Sheila nudged her playfully in the ribs and gave her a knowing smile. "Katherine Hunter is very attractive," she said.

"Mmm." It took much more effort than she thought it would to pull her eyes away from Kat's. "Will you excuse me please? I think I need to talk to Chris."

"Behave yourself," Sheila said, but Dev just waved a hand over her shoulder.

Dev took a deep breath and another drink of her wine before knocking once on the office door. After a split second, she grabbed the knob and turned it, but it was locked. She knocked again and waited. A moment later the door opened and a tall blonde walked out, a smile on her face. Dev watched her join the crowd in the main gallery, and then turned to Chris, not even trying to hide her anger.

"What the fuck is wrong with you?" she asked as she walked in and closed the door behind her. She took great care in trying not to slam it. "Rhonda's not twenty feet away from this room."

"I don't have to answer to you," Chris said as she took a seat at the desk.

"You damn well have to answer to someone. Rhonda may not be related by blood, but she *is* my sister nevertheless. *You*, on the other hand, are nothing but a slut, and I cannot believe that she puts up with your shit."

"What the hell did you come in here for?" Chris asked.

"I just wanted to thank you for your thoughtfulness in telling me about this opening," Dev said. She took a seat as she willed her pulse to slow. It wouldn't do anyone any good to get all worked up about things she couldn't change. Chris was who she was, and Rhonda knew what she was getting into before they ever got together.

"I knew you wouldn't come if I told you," Chris said. She leaned back in her chair with a smug smile. Dev suddenly had the urge to reach across the desk and wipe it off.

"For your information, I *did* know—Kat told me this afternoon," Dev said, determined not to let her rage get the best of her. "And I still showed up, Chris. Give me a little credit next time. Something like this should be *my* decision, don't you think?"

"Well, you do have a habit of running away."

"Once does not constitute a habit, and you know damn well why I left." She leaned forward, her hands clenched into fists. "Does Rhonda know why?"

"No." Chris shifted in her seat and looked at a point over Dev's head. "She can't ever know what happened."

"Trust me, I have no desire to hurt her," Dev said, counting her blessings that Sheila had talked her out of it that morning. "But I will not put up with this animosity between the two of us. I'm here to stay, Chris, and you and I will no doubt be running into each other quite often. We need to come to some kind of understanding."

"Are you sleeping with Katherine?" Chris asked.

Dev blinked in confusion at the complete change of subject. She shook her head and let out a chuckle that held no humor.

"It's none of your business who I sleep with, Chris, and it never was, in spite of what you think," Dev said once she had recovered. "And besides that, I just met Kat this morning when I was here."

It wasn't a complete lie—they had decided to start over, so the night before didn't count in Dev's mind.

"You brought her here tonight," Chris said with a shrug,

refusing to look away from Dev's intense gaze. "Rhonda said that she left here with you this afternoon. Is this a date?"

"Not that either one of us planned, but I really can't say for certain what might happen later. But again—it's none of your business."

"Just like it's none of your business what I do," Chris said with another smirk.

"It is my business because you're supposedly in a committed relationship with my sister." She knew no one was close enough to the office to hear them, but she lowered her voice nonetheless.

"I don't owe you a damn thing, but that buyer was in here putting down a deposit on a painting," Chris said. "There was nothing going on. I love Rhonda, and I've done nothing in the past three years to jeopardize our relationship. You have no right to waltz in here after all this time and accuse me of things you know nothing about."

"I know you," Dev said, not believing a word of it. She knew Chris too well. "And that gives me the right. I'm cancelling our plans for a late dinner. A better offer came along."

"What the hell is going on in here?" asked Rhonda as she and Sheila walked in. Rhonda glanced from Chris to Devon and back again, waiting for an explanation. "We can hear you outside the door. What's the problem?"

"No problem," Dev said as she stood up to leave. This was turning into a horrible night, and she wanted nothing more than to leave the gallery.

"Did you give it to her?" Rhonda asked Chris, grasping Dev's wrist when she tried to walk past her.

Dev stood in silence, knowing from experience to not challenge Rhonda when she was angry. They had that in common, and it had made things rather interesting in the Franklin household until they each learned the other's limitations. She glanced over her shoulder when she heard Chris open a drawer in the desk and toss an envelope on top of it.

"What's that?" Dev asked warily.

"Open it, honey," Rhonda said with a slight squeeze before she released her grip on Dev's wrist. "It's for you."

Dev looked at the women around her briefly before turning back to the desk and picking the envelope up. She knew before she even opened it that it contained money—a rather substantial sum, if the thickness of it was any indication.

"I don't understand."

"It's for the paintings of Jo's that we've sold since her death," Chris said, letting her head rest against the chair. "The gallery kept the standard commission, and what's there is the difference."

Dev was at a loss for words. The thought that they would have done this for her was a little overwhelming. She didn't count the money but could see that there were more hundred dollar bills than she'd ever seen in one place in her life. She directed her gaze to Rhonda.

"I can't take this," she said around the lump in her throat.

"Of course you can." Rhonda embraced her tightly for a moment. Before releasing her, she said quietly, "Jo would have wanted you to have it. I know that in my heart."

"I want that painting that you finished," Dev said when she finally regained some of her senses. She turned to look at Chris. "I can certainly afford it now."

"It's been sold," Chris said with a shake of her head.

"What?" Rhonda asked in disbelief. "Who bought it?"

"They wanted to remain anonymous," Chris answered. "The details were worked out last evening."

"Why didn't you tell me?" Rhonda was livid, but Dev knew she wouldn't show the extent of her anger until she and Chris were alone. "I own half of this gallery. Why didn't I know that painting was sold?"

Dev took Sheila's arm and led her out of the office, making sure to pull the door closed behind them as they left.

"That's not going to end well," Sheila muttered under her breath.

"Does it ever?" Dev asked.

❖

"You look a little lost," Kat said as she walked up next to Devon and handed her a fresh glass of wine. "Can I help with anything?"

What a loaded question, Dev thought as she turned to look at Kat. Her head was beginning to hurt from thinking about the exchange in the office about a half hour earlier, and she made the conscious decision to focus her attention on her date.

"I'm fine," Dev said with an easy smile. She glanced briefly at the people milling about before returning her gaze to Kat. "But I am a little bored of the conversations that seem to be about the same things they were about the last time I was at one of these things."

"No, things don't change too much, do they?" Kat said before she took a sip of her wine. Dev looked across the room, and Kat felt her heart rate speed up as she took a moment to study her profile. She shifted her weight from one foot to the other nervously. She leaned close enough so that their shoulders touched, and Kat spoke before she could think too much about what she was saying. "What do you say we get out of here?"

"What did you have in mind?" Dev asked, a sly grin slowly forming.

"Well, based solely on the look in your eye," Kat said with a slow smile of her own, "not what you're thinking, I'm sure."

"Too bad," Dev murmured so softly that Kat almost didn't hear her. Almost.

"How about just a late dinner?" Kat said when she finally turned back to Dev without her face feeling warm.

"Give me just a minute, all right?" Dev asked. She'd known

enough women in her lifetime to know that what she saw in Kat's eyes was lust. She handed her wineglass to Kat. "I'll be right back."

Kat watched as Devon turned and headed toward Rhonda. She knew she was headed for dangerous territory with Dev, but she couldn't deny there was a part of her that wanted it. There hadn't been anyone since Paula died—no one had interested her enough to be more than friends. And now here was Devon Conway, who took her breath away without even trying.

"Rhonda, do you have a minute?" Dev asked as she smiled politely at the couple Rhonda was speaking with. Dev silently thanked whoever was responsible for not allowing her to get sucked into conversations with any of the people she had known before. However, she knew it would only be a matter of time before someone cornered her. That was another compelling reason to leave with Kat now. Dev waited patiently while Rhonda wrapped up her discussion with the two men, and then took her aside.

"Is something wrong?" Rhonda asked.

"No," Dev said. "I already told Chris, but I won't be able to make it to dinner tonight. I'm sorry."

"What's the matter, honey? Did Chris say something to upset you?" Rhonda asked her as she placed a hand gently on her forearm.

"I'm just a little overwhelmed by everything," Dev said, which wasn't really a lie. Being here with so many of Jo's pieces on the walls was a bit daunting. "I just want to go home and unwind a bit."

"Okay," Rhonda said, sounding relieved. "We can give Kat a ride home, so you don't have to worry about her."

"Actually, she's coming with me."

"I see." Rhonda looked worried all over again. "Look, Devon, be careful with her, all right? I really don't think she's your type."

"What the hell is that supposed to mean?" She raked her

fingers through her hair and glanced over her shoulder at Kat, who was talking with an elderly couple across the room. She turned her attention back to Rhonda as she waited for an answer.

"She's just not into one-night stands."

"Christ, Rhonda, you know me better than that," Devon said.

"Do I?" Rhonda asked. "I know how wild you were before Jo settled you down, and I have no reason to think that you're any different now. Just be careful with Katherine. She's had a pretty rough time of it."

"And I haven't?" Dev asked angrily. "Don't worry—I *am* capable of having friends without bedding them. Besides that, it was her idea for the two of us to leave."

Without giving Rhonda the opportunity to respond, she turned and walked back to Kat, who was standing alone waiting for her now. Her breath caught at how beautiful Kat was. Dev mentally shook herself, hoping that what she was feeling didn't show in her face or in her demeanor.

"Are you ready?" she asked a bit more sharply than she had intended.

"Sure," Kat said, wondering at the abrupt change in Dev's attitude. She glanced back at Rhonda, who was watching as they headed toward the door.

Chapter Seven

They returned to Kat's house and she ordered a pizza with no input from Dev as to what she liked on it. It wasn't for a lack of trying on her part, but Dev had been completely silent on the ride home and still was not speaking. Kat went upstairs to change into jeans and a sweatshirt and then took Buddy for a walk while Dev went to her apartment to change as well. They returned to the front door at the same time as the delivery driver, and Dev pulled money out of her pocket to pay for the pizza.

Kat wished she could help Devon with whatever was bothering her, but she figured it was probably better to just let Dev come out of it on her own. The silence was a bit uncomfortable, but Dev *had* come back for dinner, so obviously she didn't want to be alone, right? Kat hoped that she was right, and also that she wouldn't say the wrong thing. There was something about Devon that pulled at her, and she knew it was more than just the fact they had both lost someone. Devon made her feel good about herself, even if she had dismissed the compliment Dev had given her at lunch.

Once inside, Kat went to the kitchen to get paper plates, napkins, and a couple of beers as Dev settled on the floor in front of the couch, the pizza box resting on the coffee table. Kat took in the sight of her threadbare jeans, taking note of the tanned thigh she could see through one of the many holes. Kat sighed as she took a seat on the floor next to her.

"This is nice," Kat said as she took a drink of her beer and helped herself to a slice of pizza. Dev merely grunted, but it was the first sound she had made since they left the gallery, and Kat took it as a positive sign. After a moment, not able to handle the silence any longer, Kat leaned back against the couch and turned her head to look at her. "What's wrong, Dev?"

Dev thought for a moment about not answering but decided she might as well talk to Kat, since she was the only person available.

"I found out tonight that Chris and Rhonda had been saving all of the profits from Jo's sales to give to me," she finally said without looking at Kat.

"And that's a problem?" Kat asked carefully. When Dev didn't answer, Kat chuckled and shook her head. "I think that you desperately want to dislike Chris, but for some reason, you just can't bring yourself to do it."

"I think that you see too much, Ms. Hunter," Dev said with a chuckle of her own. She risked looking into Kat's face, and was surprised to see compassion there. Dev redirected her gaze to her beer bottle and tried to fight the need she felt to touch Kat's cheek. *I need to either sleep with her or stay the fuck away from her.*

"Why do you want to dislike her so much, Devon?" Kat asked.

"I knew Chris before I ever met Jo," Dev finally said after a few moments of silence. This sensation of wanting a connection with another human being was alien to her. For some reason, though, she was powerless to stop the feeling. "We actually dated for a couple of weeks, and then she set her sister up on a blind date with us, and that was when I met Joanne. She had the same beauty and sultry voice, but was completely devoid of the abrasive personality that I found so extremely irritating in Chris. Suffice it to say that Chris was not happy when Jo and I started to spend more and more time together."

"So you dumped Chris for her twin sister," Kat said, trying to prod Dev to go on.

"I guess you could say that, but I never saw it that way," Dev said with a shrug. She took a drink of her beer and leaned her head back. "We never had any kind of agreement between us—we went out a few times, that's all. When I started to see Jo, Chris kind of freaked out. After a few weeks, she even tried to convince Jo that I was cheating on her."

"I take it that Jo didn't believe her?"

"Actually, she did," Dev said, laughing at the memory. She saw what Kat was trying to do, and she appreciated it. Living inside herself for the past three years, she'd never allowed for the opportunity to revisit the good times she and Jo had shared because she'd been too busy feeling sorry for herself. "Jo wouldn't talk to me for weeks. One day she finally called me and apologized for reacting the way she did, and then said she needed to see me. We met for dinner, then we wound up at my place, where she proceeded to seduce me. Now, you have to understand that even though we'd only been seeing each other a short time, I knew that she wasn't very aggressive when it came to sex. I had the feeling very early on that night that it was actually Chris I was with."

"Did you sleep with her?"

"No, but we were certainly getting pretty hot and heavy kissing on the couch," Dev said sheepishly. She looked up at the ceiling as she ran her fingers through her hair, a motion that Kat was coming to find thoroughly sexy. "I knew it was risky, but at a pretty crucial moment, I called her Chris."

"Oh, my God." Kat laughed, and without thinking put a hand on Dev's thigh. She quickly removed it, and neither of them said a word about it. Kat felt a rush of warmth course through her body at the contact, and she unconsciously rubbed her palm along her own thigh. "What would you have done if it had been Jo?"

"Beg for my life, no doubt, and then plead with Jo to give

me another chance." Dev tried to laugh along with her, but the spot on her leg where Kat's hand had been felt as if it were on fire. She cleared her throat and leaned her head back again. "I was positive it was Chris, though—Jo was a much better kisser. And I never did have a problem telling them apart."

They were both silent for a few minutes as they ate their pizza, and Kat got up once to get them each a fresh beer. When she returned, she took a seat on the couch after handing a bottle to Dev. Buddy jumped up next to her, and after a moment, Dev joined her as well.

"I'm a little bit confused about something," Dev said after a few more moments of silence. Kat turned her head to look at her, and Dev waited to make sure that she had her full attention before going on. "I know you didn't want it to, but I get the feeling this evening turned into a date at some point."

"You too?" Kat asked with a nervous laugh. She leaned back and felt herself relax ever so slightly. At least now she knew she wasn't the only one feeling that way. "I'm not really sure how that happened."

"Neither am I. I told you before that I don't date, and I haven't since Jo. Before her, I played the field. I'm not proud of my promiscuous past, but it's a part of who I am. So, a date is definitely not the norm for me, and I wanted to thank you."

"For what?" Kat asked, unable to look away from Dev's lips.

"For putting up with my reminiscing."

"You don't have to thank me. I really don't mind, and Jo was a huge part of your life, Dev. It's only natural that you think about her, and talk about her too. I really wouldn't expect that to change any time soon."

"Are you for real?" Dev asked in amazement. She didn't resist when Kat reached over and took her hand. She squeezed it gently. "Next time you'll have to tell me something about yourself."

"Next time?" Kat asked. "You mean a second date?"

Dev smiled as she looked down at their hands, and she shook her head in surprise. Dev wasn't even certain she knew what to do on a date, but she was more than willing to try.

"Yeah." Dev nodded. "At this moment, a second date with you sounds pretty nice to me."

"Tell me something," Kat said, not fully believing they were having this conversation. A few women had asked her out since Paula's death—her best friend Laura being one of them—but she'd never been compelled to accept. At least not until now. Dev was waiting patiently to find out what it was Kat wanted to know. "Since you don't really date, you may not have an answer for this, but do you kiss on the first date?"

Dev laughed as she leaned her head back to stare at the ceiling. Buddy nudged her arm, but when she didn't respond, he sighed loudly and jumped off the couch.

"How should I answer that in order to get a *second* date?" Dev asked teasingly.

"Honestly."

"Well, in that case," Dev said slowly as she turned her head to look at Kat once again, "yes, I do kiss on the first date."

"I don't," Kat said with a smile as she pulled her hand away. In reality, she didn't know if she kissed on the first date. There had never been anyone other than Paula, and it hadn't been Kat who'd refused to kiss on their first date. Their relationship had started as an affair, and they were afraid to be seen out, lest they got caught.

"Well then, I guess we cleared that up."

"What was it that Rhonda said to you before we left tonight?" Kat asked after a moment of silence. "You seemed a little angry about whatever it was."

"Nothing," Dev said far too quickly.

"Bullshit," Kat said with a short laugh. "It was something about me, wasn't it?"

"She just wanted to let me know that you're not my type," Dev said after another moment of silent contemplation.

"Really? What is your type?"

"I never knew I had one, but apparently Rhonda thinks I do," Dev said. She shrugged as she continued, "She made sure I knew that you weren't into one-night stands."

"How dare she get involved in my personal life," Kat said incredulously.

"Was she wrong?" Dev asked. This possibility didn't excite her like she thought it would, and in fact it brought up a new emotion that she was completely unprepared for and couldn't deny—jealousy.

"No, but that's beside the point." Kat leaned forward and shook her head. "I'm perfectly capable of making my own decisions. I don't need someone else looking out for me. I can't believe she'd say that to you." A thought suddenly occurred to her, and she turned her head to look at Dev. "Is that what you want from me?"

"If that was what I wanted, I would have already made my move," Dev said with more confidence than she felt. "And I sure as hell wouldn't be asking for a second date."

Kat didn't have a clue as to how she should respond. Never in her life had she even considered the possibility of sleeping with someone casually, but Dev's appeal was undeniable. If one night was all Dev was willing to offer, then Kat was almost certain she would take it, and that realization scared her more than she cared to admit.

"I should be going," Dev said as she stood. It hadn't escaped her notice that Kat had never responded to her request for a second date. It was disappointing, but she figured she'd give Kat time to think about it. Dev didn't want to leave, but it was obvious that Kat was one to take things slow. For the first time since Jo died, that prospect actually held some appeal for her.

Kat got up and walked toward the kitchen, and she returned with a pen and paper. She stopped at the dining room table and wrote something down. She held the paper out to Dev as she approached her at the door.

"Call me if you're serious about a second date," she said quietly.

"I will," Dev said. She folded the paper and stuffed it in her pocket, mostly to keep her hands busy, because she wanted nothing more than to kiss Kat until she begged her to stop.

"There's just one other thing," Kat said seriously.

Dev braced herself for what was coming. *There's a girlfriend, right? Please don't tell me there's a girlfriend.* Kat took both of Dev's hands in hers.

"What is it?" Dev asked.

"Since this really wasn't an official date," she said with a shy smile. "I don't see any reason for us not to kiss. Unless of course *you* don't want to."

"Oh, I want to," Dev said. She'd never been hesitant about this sort of thing before, but she waited for Kat to make the first move. It somehow seemed important to Dev that she hold back. When Kat's hands moved slowly up her arms, Dev placed her hands tentatively on Kat's hips, urging her closer. Their lips met in a chaste kiss, and Dev pulled slightly away, an eyebrow raised in question. "Okay?"

"No," Kat murmured. "It's not nearly enough."

She kissed Dev again, and this time her tongue slid lightly along Dev's lower lip, causing Dev to groan and pull her even closer. Dev moved her hips slightly and was surprised to feel Kat's thigh insinuate itself between her own. Dev acted on pure instinct when she moved her hands up and underneath Kat's blouse. When she skimmed them slowly up Kat's bare torso, Kat placed both of her hands firmly on Dev's chest and pushed her away slightly, resting her forehead against Dev's, both of them taking ragged breaths.

"Just a little something to remember me by until our next date," she said quietly.

"I don't really think there was ever any danger of me forgetting you," Dev said. "Unless you don't like action movies and Italian food. Any problems there?"

"Nope. Please tell me you like sports."

"Love them. Well, except for basketball. You don't root for New York teams, do you?"

"Philly all the way. Good night, Devon," Kat said as she reluctantly pulled away from Dev and reached behind her to open the door. Dev walked out without another word between them, and when the door closed, she waited to hear the deadbolt click into place before heading toward the garage.

There was no doubt in Dev's mind that she wanted Katherine Hunter, and it was pretty clear from Kat's actions that the feeling was mutual. Dev shook her head in bewilderment as she opened her door and went into the apartment without turning any lights on. There was enough light coming through the skylights that she didn't need any artificial illumination as she made her way to the bathroom.

A nice cold shower was in order, but Dev really didn't think it would do much to quell her craving for Kat's touch. A couple of knowing strokes from her own fingers would probably help to reduce the desire she was experiencing, but Dev found that prospect unappealing.

She settled for the cold shower and went right to bed.

CHAPTER EIGHT

The following morning brought Dev some clarity. What the hell was she thinking asking someone out on a date? *I don't date. Maybe Rhonda was right—I should just leave Kat alone. She's too sweet to get mixed up with somebody like me.*

"When the hell did you get so fucked up?" she asked her reflection in the bathroom mirror. She laughed humorlessly as she shook her head. She knew exactly when that had happened—in the middle of those twelve hours that had sent her life straight to hell. She'd been running from everything ever since. Kat had been right—sex was nothing more to her than a way to escape the realities of her existence.

Dev showered, and when she walked out to the kitchen, she saw the piece of paper with Kat's phone number on it lying on the counter. After staring at the numbers for a few minutes, she shoved the paper into the front pocket of her jeans.

❖

Kat pulled the chicken breasts out of the oven just as the doorbell rang. Buddy began jumping up and down, barking wildly and running ahead of her to the door.

"You're going to give yourself a damn heart attack one of these days if you don't learn to calm down," she said, bending over to pick him up.

"Am I late?" Laura asked, walking into the house without an invitation. She reached out and scratched Buddy absently behind the ears as she passed.

"No, you're right on time, as usual." Kat closed the door and set the dog down. She laughed when Buddy immediately went to Laura and sniffed noisily at her feet, no doubt smelling all of the animals that had gone through the veterinary clinic that day. "Busy day?"

"No more than usual." Laura shrugged and made herself comfortable on the couch. "There are far too many clients that refuse to let anyone but you treat their animals. What the hell do you do to those people?"

"I've simply succeeded in captivating them with my overwhelming beauty and charm," Kat said sarcastically. She went to the kitchen and poured them each a glass of wine before returning to sit with her colleague on the couch.

"You're joking, but I believe it's true," Laura said with a laugh.

Kat watched Laura take a sip of her wine and took the opportunity to wonder why she wasn't physically attracted to her. Laura was beautiful, and she was fun to be with, but there was no spark between them. Until she'd met Devon, Kat had begun to think that she would never be attracted to anyone again.

"I'm sorry?" Kat asked when she finally realized that Laura had asked her a question.

"I wanted to know if you met anyone at the bar the other night," Laura asked again.

"You know, you really pissed me off, leaving the way you did," Kat said, but she was unable to keep the grin off her face. "How in the world can you go home with someone different every time you go out?"

"I captivate them with my overwhelming beauty and charm," Laura said, smirking.

"You know what I mean." Kat laughed and leaned back

into the couch. "Don't you get tired of it? Don't you ever want more?"

"I offered to change for you, but you made it clear that you weren't interested." When Kat didn't say anything in response, Laura looked down at her wineglass and shook her head. "There are times that I think I might want more than a one-night stand, but then I remind myself of what happened the last time I tried to have a relationship. It was a disaster, and trust me, I'm being kind. I ended up cheating on her, and she ended up hating me. Unfortunately, that doesn't stop me from wanting to try it again from time to time."

Kat didn't say anything in response, just stood and went to the kitchen to dish up their dinner. She found herself wondering what Devon was doing at that moment, and was struck by the thought that perhaps she should have pursued more with her the night before. *Maybe it would do me some good to get laid.*

"You never answered my question," Laura said from where she stood just a few feet away, leaning against the wall as she studied Kat. "Did you meet someone the other night?"

"No," Kat said after a slight hesitation. She took both plates to the dining table and took her seat, but Laura stood where she was, watching her. For some reason she couldn't explain, she wasn't ready to share the fragile beginnings of what she and Dev had. Whatever that was.

"Bullshit." Laura took the seat next to her. "Honey, I know you too well. What's her name?"

"I didn't meet anyone."

"Fine," Laura said in defeat as she picked up her fork. "Come out with me tonight. You need to get back into the swing of things."

"Going to lesbian bars was never my thing, Laura," Kat said. "If I want to meet anyone who's going to be relationship material, it isn't going to be in a bar."

"You have to work your way up to relationship material,"

Laura said with a playful nudge. "You can't just meet someone and jump right into it."

"I did with Paula."

"I'd be willing to bet that there isn't anyone out there quite like Paula," Laura said. "So if you're waiting for someone to come along and sweep you off your feet like she did, you're no doubt going to be waiting for a hell of a long time."

"I'm not going out with you tonight, but thank you for asking," Kat said with a smile. "Nessa is coming by later."

"Good. Maybe she can talk some sense into you."

And if I'm lucky, maybe Dev will call, Kat thought as she made the futile attempt to concentrate on her food.

❖

It was almost nine o'clock when Dev pulled into the driveway that night. She'd spent the day driving to New Hope, and from there made the trip to the Poconos. After doing nothing but thinking about Kat the entire day, she finally decided that as soon as she got home, she would call her and ask for that second date. She could just go knock on the door, but that might make her seem desperate. The phone would be better.

As she walked up the steps to her apartment, she pulled the cell phone from her pocket and flipped it open. Her steps faltered when she reached the door, and she heard voices coming from the front door of the house below. She sat on the top step and watched for a moment.

There was a woman standing on the porch with Kat, and they looked to be rather friendly. It was difficult to make out any features in the dark, and she could only hear murmuring from where she sat, but there was no mistaking the quick kiss on the lips they exchanged before she walked away from Kat to the car parked outside of the garage. The outside lights weren't on, and Dev couldn't see Kat's visitor clearly. *Girlfriend? Would she have kissed me like she did last night if she had a girlfriend?*

Dev closed her cell phone and let herself into the apartment. It would be pointless to call after what she'd seen, wouldn't it? She sat in the dark for a while nursing a bottle of beer, and just when she had made up her mind to go to bed, she heard another car pull into the driveway. Morbid curiosity made her go to the window.

She had absolutely no problem determining that the new visitor who got out of the car was very pregnant. Dev watched in silence as the she walked to the front door and rang the bell. When Kat opened the door, Dev's heart sank when she saw the affectionate hug and kiss, and then Kat ushered her guest inside, one hand firmly on the pregnant, protruding belly.

Dev took a deep breath as the door closed, trying not to acknowledge the quick jolt of jealousy that rocked her. To admit to that emotion would mean that she would have to confess that she felt something for Kat, and she was definitely not ready for that.

She went to bed, but after forty-five minutes of tossing and turning, she threw the covers off in frustration. She sat on the edge of the bed for a moment, wishing that she had thought to make a stop at the liquor store earlier. Katherine Hunter simply would not get out of her head, and that was making the attempt to sleep futile. Dev chuckled humorlessly, remembering a time when she thought that she would have been happy to not have Jo's ghost keeping her awake at night. Somehow this seemed worse. She wanted Kat, and it was becoming increasingly obvious, with the women coming and going from her house, that she was probably unavailable. What would a person like Katherine want with someone like her, anyway? A greasy mechanic with a heap of baggage from her dead lover. She sighed.

A shower and a few drinks at the bar. That's what I need right now to get her out of my head.

❖

As Dev walked into the bar, she glanced around quickly, easily identifying the women who were there looking for a quick hook-up. Knowing that wasn't really what she wanted, she made her way to the opposite end of the bar and found an empty stool.

"Shot of whiskey," she said to the bartender as she placed two twenties on the bar in front of her. She looked around but didn't see Leigh, which meant she was either off or busy in the back office. It was just as well, because Dev really wasn't in the mood to talk. "And keep them coming."

She was on her third shot and hitting a nice buzz when a woman came and took the stool next to her. Dev turned to look at her and was greeted with a dazzling smile.

"I've never seen you here before," she said, leaning close to Dev with her hand resting gently on her forearm. Dev made no attempt to move away from her touch.

"I guess you could say that I'm new in town." Dev shrugged indifferently.

"Looking for company?" she asked.

Dev turned on her bar stool. She took in the blond hair, blue eyes, and incredible body. Something about her was familiar, but it stayed just out of reach of her memory. She smiled seductively as Dev looked at her, obviously not bothered by the scrutiny she was receiving. Dev noticed that the cargo pants she was wearing were a bit baggy, but the blouse was tight, and clearly meant to show off her ample cleavage.

"I guess that would depend on who's offering," Dev said as she picked up her newly filled shot glass, refusing to acknowledge the nibble of guilt when she thought of Kat and their conversations about one-night stands.

"My name is Laura."

"Devon," she said, extending her hand which Laura took, holding onto it a little longer than was necessary.

"It's a pleasure to meet you, Devon."

Dev stared at her as Kat's face invaded her thoughts, and

the words she had spoken just before walking away from their first meeting came back to her. *I wish I could say that it was a pleasure meeting you.*

Dev shook her head to chase those memories away and then forced a smile.

"The pleasure is mine."

"It certainly will be," Laura said, with total confidence. "So…your place or mine?"

This had definitely not been Dev's intention when she made the decision to come out tonight. All she'd wanted was to have a few drinks and to get Kat out of her head. She studied Laura's face as she contemplated her options. She could simply go home and *try* to fall asleep with images of Kat running rampant through her mind, or she could lose herself in a few hours of passion with this extremely alluring—and very willing—woman.

"Yours," Dev said quietly after a moment. Without waiting for a response, she shoved her money across the bar and downed her last shot. When she turned to face Laura again, she saw that Laura was already halfway to the door. Dev made her way through the crowd.

❖

"Jesus, that was incredible," Laura murmured, her lips pressed to Dev's neck and her legs wrapped tightly around Dev's thighs—which effectively trapped Dev's arm between their bodies, her hand still between Laura's legs. She slowly loosened her hold on Dev as her breath came in ragged gasps, and her muscles slowed their reactions to the orgasm that had shaken her only moments before. "I want you to feel the things that you made me feel."

Dev flinched when she felt Laura reaching for her, and she took a firm hold of Laura's wrist as she rolled off her.

"What's the matter, baby?" Laura asked as she propped

herself up on one elbow and ran her hand slowly across Dev's abdomen. "Don't you want me to touch you?"

"I should go," Dev said. *What the hell is wrong with me?* She'd never had a problem being with a one-night stand before, but for some inexplicable reason, Kat was invading her every waking moment. No one had ever affected her that way—other than Jo, and Dev really did not want to consider what that might mean. When she felt Laura's hand moving toward her center, she grabbed her wrist again to stop her. "I really need to go."

"I know you have to be close, baby," Laura said as she leaned in to put her lips close to Dev's ear. "You gave me three mind-blowing orgasms. Let me help you get there."

"I'm fine, really," Dev said as she pulled away and got out of the bed.

"What's her name?" Laura asked, falling back against the pillows with her arms crossed over her stomach.

"Excuse me?" Dev asked, faltering slightly as she pulled on her jeans. She glanced over her shoulder and saw that Laura was sitting up, the sheet only up to midthigh. *There really is something wrong with me,* she thought. *Why in God's name am I walking away from this?*

"I have to admit that I've never been rejected like this before," Laura said. "So I figure you must have someone at home waiting for you."

"I'm not rejecting you," Dev said with a nagging annoyance that she knew she had no right to be feeling. She allowed the silence to settle over them as she finished getting her clothes on, and then she sat down on the edge of the bed. "There's not someone at home. I'm just not in the right frame of mind to be doing this tonight. I probably should have never gone to the bar in the first place."

"Can I see you again?" Laura asked quietly.

"I kind of got the feeling that you don't see people more than once," Dev said with a slight smile. "Honestly, I don't either.

It's probably better if we just leave things the way they are, all right?"

Laura didn't answer, but simply watched Dev as she stood and left the bedroom.

Jesus, I am such an ass, Dev thought as she walked out the front door.

Chapter Nine

D ev opted to stay in her apartment on Sunday, mostly because she knew that if she went out, she would have gone straight to Kat's. And as much as she wanted to see Kat, that was precisely where she did not want to end up. A little distance at this point would no doubt be a good thing.

Monday morning Dev awoke to the sound of rain pelting her bedroom window, and she groaned as she pulled the covers up over her head. Normally, she didn't care about riding the bike in the rain, but it was mid-October, and the air had a slight chill to it. Since she had to get to the garage to place an order for the parts she needed to fix Kat's car, she wanted to be dry. Dev sighed when she realized that meant she would need to take the Harley to Sheila's in order to pick up the Durango. At least she had left some of her clothes there, so she could change after riding the bike in the rain. It was raining even harder when she emerged from Sheila's house dressed in dry clothing—at least, it had been dry when she put it on. The Durango was parked outside the garage now, since Rhonda knew that she was back, and she made a run for it but stopped short when she saw something on the ground behind the right front tire.

"What the hell?" She kneeled down to see what it was. The small gray and white kitten turned its head to look at her as she reached out to touch it. "Shit. Are you all right, little guy?"

It was obvious that the cat was injured because it didn't even try to move away from her. Dev turned and ran back into the house to retrieve a blanket and then hurried back to get the cat. She carefully picked it up and wrapped it in the blanket before walking around the truck and placing it on the passenger seat.

"So much for not wanting to look like a drowned rat," she mumbled as she glanced at her reflection in the rearview mirror. As she turned the key in the ignition, she looked down at the ball of fur that was making soft mewling noises as it tried to shift its little body inside the blanket. She reached over and placed a hand gently on its side. "Hang in there, tough guy. I'm going to take you to see a doctor who's going to make everything better."

Dev was pretty sure that she had seen a veterinary office a couple of miles down the road from Kat's house, and that was where she headed. A few minutes later, she found herself standing in the reception area with a wet bundle crying in her arms.

"Sign in on the sheet there, and then have a seat," the receptionist at the front desk said without looking up from her computer screen. "Someone will be with you in a moment or two."

"I don't have an appointment," Dev said. She ignored the look of irritation on the woman's face and said, "It's a bit of an emergency. I found this little guy under my truck, and he's hurt. We need to see a vet."

Dev filled out all of the information she asked for, but hesitated when she asked for the cat's name.

"I found him. He doesn't have a name."

"Make something up," she said with a bored sigh.

"Listen." She glanced down at the receptionist's nametag before trying again her with a forced smile. "Stella, he doesn't belong to me. I found him this morning, and he's hurt. I honestly don't think I'm going to be keeping him, but I just wanted to make sure he's all right."

At that moment, Dev made the mistake of looking down at the bundle she held in her arms. The cat was looking at her as if he trusted her completely, and she felt her heart break a little at how fragile he looked. Maybe she could manage to find room in her life for a little fuzzball.

"Baxter," she said.

"Excuse me?"

"His name is Baxter," she repeated, and he snuggled deeper into the blanket as she scratched his head.

"Please have a seat, and one of the doctors will be with you shortly."

Dev didn't have time to sit down before a technician called her name. She followed the young man into an exam room, and he closed the door behind her.

"You can have a seat," he said pleasantly as he gently took Baxter out of her arms. "I just need to take his temperature and jot down a few notes for the doctor."

Devon stood next to the cold metal table and grinned when Baxter nestled his face in the crook of her arm as the tech did what he needed to do and got what little information from her that she could give.

"Dr. Hunter will be right with you," he said as he opened the door and disappeared into a hallway running through the middle of the building. Dev nodded in response, not paying attention to anything but the ball of fur in her arms.

Not until the door opened again, and Kat stepped into the room.

Dev felt her heart rate speed up a bit at the sight of Katherine in her scrubs and her spotless white lab coat.

"Devon?" she asked in bewilderment. Kat silently scolded herself for not looking at the file to see the name of the person who owned the pet. She had been too preoccupied with the symptoms of the animal. "You have a cat?"

"No," Dev said with a sheepish smile. "At least I didn't until about half an hour ago. He was curled up behind the tire of my truck, and I have no idea where he came from."

"Your truck?" Kat asked. "What truck?"

"As much as I love the Harley, I won't drive it in the winter," Dev explained with a wry grin. "I bought the Durango right after I moved back here. I've been keeping it at Sheila's."

"You can use the garage," Kat said without thinking. She set the chart down on the counter behind her and turned her attention to the cat. "Let's see what we have here. Hello there, Baxter. Looks like you've had a rough morning, little guy."

"I completely forgot you were a vet," Dev said, watching her as she worked. "I'm sorry, I kept thinking the gallery was your main job."

"No need to be sorry," Kat said, trying her best to not let Dev see how her presence affected her. "I did mention that I was a veterinarian, though."

"I'm also sorry that I didn't call you," Dev said as she felt her cheeks flush in embarrassment. *Crap, how could I have forgotten that she was a vet?* Kat looked up to meet her gaze, and Dev thought she saw disappointment in Kat's eyes in the split second before she turned her attention back to the cat.

"Again, there's no need," Kat said with a shrug. "I've been pretty busy the past couple of days anyway."

"Have dinner with me tonight," Dev said quietly before she could think about what she was saying. She looked down at Baxter in an attempt to avoid seeing Kat's reaction. She put her hand under Baxter's chin as she chuckled into the uncomfortable silence. "I completely understand if you're not interested."

"I don't recall turning you down. I'm done at five tonight."

"Great." Dev returned the smile and tried her best not to stumble over her words. It was more than a bit disconcerting that being around Kat could make her so nervous. No one had ever made her feel this way—not even Jo. "Maybe we could go out to dinner, and if you're feeling up to it, a movie after? I could be at your place around six."

"Sure," Kat said. She looked back down at the cat on the exam table between them. "I'll need to run some x-rays on him.

You're welcome to wait here, and I'll bring him back in a few minutes."

Dev sat down, waiting rather impatiently for Kat to return, and all she could think about was the kiss they had shared. In fact, if she was being totally honest with herself, that had been pretty much all she'd been able to think about since it had happened.

This is so not like me. Since Jo died, Dev had never even entertained the possibility of dating someone. What was it that made Kat so different? It was a question she'd been pondering ever since they'd gone to the gallery opening Friday night.

"It will be a few more minutes before I get the results of the x-rays back," Kat said, startling Dev out of her contemplative state. "Sorry. Did I wake you up?"

"No—just thinking," Dev said as she stood. There were so many questions running through her mind, but she wasn't sure that she had any right to ask them. Instead, she reached out and placed a hand on Baxter's side. He looked up at her and blinked lazily before closing his eyes again.

"Are you going to keep him?" Kat asked.

"I'm not sure my landlady allows pets."

"Well, unless your landlady is a coldhearted bitch, I don't see why she would mind."

"Well then, since I'm fairly certain she's *not* a coldhearted bitch, I think I have to keep him," Dev said. "I think he's gone and gotten himself attached to me. Besides that, I can't see spending this much money on him just to give him away to someone else."

"Most people wouldn't have even taken the time to bring him in for treatment," Kat said as they both looked down at the defenseless kitten. "I think it was incredibly sweet of you to have taken care of him like this."

Much to her consternation, Dev felt the heat rise in her cheeks. She shifted her weight from one foot to the other as she reached up to scratch at her neck nervously.

There was a knock on the door that rescued Dev from further embarrassment, and Kat went to slide it open. The tech handed her the x-ray films, and she placed them over the light box so they could look at them.

"It looks like he's got a break in the pelvic area." Kat pointed to a small fracture that Dev had difficulty seeing. "It's not incredibly severe, but it will probably affect him in some way for the rest of his life."

"What can I do to help him?" Dev asked, acutely aware that she was standing close enough to Kat that their shoulders were touching.

"He should be kept confined for a week or two to limit his movements," Kat said as she eased away from Dev. "It will also give him time to heal. You'll have to keep an eye on him for the next couple of days to make sure that he's able to urinate on his own."

"And if he's not?"

"We can discuss the options if the problem arises." Kat switched off the light before turning to face Dev again. "I'll give you some pain pills for him, and I can take a look at him tonight if you want."

Dev found herself wondering if the elation she was feeling at having a date with Kat was at all evident. She was helpless to stop herself from reaching out and grasping Kat's hand.

"Thank you," she said quietly. She stared at Kat's lips, and when Kat's tongue made an appearance to wet those lips, Dev thought that her knees might give out. She quickly pulled away and busied herself with wrapping Baxter in the blanket again.

"Let me give you a dry blanket for him," Kat said.

"I'm going to have to leave him alone for a little while," Dev said, suddenly remembering that she needed to order the parts for Kat's car. She looked back at Kat, her concern evident. "Will he be all right?"

"He'll be fine," Kat said. "Just put him in a box that's tall enough so he can't get out of it. Make sure that he has some food and water—preferably canned food—and a small litter box. I'll be right back with a blanket for you."

After Kat left the room, Dev stood there looking at Baxter, who appeared to be sound asleep. She chuckled as she reached out to gently stroke his head.

"I'm certainly glad that one of us is able to relax around her," she murmured. "I can't seem to think of anything but kissing her."

❖

"How about grabbing a drink with me?" Laura asked when they were getting ready to leave the veterinary clinic.

"I can't," Kat said. "I have a date."

"What?" Laura asked, placing a hand over her heart in mock surprise. "Katherine Hunter has a date? An actual honest-to-God date? What is this world coming to?"

"Very funny."

"So who has finally managed to break through your defenses? She must be something special to get you to agree to go out with her. God knows I've been shot down enough."

"She's renting the garage apartment," Kat said, pointedly ignoring the last remark. "I just met her last week."

"Do you really think that's a good idea? What if it doesn't work out, and you still have to live on the same property together?"

"Thanks for the vote of confidence," Kat said. But what if Laura was right? *What if it doesn't work out? But what if it does?*

CHAPTER TEN

Dev was showered and dressed by five thirty that afternoon, and she didn't think she'd be able to sit down and wait for another half hour. The day seemed to take forever to pass, but she had managed to get some things done at the garage, which she was happy about. She'd tried to nap when she'd gotten home, but images of Kat's lips, her luscious body, and the smell of her musky cologne invaded her thoughts. She'd quickly given up on sleep.

"I told her I'd be there *by* six," she said to the cat as she looked in on him in his little jail cell. "I didn't tell her I'd wait *until* six to show up."

Baxter meowed his agreement, and she grinned as she reached in and scratched under his chin. Satisfied that he had enough food and water, and more ecstatic than she thought she'd be that he had used the litter box on his own, she grabbed her keys and headed across the driveway to Kat's front door. The moment she found herself standing at her destination, though, she felt incredibly foolish. *I'll seem too anxious. I should just go back home and wait.* Taking a deep breath, she pushed the bell.

She looked around the yard and shoved her hands into her pockets, not wanting Kat to see that her hands were trembling. *Christ, I feel like I'm sixteen and going out on my first date.*

"You're early," Kat said with a genuine smile when she opened the door.

"I can go back home," she said, uncharacteristically nervous. She hated the way Kat made her feel, but there was also a part of her that was beginning to enjoy it immensely.

"No, it's fine." She took Dev by the arm and led her into the house. After she had closed the door, she turned to face Devon. "I have some unexpected company, though. Come on into the kitchen with me."

Dev cursed herself for not paying attention to the strange car that had been parked in the driveway.

"Hi." It was the very same, *very young* pregnant woman Dev had seen at the house the other night. She began to stand, but Dev motioned to her to not bother because she could see she was having difficulty managing the feat. "My name is Vanessa, but I prefer Nessa."

"I'm Devon," she said as she held out a hand in greeting. Nessa gripped it firmly, and Dev managed a smile in spite of the anxiety she suddenly felt. She wondered if she could make an escape without too much fuss. Was it possible this was Kat's girlfriend? Nessa looked like she could be twenty years younger. "You can call me Dev. I'm just a friend. I live in the apartment above the garage."

Nessa simply smiled at her before turning her attention to Kat. "Really?" she asked, her head tilted to one side. "Why is it that you haven't mentioned this *friend* to me before, Mother?"

Dev was confused as she looked back and forth between the two of them. She must have heard wrong. Her first reaction was relief to find out that Nessa was not a girlfriend. Then her attention turned back to Nessa's protruding belly. Panic soon set in as the realization dawned on her that Kat was going to be a grandmother. She hoped to God that the shock wasn't obvious in her expression.

"Actually, I just met her a few days ago, Nessa," Kat said as she watched the change of emotions on Dev's face. She went to the refrigerator and returned with beers for herself and Dev and a bottle of spring water for Nessa. Kat glanced at Dev, who looked about as nervous as the proverbial cat in a room full of rocking chairs.

"I can come back later," Dev said as she set the beer down and turned toward the door.

"Don't be silly." Kat reached out and placed a hand on her arm. This was not the way that she had wanted Dev to find out about Nessa, but her daughter had shown up unexpectedly a few minutes after Kat had gotten home from work. Now that Dev had met her, there was no reason for her to leave. "Come sit with us."

"So, you two have plans for the evening?" Nessa asked, looking from Kat to Dev and back again. Kat shook her head at her daughter's question. Nessa reached for her purse and started to stand. "Mom, you should have told me. I can come back another time."

"You don't have to leave," Kat said quickly.

"We were just going to grab some dinner," Dev said, sounding to Kat as if it meant absolutely nothing to her other than a meal.

"Nonsense," Nessa said with a smile as she finally got to her feet. "You two go out and have fun. I'll call you tomorrow, Mom."

"I'll be right back," Kat said as she brushed a hand across Dev's shoulders on her way to walk Nessa to the door. "Honey, you don't have to go."

"Mom, how often do you go out on dates?" Nessa asked in a low voice.

"Never," said Kat.

"Exactly, and she's gorgeous, Mom," Nessa said, grabbing Kat's arm and smiling. She glanced over her shoulder toward the dining area as if to make sure Dev wasn't paying any attention to them. "You know I'm going to want to hear about your date, right?"

"Nessa…"

"Paula would approve," Nessa interrupted before Kat could protest too much. "God, Mom, you know she didn't want you to spend the rest of your life alone, right? Just go out and have some fun. Let whatever happens happen."

"Isn't that the attitude that got you into this condition?" Kat asked. She placed a hand on Nessa's belly.

"Yes, it is," she said with a grin. "But you won't have to worry about this happening to you again, will you?" Nessa laughed at her expression and then said in a louder voice, "It was nice to meet you, Dev. I hope to see you again soon."

"You too," Dev said as she stood and faced their direction. She watched in silence as Kat kissed Nessa on the cheek, and then they were alone in the house.

"I didn't mean for you to find out about her that way," Kat said apologetically as she walked toward Dev, stopping about a foot in front of her.

Dev closed the remaining distance between them and placed her hands tentatively on Kat's hips. When Kat leaned into her, her arms going around Dev's shoulders, Dev relaxed into her.

"I've wanted to do this ever since you left here the other night," Kat said as she moved a hand to the back of Dev's neck and pulled her closer. Kat moaned when Dev pulled her even closer, and she was certain her legs would give out completely when she parted her lips to allow Dev's tongue the access it was seeking.

"I haven't been able to think of much else myself," Dev said breathlessly when they finally came up for air. She shook her head. "I may need to do more than kiss you if we don't stop now, though."

"I know the feeling." As soon as the words were out of her mouth, she was mortified. This was not like her at all. She sat on the couch and patted the cushion next to her. Dev grabbed their beers from the table and sat down just as Buddy jumped up on Kat's lap. "Would you mind very much if we didn't go out tonight?"

"What did you have in mind?" Dev took a sip from her bottle.

"There are some things I want to talk to you about," Kat said slowly. She absently scratched Buddy behind the ears and refused to look at Dev.

Dev reached over and cupped her jaw, gently turning her head to make Kat meet her gaze. "You don't have to tell me anything."

"Thank you for that, but I want to." Vanessa was the only one who truly knew what Kat had gone through, and she had always been her strongest supporter—in spite of the fact that she had only been sixteen at the time. Rhonda knew only what Kat had chosen to tell her. Chris knew absolutely nothing, unless Rhonda had shared any information, because for reasons of her own, Kat didn't trust Chris. "It doesn't bother you that I'm going to be a grandmother?"

Dev set her beer on the coffee table. Leaning back, she let out a deep breath and put her hands behind her head, her fingers interlaced. "I will admit that it did catch me a little off guard. Maybe it hasn't really sunk in yet."

"Well, when you jump up and run screaming from the house, I'll know it's sunk in," Kat said with a small laugh.

"That's not going to happen." A smile tugged at the corners of Dev's mouth. "Just how old are you, anyway?"

"I'll be forty next month. I got pregnant when I was a senior in high school," Kat said with a sigh. *God, it seems so long ago. Almost as though it was a totally different life.* "I got married that summer because it was expected in situations like that. Vanessa was born in October, and she just turned twenty-two. I guess that I should just be thankful that she didn't end up pregnant as young as I did."

"What happened to your marriage?" Dev asked, gently prodding her to continue.

"We were divorced a year later." Kat pushed Buddy off her lap before leaning forward and setting her beer on the coffee table. "He cheated on me. But in all honesty, I cheated on him too. I always knew that I liked women, but that wasn't something you talked about in my family. I so envy people who know who they are and embrace it. I always wished that I could have been that way. You were, weren't you? You always knew you were a lesbian?"

"Pretty much." She reached over and took Kat's hand gently in her own. "But we aren't talking about me tonight, remember?"

"Vanessa was six months old when I decided that I was going crazy sitting around the house all the time, and I got a job as a checker at the grocery store," Kat said. "That was when I met Paula." She stopped to take a sip of beer and steady her voice. "She was incredible, Devon. We hit it off right away, and we started spending a *lot* of time together. The first time she kissed me, I felt as though my world had finally righted itself. Everything in my life became so perfectly clear to me in that single moment. We ended up having an affair for about three months, and I was desperately trying to figure out how to get out of my marriage. Then one day he came to me and told me he wanted a divorce because he'd met someone else. It all worked out perfectly. I moved in with Paula, and we raised Vanessa together. Nessa's father had her every other weekend, and for two months during the summer. He never had a problem with Paula and me being together."

"You're lucky in that regard," Dev said when Kat paused to take another drink of her beer. Kat settled back into the couch and took Dev's hand again, holding it in her lap, her thumb stroking Dev's palm slowly. "What happened to Paula?"

Kat hesitated. If she had spoken about this to anyone other than Vanessa and Rick over the years, she probably wouldn't be feeling as if she were going to cry. Without releasing her hold on Dev's hand, she reached for her beer again and finished what was left in the bottle. It still hurt to think about Paula, but five years after her death, Kat had finally managed to at least stop thinking about her all of the time.

"In two thousand she was diagnosed with brain cancer," Kat

said, somehow forcing herself to hold back the tears that were threatening. Dev tightened her grip slightly on Kat's hand. Kat lifted Dev's hand and held it to her lips for a moment as she tried to steady herself. "They only gave her one year to live when they diagnosed it. She managed to make it two years, although she spent the last eight months of her life in the hospital. So it seems as though you and I have something in common."

"Jo died in a car accident." Dev moved closer to Kat and put an arm around her, pulling Kat's head against her shoulder. Losing the person you loved was certainly not something she had ever wanted to have in common with anyone.

"I'm sorry," Kat said quietly. "I would never kid myself into thinking that it was anywhere near the caliber of what you went through."

"No, I think what you went through was worse, in a way. That will take a toll on anyone, no matter how strong they are. At least with Jo it happened fast. I was in too much emotional pain to be able to realize it at the time, but I truly think it was a blessing. She didn't have time to suffer. With the cancer, you *both* had to suffer through it for those two years. And Vanessa. God, it must have been rough on her too."

"It was," Kat said, allowing Dev to hold her, and acknowledging to herself how good it felt to be in her arms. She realized for the first time how much she had cut herself off from people after Paula died. She'd never talked to anyone other than Nessa and Rick about it, because when she had tried to talk to colleagues, they just stared at her like she had two heads. She came to the understanding rather quickly that most people would never truly understand what the loss had meant to her, and to her daughter as well, no matter how tolerant they seemed to be of homosexual relationships. But Dev understood how deep that kind of loss cut, and it seemed to be so easy to talk to her about it. Much easier than she had thought it would be. "She loved Paula as much as she loved me. As far as she was concerned, we were both her mothers. There was no distinction in her mind."

"I can't begin to tell you how sorry I am for what you went through, Kat," Dev said quietly as she pressed her lips to Kat's temple. Death was difficult no matter how it chose to present itself. "So it's been five years since she died?"

"Yes." She leaned back and looked into Dev's eyes. "You're incredible, do you know that?"

"No, I'm not. I just know what it feels like to mourn. I know that for me, after three years, I'm tired of feeling this way—like I have to force myself to face each day. I want to live again."

Kat stared at her, wondering how it was that Dev could be making her feel the things that she was feeling. Arousal was only a part of it, but even *that* she hadn't experienced in over five years. She opened her mouth before her brain engaged.

"I want to sleep with you, Dev," Kat said. She laughed nervously as soon as the words left her mouth. "You have no idea how totally unlike me that is."

"Yes, I do. I heard you and Vanessa talking before she left. I was trying not to listen, but the dining room is way too close to the front door."

"You heard everything?" Kat felt her cheeks flush as the conversation came back to her.

"Pretty much." Dev leaned in to kiss her on the corner of her mouth. "I heard you tell her that you never date. There really hasn't been *anyone* since Paula?"

"No. There really hasn't been anyone that I've been interested in for more than friendship."

"Why me, then? Why do you think I'm the one?"

"You think it's just because we both lost someone, don't you?" When Dev simply shrugged and nodded in response, Kat turned contemplative. "I'll admit that was probably why I was so comfortable with you at first, but I also find you to be extremely funny, charming, and easy to talk to. And you kind of, well, balance me. I mean, you work with your hands, fixing things. I do the same, but with animals."

"And I'm gorgeous too, don't forget that part." Dev flashed

the sexy grin that made Kat's heart feel as though it was going to burst out of her chest.

"My God, you really did hear everything we said, didn't you?" Kat asked as she pulled away and sat up straight. "I'm so embarrassed."

"Why? You weren't the one who said it."

"No, but I do agree with her assessment." She turned serious. "Why do you think it is that we're attracted to one person and not another?"

"I really don't know," Dev said. "I've wondered that myself sometimes. Take Jo and Chris, for example. They were identical twins, but I never had any real interest in Chris. But from the moment I met Jo, I couldn't think of anything else other than the next time I would see her. She tried to resist my charms at first, because she said that she didn't want to date someone who had gone out with her sister. But she had to finally admit that she was falling in love with me."

"Had you slept with Chris?" Kat asked casually.

"Yes," Dev said after only a slight hesitation. "Remember, I told you that I was a little wild in my younger days."

Kat put her hand on Dev's thigh, and Dev tensed slightly when she felt the hand move slowly up her leg. With reluctance, she reached down and stopped the movement before Kat could make it all the way to her crotch.

"I want you, you have to know that."

"But…?" Kat asked slowly.

"But I really think we should wait. All we've really talked about is Jo and Paula. I'm just not sure that we would be alone if we went to bed together right now. Too many ghosts in the room, so to speak, and I don't want that. I want it to be just the two of us, Kat. I want to get to know *you*. I want to know what makes you happy, and I want to know what makes you angry. You have absolutely no idea how much it's killing me to say this, but I really do think we should wait."

"You really are incredible," Kat said. She didn't have to

like it, but she certainly respected Dev's viewpoint. Kat would never have admitted it to anyone, but she had always been afraid that if she were to go to bed with another woman, all she would be able to think about was Paula. It was a double-edged sword, really. She was afraid she wouldn't completely be with the other person, but on the other hand, she was terrified to feel anything but her love for Paula. Dev seemed to take all of her fears away without even realizing it. "Well then, we should at the very least get something to eat, right?"

"Sounds good to me." Dev grinned as they both got to their feet. When Kat reached for the beer bottles, Dev stopped her by taking her hand. She waited until Kat looked at her before she spoke again. "You do know it has nothing to do with you, right?"

"Yes. I think that I might like you even more because you want to wait. Knowing you want me is enough for the time being—but it won't be enough forever."

"Understood." Dev nodded solemnly as she released her hand so Kat could get rid of the empty bottles. *Trust me…it won't take forever.*

Chapter Eleven

After dinner, they decided to take in a movie after all, mostly because neither one of them wanted the evening to end. Dev enjoyed sitting in the theater holding Kat's hand. They had talked more during dinner, and surprisingly, neither Jo nor Paula came up in the conversation.

When they got back, Kat offered to take a look at Baxter, and followed Dev up to her apartment and back to the bedroom, where Dev had him set up in a box in the corner.

"He looks good," she said as she stood again. "I'm glad that he's urinating and able to have bowel movements on his own."

"What would have happened if he couldn't?" Dev asked, not sure she really wanted to hear the answer.

"More than likely, he would have had to be put on a catheter," Kat said. "I know most people don't want to have to deal with that, especially when you're talking about a kitten you really didn't want in the first place. I've found that it's easier for most people to opt for euthanasia in cases like that."

"I don't think I could do that," Dev said, glancing down into the box to hide the emotion that welled up inside her. It was true that she hadn't gone looking for a cat, but now that she had him, she was becoming attached. *God, when did you become so soft? You haven't even had him for twenty-four hours.*

"Well, you don't have to," Kat said, placing a hand gently on her arm.

"I'd offer you a drink, but I don't have anything here," Dev said as they went back to the living area.

"Come back to my place for a drink. I promise to behave myself. At least I promise to *try* to behave myself."

"I really shouldn't leave him again," Dev said, knowing it was a lame excuse. Kat was the doctor, after all. The truth was that she wanted to go back to Kat's.

"Bring him."

"What about Buddy?"

"Believe it or not, Buddy loves cats."

"For dinner?" Dev smiled when Kat shook her head at the attempted humor.

"I'll go walk Buddy, and you can get Baxter ready," Kat said without waiting for an answer.

Fifteen minutes later, they were sitting on the couch once again, and Buddy was on a chair looking down into the box that contained the kitten, whining his displeasure at not being able to play with his new friend.

"They'll be fine," Kat said when she saw how nervous she was about Baxter. "I had a really good time tonight, Dev."

"So did I," Dev said distractedly. When she felt Kat's fingers moving slowly along her forearm, she finally looked away from the animals and gave Kat her full attention. She made the decision to bring something up that Kat had merely touched upon over dinner. Dev was aware it was a sensitive subject, but she really wanted to know. "Tell me what happened with your parents."

"Oh God," she said with an exaggerated groan. "Do we have to talk about them?"

"No, we don't have to, but I would like to hear about it," Dev said. Kat moved closer to her, and Dev automatically put an arm around her as Kat rested her head on Dev's shoulder. Dev smiled at the realization that this was becoming a comfortable position for both of them.

"They were none too happy when I ended up pregnant at seventeen," Kat began with a humorless laugh. "They were even less thrilled when I ended up divorced less than two years later and told them I was moving in with another woman. For all intents and purposes, I haven't seen or talked to them since Vanessa's first birthday. I was living in California with Paula, and when she died, I ended up moving back here. My brother is the only one I could talk to about all of it, other than Nessa."

Dev said nothing, sensing that Kat was gathering her thoughts. Whether it was something to make her parents sound better or worse, she wasn't quite sure.

"My grandmother died a couple of years ago," Kat said after a moment. "I guess they didn't expect me to show up at the hospital, because I always did everything I could to avoid them. I will never forget the look on my mother's face or the ugliness in her voice when she said, *What the hell are you doing here?*"

"Damn, that's harsh," Dev said quietly.

"Well, I ended up having the last laugh," Kat said. At the time, she had wanted nothing more than to strangle her mother. Time had created a buffer so that she could recount it without feeling anything. "My grandmother left me this house in her will. They still haven't gotten over that."

"So you own this house free and clear?" Dev asked.

"This and the veterinary clinic," Kat said. "My parents were pissed at me because not only did I *choose* to be a lesbian, but they gave Nessa's father and me a house as a wedding present. When we divorced, I sold it and split the money with him. I didn't see any reason to give them the money, because it *was* a gift. I used that money to go to veterinary school and to start investing in real estate."

"How much property do you own?" Dev asked warily, wondering if perhaps she hadn't gone and gotten herself involved with the female version of Donald Trump.

"Well, I own two apartment complexes," Kat said slowly. "I also own a couple of houses that I rent out. Paula and I used to buy houses and fix them up to resell for a profit. I stopped doing that when she got sick, because there just wasn't enough time to devote to what needed to get done. Other than the veterinary clinic and this house, all the property I own is in California."

"So, how much money do you have exactly?" Dev asked, and then she laughed out loud. "I'm sorry—I know better than to ask a woman her age, or how much money she has, and I believe I've now asked you both questions in the span of about six hours."

"I have enough that I don't *have* to work," Kat said. If this thing with Devon was going to work out, she wanted to know that Dev was with her for her, and not for her money. "I only work at the clinic three days a week. I do that because I love animals, and I couldn't imagine not doing it. I also have enough that I don't really need to worry too much about the future. But since you just got a tidy sum from Rhonda and Chris, I'm guessing that you don't want me for my money."

"Whatever money you may or may not have has never entered my mind. Jesus, I just realized that my landlord wants to sleep with me," Dev said with a laugh, willingly changing the subject.

"Speaking of that," Kat said as she pulled away from Dev and sat up. She wanted to see Dev's face when she confessed something she'd been worrying about all evening. "I should probably tell you that Paula is the only woman I've ever been with."

"I kind of figured that," Dev said. "I sort of did the math as you were telling me about her earlier. So, am I right in assuming that you've only been intimate with two people in your life?"

"Yes," Kat answered sheepishly. "Does that bother you?"

"No, actually, it's kind of a relief. I won't have too much to live up to. I could be really bad, and you wouldn't know any better."

"Trust me, I'd know," Kat said with a sly smile.

"Why me?" Dev asked once again, turning serious as she

took Kat's hand. She watched as their fingers entwined, marveling at how right it felt to hold her hand while they talked. It did not escape her notice that Kat had never answered this question earlier. "After all this time, what makes you think I'm the one you want to take this step with?"

"Honestly, I can't explain it. I've been wondering that myself for the last couple of days, and I can't come up with anything other than the fact that you stir things in me that no one else has been able to." She watched in amazement as Dev's eyes turned the color of the sea at night. "I've felt dead for so long, and here you are, able to make me feel alive without even trying. I want you, Dev, and I can see by the way you look at me that you want me too."

"I do," Dev said. "You have no idea just how much I want you. I still think we should wait, though."

"Can I just tell you that you scare the hell out of me?"

"Why is that?"

"There are women I've known for months, and some for years," Kat said as she studied Dev's face. "More than one of them have made it perfectly clear that they would like to sleep with me, but I've turned them all down. Then, just a few days ago, you walk into my life, and I can't seem to get you out of my head. I have *never* made the first move with anybody, and I feel like I'm throwing myself at you, but I can't seem to help myself. In all honesty, I've never understood the casual sex thing, but if you were to tell me that a one-night stand was all you wanted from me, I'd probably drag you upstairs right this minute."

Dev had no clue what to say in response to that. Kat was incredibly beautiful, and it was definitely not like Dev to turn down an open invitation for a night of pleasure. The problem was, since Jo died, her one-night stands had been all about trying to forget the pain she was dealing with. With Kat though, she actually wanted—no, *needed*—to really *feel* again. Dev knew instinctually that Kat wouldn't want her to forget Jo, just as she would never expect Kat to forget Paula.

"You scare me just a little bit too." Dev rested her forearms on her knees. "The way I feel about you is so totally foreign to me, Kat. I'm having the same problem of not being able to get you out of my head. There wasn't anyone I was serious about before Jo, and there hasn't been anyone since. I can't explain the way I'm feeling, but then again, maybe I don't want to." She turned her head so she could look at Kat, who was watching her intently. "I think I kind of like feeling as though I have something to look forward to with you."

"Me too," Kat said, sounding a little choked up as she reached out to brush a lock of hair from Dev's forehead. Kat let her hand linger for a moment on Dev's cheek, and Dev turned her head to press her lips to Kat's palm.

"You are so beautiful," she whispered. She knew if she didn't put an end to this moment, she'd be the one dragging Kat upstairs. "I should go. It's getting pretty late."

"Okay," Kat said, looking at her feet for a moment. She stood and walked with Dev to get the box where Baxter was sleeping soundly under Buddy's watchful eye. "Dev?"

The tone of Kat's voice made Devon stop and turn, only to be met with a palm squarely in the center of her chest. Dev raised her hand to cover it as she waited for Kat to say what she had to say.

"Stay with me tonight," she whispered. "No sex. We can even leave our clothes on. I just have this incredible need to fall asleep with you next to me. I promise to behave myself."

"I'm not so sure that I can make that promise, Kat," Dev said with a slight smile and a shake of her head. It was becoming increasingly difficult to think rationally with Kat's hand on her chest, but she made no attempt to move it.

"Would that really be so bad?" Kat asked, her voice low and seductive.

"It might be." Dev's hands went to Kat's hips, but she resisted the urge to pull her closer. Kat, however, slid her hand up to Dev's shoulder and closed the gap on her own. "But honestly, at this moment, I can't think of a single reason *why* it would be bad."

"Then you'll stay?" Kat asked hopefully as she slid both arms around Dev's neck. There was no mistaking that Dev's heart was beating just as wildly as hers.

"Yes, but only because Baxter is sound asleep, and I don't want to wake him up," Dev said, trying to inject some levity into the situation. Her eyes closed when Kat's hand moved up her neck and into her hair, pulling her closer for a kiss. When Dev finally pulled away, she was breathing heavily. "Damn, Kat, you have no idea what you do to me."

"I think I have a pretty good idea," Kat said, her own breath ragged. She tried to ignore the insistent throbbing between her legs as she turned and led Dev up the stairs to her bedroom.

❖

Dev awoke the next morning to the feel of a cold, wet nose sniffing rather energetically in her ear. She raised her hand absently to wipe away the offender, and was rewarded with a sloppy tongue on her neck. Buddy was sitting on the bed staring at her when she opened her eyes to unfamiliar surroundings. She stared back defiantly as he cocked his head to one side and lifted his ears slightly. If she didn't know better, she would have thought he was smiling at her.

"I am so not a dog person," Dev said under her breath, but the admission only seemed to excite Buddy, who whipped his tail back and forth on the mattress as he covered her face in doggy kisses.

"Neither am I, really." Dev rolled over to look at Kat, who was propped on one elbow looking at her. "Just don't tell him that. I much prefer cats."

"Good morning," Dev said. She glanced down to take a quick inventory of her clothing. It was all still there, and still intact. Kat had kept her word about behaving herself, and Dev felt an involuntary pang of regret. *Nothing was stopping me from making a move, though. What the hell am I doing?*

"Good morning. Did you sleep all right?"

"Not really." Dev sat up and swung her legs over the edge of the bed and ran a hand quickly through her hair. "I think I woke up every time you moved. I guess I'm just not used to sleeping with someone else in the bed anymore."

"Neither am I, but I have to admit that I slept better last night than I have in a very long time." Kat got out of bed and motioned for Buddy to get down. He ran back out the door, no doubt on his way to check on his new friend, who was still in the box downstairs in the living room. "Thank you for staying here last night. I have to tell you, though, it wasn't easy to keep my hands to myself."

"I know what you mean." She walked over to Kat and slid her arms around her from behind. Kat leaned back against her and rested her head on Dev's shoulder. Dev couldn't resist the exposed neck, and leaned down to kiss her where her pulse was beating erratically. Before things moved any further, Dev took a step backward—holding Kat was beginning to feel almost *too* good. "So...why do you have a dog if you prefer cats?"

"Smooth," Kat said, stifling a laugh. She watched as Dev took a seat on the edge of the bed to pull her socks on. "His owners wanted me to put Buddy to sleep because he was too wild for their young children. He was just a pup—not even eight months old. I never understood people who get puppies like that and then expect them to behave like they're fully grown and completely trained animals. I decided to take him in, and he's kind of grown on me since then."

"You're just a big softie, aren't you?" She looked into Kat's face as Kat took a seat next to her and reaching out to rest a hand on Kat's thigh. "I should really be getting home."

"Why?" Kat asked. She held Dev's gaze as she waited for her to answer the simple question. She was sure the desire she saw in Dev's eyes mirrored her own. She was also sure she had never seen anything quite so sexy. It caused her pulse to quicken even more.

"Because if I stay here much longer, I may just forget why it was I wanted to take things slow with you," Dev said.

"I wouldn't mind."

Dev held her breath for a moment, wondering how in the world she could even begin to explain all that she was feeling. After a moment, she took Kat's hand and focused on it as she tried to express herself.

"I love this feeling—the anticipation, the way my heart speeds up whenever you look at me, the wanting that is so deep in my being that it's almost a tangible presence." Dev ran her thumb gently along Kat's forearm.

"Go on," Kat said, her voice almost a whisper.

"Since Jo, all I've wanted was a quick fuck with someone I knew I'd never see again," she said, silently cursing herself for the tears she felt threatening, but she never looked away from Kat's face. "And then I met you. Now it's suddenly like the rules changed on me overnight. I can't seem to think straight, and when you touch me, I feel as though I might actually melt. It's like you've reached deep inside me and latched on to everything about me. I really don't know how to explain it."

"I think you're doing a pretty good job," Kat said, reaching up to draw a finger along the outline of Dev's jaw. Dev closed her eyes for a moment before putting a hand on Kat's wrist and pulling it away.

"Knowing you want me just as much as I want you only makes the anticipation that much sweeter," Dev said. "The reasons I gave you for wanting to wait are valid—I honestly don't think we would be alone at this point. But I also feel like there's something different about you—something special. I really want to get to know you better."

"So do I."

Dev was amazed at how comfortable she was with Kat. She felt like she could be herself, and after Kat had opened up to her

about what had happened to Paula, she felt that it was time to tell
her own story. She'd never talked about that night, and she took
a deep breath to settle her nerves before she began.

"Jo had been in Baltimore that night for an opening of a
group show that she had a couple of pieces in," Dev said slowly.
She took another deep breath and forced herself to continue.
"She was supposed to spend the night there, but the next day was
our anniversary, and she wanted to come home. I went to bed
knowing that she would be there with me when I awoke in the
morning."

"Dev…" Kat began when she saw the tears welling up in her
eyes. Dev just shook her head.

"You asked me about it the other day, and I ignored it. Please,
just let me finish, because I want to tell you," she said as she met
Kat's concerned look. She glanced down at her tightly clasped
hands, not surprised at all that she wanted to share this with Kat.
"She was almost home. In fact, she'd started onto the off-ramp of
our exit. She was going about five miles over the speed limit, but
the drunk guy who decided to drive onto the freeway going the
wrong way was doing about sixty when they hit head-on."

"Oh, Jesus," Kat murmured under her breath.

"They told me that *he* died instantly," Dev said. If she didn't
finish this now, she might never do it, and she knew she needed
this. It was time to talk about it. "Jo, however, was in critical
condition, totally unresponsive when the medics arrived on the
scene. She had her seat belt on, but it malfunctioned somehow,
and her head went right through the windshield. The engine had
been pushed back into the front seat, and her legs were crushed.
The airbags deployed but were pretty much useless in the impact.
They had to use the Jaws of Life to get her out of the car, and a
helicopter took her to the hospital. She'd been there for about
half an hour before they called me, but my decision to stop
treatment was nothing more than a technicality really. There
wasn't anything they could do for her. She'd lost so much blood

at the scene—they were lucky they even got her stabilized for the helicopter ride."

"I am so sorry," Kat said, and Dev looked up to see tears in her eyes. Dev gently brushed them away with her thumb. Kat laughed shakily. "You shouldn't be comforting me."

"I don't need to be comforted," Dev said, her voice almost a whisper. "I came back here because I need to face what happened, and I've finally realized that I can't change any of it, as much as I may want to. I know that Jo isn't coming back—and neither is our baby."

Kat just stared at her for a moment, obviously letting the words fully sink in. "She was pregnant?"

"Seven months." Dev took a deep shuddering breath before she trusted herself to speak again. "I think that was probably the only reason they tried to save Jo in the first place. They were able to deliver the baby by c-section before I got to the hospital, but she'd been gravely injured in the accident too. I had to make the decision to end treatment for both of them."

"Jesus, I don't know what to say." Kat shook her head in disbelief. She took Dev's hand, watching as their fingers entwined. "I just can't imagine what you must have gone through."

They were both silent for a few long moments, and Dev found herself wanting to take Kat in her arms. The feel of Kat's hand in hers sent a tingle down her spine. Dev squeezed her hand gently, causing Kat to look up at her.

"It's okay. It was three years ago, and while I don't think I'll ever completely get over it, I think I'm finally moving beyond it. Sorry to bring up something so heavy so early. I've certainly gotten the day off to a great start, haven't I?"

"I'm glad you shared this with me." Kat squeezed her hand gently. "I'm glad you feel comfortable enough to share it."

"You're very easy to talk to." Dev leaned over, intending to kiss Kat's cheek, but Kat turned her head so that their lips met briefly instead. "And very easy to kiss too."

"You are so incredibly sexy."

"You keep saying things like that," Dev warned with a sly smile, "and I might just change my mind tomorrow about waiting."

"Or tonight?" Kat asked hopefully, a seductive smile playing at the corners of her mouth.

"Maybe," Dev said in a moment of weakness.

"Mmm," Kat murmured. "Something to look forward to."

"Wait, did I miss something?" Dev asked. "What's tonight?"

"You're going to cook dinner for me," Kat said with a grin. "Did I forget to tell you?"

"Yeah." *Jesus, I can't cook. I hope to God that Sheila can help me out.* "I hope you like stew out of a can."

CHAPTER TWELVE

Dev was worried about what she had gotten herself into. Rhonda and Chris would be there when she stopped by to pick up the dinner Sheila had made for Dev and Kat. That alone was enough to cause worry, but as Dev turned onto Sheila's street, she saw Rhonda driving away from Sheila's house, and she did not appear to be very happy. Dev was grateful that her truck was new and therefore unfamiliar to Rhonda, who never gave her a second glance as they drove past each other.

Dev parked in the alley behind Sheila's house and made her way to the back door that led into the kitchen. She shut the door quietly behind her and took a few steps toward the front of the house, but she stopped when she heard Chris and Sheila, who were obviously arguing.

Dev stopped just inside the door, where she couldn't be seen, and listened.

"I really don't need this shit from both of you, Sheila," Chris said.

"Apparently you do. I don't give a good goddamn about what's happened between you and Devon in the past, but it's time for you to let it go. She's made it clear to you that she isn't interested, and you have no right to get pissed off because *I* think that she should start dating again. If you want to vent your anger at someone, then direct it at me. Rhonda isn't stupid, and sooner or later she's going to put two and two together and realize you're in love with Devon. You need to get a grip on things, because if you *ever* hurt either one of my girls, you'll have me to deal with. Do you understand?"

"For your information, I told Devon the other night at the opening that I thought she should start dating again." Devon didn't miss the fact Chris neglected to deny that she was in love with her. She wanted nothing more than to peek around the corner, but somehow she resisted the urge, and simply took a deep breath instead.

"Then what exactly is your problem?"

"I'm just not sure that I can handle seeing Dev with someone new. It would be like she was cheating on Jo."

Dev clapped a hand over her mouth to stifle the sarcastic laugh that wanted to escape. *You couldn't even stand to see me with your sister, you lying bitch. Just tell Sheila that the reason is because* you *want to be with me.*

"Don't you want to see her happy?"

"Of course I do, Sheila, but seeing her happy with someone other than Jo would be a little unsettling."

Dev hurried to the refrigerator and opened it when she heard the floorboards creak, indicating that someone was walking through the dining room toward her. She pulled out a soda and shut the door just as Chris entered the kitchen.

"Jesus…" Chris about jumped out of her skin at the sight of her.

"Hey, Chris." Dev forced a smile and tried to act nonchalant as she opened the can and took a long drink.

"How long have you been in here listening?"

"I don't know what you're talking about." Dev smiled at Sheila, who stepped in behind Chris, and then she pointed at the back door. "I've told you before not to leave this door unlocked, Sheila. You don't live in the nicest of neighborhoods."

"I've lived here for forty-five years, Devon," Sheila said with a dismissive wave. "It's a little late to be expecting me to change my ways now, don't you think?"

Dev didn't answer, but glanced at Chris briefly before turning her attention back to Sheila, who was putting the dinner that she'd made in a plastic shopping bag.

"Thanks for this, Sheila." If she hadn't cooked for her, Dev really would have had to make stew out of a can for Kat. Or maybe one of those horrid frozen meals. Not exactly romantic.

"Here's some fresh bread, and a nice bottle of red wine." Sheila finished packing up all of the food and placed it on the counter next to Dev.

"Got a hot date tonight?" Chris asked.

"I've told you before that my personal life is none of your concern, Chris."

"Just trying to be friendly." Chris held up her hands defensively.

"I'd like to believe you, but there's too much history between us for that." Dev crossed her arms and leaned against the counter. She could tell Chris wanted to say something, but it was obvious she wasn't in the mood to deal with Sheila anymore.

"I'm going for a walk," Chris said after a moment. Neither Dev nor Sheila made any attempt to stop her, and she slammed out the back door.

"Where's Rhonda?" Dev asked when she was gone.

"She went to the store to get Chris some beer." Sheila shook her head before opening the oven and checking on her own dinner. "I wish she'd stop running around doing everything for that woman. Chris takes advantage of her."

"I should probably get home." Dev turned to pick up the bag, not wanting to get into Rhonda and Chris's drama, but Sheila stopped her.

"I think you should bring Katherine to Rhonda's birthday celebration."

"Excuse me?" Dev realized this was what they had been arguing about. "Did you tell Rhonda about this plan of yours?"

"Yes, and she didn't seem too happy about it." Sheila shut the oven door and turned to look at Dev. "She wasn't nearly as upset about it as Chris was, though. Why do you suppose Rhonda wouldn't want you seeing Katherine Hunter?"

"She thinks I'm a bad influence."

"Honey, it doesn't matter what the hell anyone else thinks. Maybe all you need is to find someone who's a good influence on *you*. Like Jo was. Personally, I think Katherine may be just what you need, and I want you to bring her."

❖

"Hey," Dev said as she opened the door for Kat that evening. She silently said a thank-you once again to whatever higher power was listening that Sheila had cooked a meat loaf for her to present to Kat as her own. As Kat stepped inside, she handed Dev a bottle of red wine.

"Hey yourself," Kat said. When Dev closed the door, Kat was waiting as she turned around, and she slipped her arms easily around Dev's waist. Her heart sped up as her lips touched Dev's, and she let out an involuntary moan. She broke the kiss and leaned her forehead against Dev's. "Oh. My. God."

"Something wrong?" Dev asked with a grin as she pulled Kat closer with one arm.

"Absolutely not," Kat said with a chuckle. She had to summon every ounce of willpower she possessed to pull away from Dev. "It's just a little scary that you seem to be able to awaken every nerve in my body with a simple kiss. It's nice, but it's a bit frightening as well."

"Then perhaps I should stop kissing you."

"Don't you dare." Kat kissed her again, and this time it was Dev who moaned and pulled away. Kat grinned. "Looks like you may be having a bit of a problem in that area yourself."

"Maybe a little," Dev said sheepishly as she stepped away and shook her head in an attempt to clear it. She took a deep breath before walking into the kitchen and opening the wine.

"Dinner smells wonderful."

"I hope you like it," Dev said. She poured them each a glass and handed Kat one as she took a seat next to her. Dev thought about Sheila's invitation to Rhonda's party. It might be nice to have Kat along—not just because she was really enjoying spending time with her, but because maybe then Chris would get the message. She turned so she was facing Kat. "What are you doing Friday night?"

"Nothing. Why? What did you have in mind?"

"It's Rhonda's fiftieth birthday," Dev said as she took Kat's hand. "A friend of mine owns the bar we met at the other night, and Sheila's made arrangements to have a little get-together there. I'd really like it if you could join us."

Kat hesitated for a moment, not because she didn't want to spend the evening with Dev, but because she wasn't sure she wanted to be around Chris. The bitterness in the air between the two of them was almost palpable, and it amazed Kat that Rhonda had never noticed it. It irritated Kat no end that Chris had come on to her about six months earlier, but she liked Rhonda, so she had kept her mouth shut about it. No doubt it would be a mistake to bring the subject up with Dev too, given the animosity she obviously felt toward her late partner's sister.

"Is there a problem?" Dev asked.

"Not at all," Kat said with a quick squeeze of her hand. "Who else is going to be there?"

"Rhonda and Chris, obviously," Dev answered as the oven timer went off. She stood and continued talking over her shoulder as she tended to their dinner. "Me, Sheila, hopefully you, and I'm not really sure who else. I hate to admit that once Rhonda got involved with Chris, she kind of lost touch with a lot of her friends." She turned to face Kat, who was still sitting on the couch, and motioned to the meat loaf on the counter in front of her. "Come on, let's eat."

❖

After dinner they returned to the couch, and Kat settled close to Dev, her head on Dev's shoulder and a hand resting lightly on Dev's thigh. Dev sighed with satisfaction as she put an arm around Kat's shoulders and ran her fingers absently up and down her upper arm. It had never even occurred to her that she could be happy in another woman's arms. It made her feel a little guilty—almost as if she were cheating on Jo—but she knew that Jo wouldn't have wanted her to go on the way she had been for the past few years. It really was time to move on.

They sat in comfortable silence for a few minutes, and Kat was enjoying just being with Dev. She felt utterly content. It felt *right* to be in her arms, and she wasn't quite sure why. They really didn't know each other very well, and Kat had always assumed that if she did find someone she wanted to be intimate with, it would certainly be someone she had known for more than a few days.

Sometime between the moment Dev had arrived the night before and the time she had asked her to stay the night, Kat had come to the realization that she was not just looking for a substitute for Paula. Paula would always be in her heart, and she believed that Devon understood that. It seemed important that she did understand that.

"Dev?" she asked quietly. She'd suddenly decided that she wanted to learn more about the mystery that was Devon.

"Mmm?" Dev murmured, rudely pulled back from the thoughts of what it would be like to wake up with Kat after a night of passion.

"What happened to your parents?" Kat asked. When Dev tensed, Kat sat up and looked at her with concern. "I'm sorry…I didn't mean to…"

"No, it's okay," Dev said. God, had it really been almost thirty years since her mother died? There were times—times like this—when it seemed as if it were just yesterday. She hadn't thought she was ever going to be able to get the picture of her dead mother out of her head. Dev took a deep breath before lifting the wineglass to her lips. "I never knew my father. She told me he died before I was born. I found out when I was fifteen that she had lied to me. Sheila told me he was alive and said she would give me his name if I ever wanted to track him down. She also let me know he didn't want to see me."

"So did you ever find out who he is?" Kat asked in disbelief. It was one thing for your parents to reject you, like hers had, but how must it feel to know that your own father didn't even want to meet you?

"No. It was obvious that there was no room for me in his life," Dev answered solemnly. She couldn't help the sarcastic grin that tugged at her lips. "I was fifteen, and I knew all there was to know in the world. For instance, I knew that if I were to track him down, it wouldn't have made one bit of difference in my life. A couple of years after I met Jo, Sheila told me that he had died. I think it was a drug overdose."

"Jesus," Kat murmured.

"Now, my mother…" Dev let out a short laugh and shook her head as she took Kat's hand and held it in her lap. "She had some serious mental problems. She was what they term now as bipolar, but I didn't really have a name for it back then—other than crazy. She committed suicide when I was ten. It just so happened that I'd been the one that found her, but I think she'd assumed it would be my older brother David. He was supposed to take her to the doctor that afternoon, but he had car problems, and he tried to call to let her know he wouldn't make it."

"You were only ten?" Kat asked, appalled that a child would be forced to deal with something so incredibly horrific. Dev only nodded her response, and Kat reached out with her free hand to stroke Dev's cheek with the backs of her fingers. "My God, Devon. What did you do?"

"I called David, because I didn't quite know what else to do," Dev said as she leaned into the touch. "He took care of calling the police and getting the body removed from the house, and he was the one who called Sheila, because he didn't know what else to do with me. He was fifteen years older than me, and he'd just gotten married. They had a baby on the way, and he'd just started a new job. It wasn't so much that they didn't want to take me in, but with everything else in his life, he just couldn't be faced with an instant family. I think I resented that for a short period of time, but we're pretty close now. In fact, I spent some of the past three years with him and his wife in Oregon. Sheila was my godmother, and she didn't hesitate to accept me into her home. I've often wondered how I would have turned out if it wasn't for her and Rhonda keeping me in line."

"I'm so glad they were there for you, Devon," Kat said. "I can't imagine going through something like that *now,* much less when I was that young."

"She hanged herself in the kitchen," Dev went on, sensing that Kat was curious but would have never asked specifically. Dev laughed without humor and shook her head. "I was so scared when I saw her there that I peed my pants."

"Baby, you don't have to tell me all of this," Kat said softly. "I'm so sorry I even asked about it."

"Don't be," Dev said. She felt goose bumps rise on her arms at the term of endearment that Kat didn't seem to realize that she'd used. "You know, most of the time, it really seems as though it happened in another lifetime. It's all a part of that past that I know I can't change. It's time for me to look forward now."

"You truly are amazing, do you know that?" Kat asked, seeing the pain in Dev's eyes, but respecting her enough to not press the issue.

"If you keep telling me things like that," she said, placing a hand on Kat's thigh, "I may just start to believe it."

"I meant it," Kat said. They gazed silently at one another, and Kat was a bit surprised to feel her pulse quicken from the need in Dev's intense gaze. She knew if she didn't look away, they would both be in serious trouble. "I should go. I need to walk Buddy, and I'm afraid that if I sit here with you much longer, I may try to talk you into taking me to your bed."

"Okay," Dev said slowly, wondering if that would really be so bad. But she had been the one who wanted to take things slow, and she reminded herself that Kat was simply adhering to her ground rules. Besides, after what they had just talked about, it didn't seem to be the right time. She stood and walked Kat the short distance to the door. "I'm not sure you ever answered me about Friday night."

"I would love to go with you," Kat said as she turned to face Dev. "I have to go with Nessa to the doctor in the afternoon, but I'll call you when I get home, all right?"

"I can't wait," Dev said, her throat constricted with desire that she was finding increasingly difficult to control. She touched Kat's cheek gently as she leaned in to kiss her good night.

Chapter Thirteen

The first thing Dev noticed as they walked into the bar was Chris standing by the front door, looking for all the world like she was waiting for them. Dev took Kat by the elbow and walked past her just as if she hadn't even seen her standing there. She guided Kat to the table where Sheila, Rhonda, and a couple of Rhonda's friends were seated.

"Kat, I'm so glad you could make it," Sheila said, aiming a smile and a knowing wink in Dev's direction.

"What's up with Chris?" Kat asked as they removed their jackets and hung them on the backs of their chairs. She smiled when Dev held her chair out for her. *And they say chivalry is dead. Obviously* they've *never met Devon Conway.*

"She's sulking," Rhonda said dismissively. "So, are you two seeing each other?"

"Ooh, so subtle, Rhonda," one of the other women at the table said. Kat felt the hair on the back of her neck stand up at the open appraisal she gave Dev. Kat reached over and placed her hand on top of Dev's, on the table top in clear view.

"Yes, we are," Kat said without giving Dev a chance to respond.

Dev's thighs clenched at Kat's possessive gesture. *How fucking hot.* She hadn't missed the look she'd been receiving from Rhonda's friend. Obviously Kat hadn't missed it either.

She turned her hand over and laced her fingers through Kat's, squeezing gently to let her know she was okay with it.

"Too bad."

"Katherine and Devon, these are my friends Mary and Tammy." Rhonda gave her overzealous friend a shove. "In spite of what it may look like, they are in a relationship."

"An *open* relationship," Mary said, holding a hand out to Dev in greeting.

"It's nice to meet you," Dev said amiably as she took the hand very briefly to avoid being rude. "And for the record...I don't play that way."

"What a shame," Tammy said. She seemed to be more taken with Kat, and Dev couldn't help her own spark of jealousy that flared up.

This is so not going to be a comfortable evening.

"Something to drink?" Dev turned her full attention to her date.

"Wine would be nice."

Dev asked the rest of the table if they needed anything and then turned to walk toward the bar. Kat watched her silently and didn't even notice when someone took the chair next to her.

"What are you doing here with her?" Laura asked, pulling Kat out of her fantasies.

Kat turned to look at her. "Excuse me?" she asked.

"Devon," Laura said, indicating who she was talking about with a tilt of her chin toward the bar. "How do you know her?"

"She lives in the apartment above my garage," Kat said, wondering why she sounded so defensive. She turned her body to face Laura. "How do *you* know her?"

"I took her home with me on Saturday night," Laura answered. She finally turned to meet Kat's gaze. "She is one fine piece of ass, Kat. I would never have thought that she'd be your type, though."

The silence that greeted the statement seemed to bring Laura out of her musings. "Oh, shit. She's the one you had a date with the other night."

Kat's head began to swim. Saturday night? The night after they had kissed and discussed the possibility of a second date? *Jesus, how stupid am I? I knew all about her, but I still believed all of the things she said to me. I was never anything more than a conquest to her.*

The room began to swim, and she suddenly felt as though she might be sick.

"Excuse me." Kat stood up and grabbed her coat. She didn't even look back as she walked out the front door. She knew it wouldn't bother Dev—she could just go home with Laura again, if that was what she wanted.

❖

"Devon, honey, you have a real problem," Rhonda said as she quickly walked up to her where she was still waiting for the bartender to get her glasses of wine.

"What?" she asked, turning her head to look at her.

"Kat just stormed out of here."

When Dev turned to look back at the table, she saw Laura sitting where she had been a few moments ago. Her heart dropped when she realized this was the friend Kat had been talking to at the gallery opening. *No wonder there was something familiar about her the night I met her at the bar.*

"Fuck."

"Then you do know her?"

"Yeah," Dev said. She decided to abandon the drinks and head back to the table, but Rhonda grabbed her arm. "I need to go after her."

"I don't think that's a good idea right now," Rhonda said, shaking her head. "Give her a little time to cool off. That woman's name is Laura, and she works for Kat at the clinic. I think I heard her tell Kat that she took you home with her the other night… please tell me I heard it wrong, Devon."

Dev suddenly felt light-headed, and gripped the bar stool beside her to hold herself upright. *Jesus Christ, I am such a fuckup.*

"Damn it," Rhonda said vehemently when Dev didn't answer. "I told you to be careful with Kat, didn't I? You fucked up bad this time, sister."

Dev swung her head around to glare at Rhonda, and the words were right there on the tip of her tongue—*not nearly as bad as when I fucked up with Chris, though. I even had to leave town for three years after that one.* She caught herself before she said anything, and felt Sheila's glare on her back without even looking over.

"Problem?" Sheila asked.

"No, Mom, go back to the table," Rhonda said quietly before returning her attention to Dev. She placed a hand on Dev's forearm as she spoke. "Look, I'm sorry. You don't need this from me right now, do you? I can see that you have feelings for her, and you're right that you need to talk to her, but not tonight. She needs to cool off for a bit."

"So do I." Dev pulled her arm away and headed for the door. She glared at Laura as she walked past the table, grabbing her jacket off the back of the chair without even slowing down.

She spent the next two hours riding around aimlessly on her bike, and when she got home, all of the lights in Kat's house were out. She toyed briefly with the idea of ringing the bell anyway, but in the end walked slowly up the steps to her own dark apartment.

❖

"Devon, there's a customer up front for you."

Devon looked up and saw Rita, her office manager, walking toward her. "He asked to speak to you personally."

"Is there a problem with his bill?" Dev tried to hide her annoyance as she grabbed a shop towel and tried to wipe the grease off her hands. Rita just shrugged, and Dev gave up with the towel because it was obvious she would need some soap to remove the grease. She headed toward the front desk, muttering under her breath as she went. Her steps faltered when she saw Rick Hunter waiting for her, but she recovered quickly as she forced herself to smile. "Hi, Rick. Is there some problem?"

"No, I just wanted to thank you for fixing the car. My wife picked it up yesterday, and it runs like a dream now." He held a hand out to shake hers, and Dev unconsciously wiped her palm on her work pants before gripping his tightly.

"Well, there is a reason they tell you to change the oil every three thousand miles."

"I'm a salesman," he said with a shrug. "Sometimes I can drive three thousand miles in a month, and it doesn't always occur to me to get the oil changed."

"That's why we put the little reminder sticker in the window." Dev didn't want to be having this conversation with him. She wanted to ask him how Kat was doing. She hadn't seen or spoken to her in almost three weeks, and it was driving her crazy. Kat was never home, and Dev hadn't felt right calling her to talk about what had happened. Kat had even come by to pick up her car on the day Dev was off.

"I wanted to talk to you about something else." Rick motioned for her to follow him outside, which Dev did after a quick glance over her shoulder into the garage area. "Kat told me that the two of you have been seeing each other. You have no idea how happy that makes me. When Paula died, she just closed up emotionally, and I had no idea what to do for her. My wife tried setting her up on a blind date or two, but they never worked out. I think that she was looking for that same instant connection that she felt with Paula. I'm glad she finally found it."

Dev didn't know what to say. She cleared her throat and shook her head as she found herself studying her filthy hands.

Obviously Kat hadn't told him about what had happened that night at Rhonda's birthday. For some reason Dev didn't want to tell him either. Maybe if she didn't say it out loud, it wouldn't be true. She forced herself to look at him and tried not to sound anxious when she spoke.

"Have you talked to Kat lately?" she asked.

"Not in a couple of weeks. I assumed that she was just busy, you know, spending time with you." He suddenly looked concerned. "Why? Is something wrong?"

"No." Dev shook her head and forced a laugh, hoping to ease his concern. "Everything's fine. I keep telling her she should call you. Family's important to her."

"I'm sure that I'll talk to her soon." Rick glanced at his watch. "I need to run, but the two of you should come over for dinner sometime. I'll have Barb give Kat a call and work it all out."

"Great," Dev said to his retreating back. *Fuck. What the hell am I going to do now?*

❖

The next few days crawled by for Dev, and she still hadn't even seen Kat. She was always gone in the mornings before Dev awoke and wasn't ever home in the evenings. The pain was tearing Dev up inside, and she didn't know how to deal with it. She'd only left the apartment to go to work and was hoping against hope that Kat would come to see her.

She'd refused to answer her phone—thank God for caller ID on the cellular—preferring to simply wallow in her own self-pity. She'd screwed up, and she had no idea of how to fix things, or if it was even possible to do so.

She was lying in bed trying in vain to get some much-needed sleep on a rare day off when there was a loud banging on her front door. She tried to ignore it, but it soon became evident that it wasn't going to stop any time soon.

"I'm coming!" she yelled as she pulled on a pair of sweatpants and a T-shirt. Actually, it surprised her that it had taken this long for someone to come and try to physically pull her out of her self-pity party. *They're just lucky I'm not going to work,* she thought as she glanced at the clock in the kitchen on her way past. She unlocked the deadbolt and yanked the door open. "What the hell do you want?"

Dev shut up when she saw Rick standing at the door. She noticed that he was holding the hand of a very young child. Dev's best guess put her at around four years old. She blinked in surprise, and then she felt her cheeks flush.

"I'm sorry," she said to Rick as she motioned them inside.

"I think I'd probably have the same reaction to being awakened at six in the morning," he said with a slight grin. "Don't worry about it."

"I don't mean to sound rude, but why are you here?" Dev asked. She went to the kitchen and started the coffeemaker as Rick and his daughter took a seat on the couch.

"Well, honestly, I should be the one apologizing," he said with a shrug. "My wife is out of town for a conference, and I've been called to go to our office in Philadelphia today. I tried to call Kat to see if she could take care of Grace today, and when she didn't answer, I drove over hoping I could catch her at home."

"She's not there?" Dev asked in obvious surprise. She looked at the clock again, as if it would have changed drastically from the last time she looked about ninety seconds earlier.

"No, she must have gotten called in for an emergency. I'm in a bind, Devon. Would it be possible for you to take care of her until Kat gets home?"

Dev panicked. Yes, she and Jo had been about to have a baby of their own, but she had secretly harbored the fear all through the pregnancy that she would be horrible with a child. She shook her head slowly.

"Trust me, I know that deer in the headlights look," Rick said with a chuckle. "She's really very well behaved. All you have to do is set her in front of the television with a DVD and it'll be like she isn't even there. I wouldn't ask if I didn't really need your help."

At least he didn't say that he wouldn't ask if he wasn't desperate. Nothing like being told that you're someone's last choice. This was crazy. What if Kat ended up being gone all day? How the hell would she be able to entertain a small child for that long?

"I don't have any DVDs that would be appropriate for her," Dev said, knowing it was a lame excuse, but hey, she was grasping at straws.

"Kat has a whole cabinet of them. I'm sure she wouldn't mind if you took Grace into the house," he said as he stood and looked at his watch. "I'm supposed to be there by eight."

"I don't have a key to the house," Dev said. She was losing this halfhearted argument, and she knew it.

"I do." He took the key off his key ring and handed it to her.

Dev knew this was wrong on so many levels, but what was she supposed to do? Rick was practically begging her to help him out. Kat would probably be more angry if she were to refuse him. She finally agreed, and she didn't have a clue how to respond when he hugged her to relay his thanks. When he was gone, she looked at the little girl who was sitting on her couch watching her warily.

"Well, Grace," she said with a sigh. "My name is Devon. Did you eat breakfast yet?"

Grace shook her head, and Dev turned to go into the kitchen. *This is going to be a disaster, I just know it.*

❖

When Kat finally walked in through her front door around noon that day, she hesitated when she went to push it closed because she heard the television in the living room. *What the hell? I didn't even turn it on this morning.* She walked slowly into the entryway and peeked cautiously around the corner. When she saw Devon sitting there drinking a soda and eating potato chips, her first reaction was to smile. Her second reaction was not nearly as amiable.

"What the hell are you doing in my house, and how in God's name did you get in here?" she asked as she stalked toward the couch. When Dev opened her mouth to answer, Kat held up her hand and shook her head vehemently. "No, never mind. I don't want to know," she said, her hands firmly on her hips. *The nerve of Devon, thinking that she could just let herself in without even asking.* Kat felt the heat rise up her neck and into her cheeks. She tried not to think about how vulnerable Devon looked as she stood above her. "Just leave, and I *do not* want you in my house again without permission."

Dev sat there unmoving for a moment as she tried to quell the anger rapidly rising inside her. After a moment, she got to her feet and walked the two steps that separated her and Kat, but stopped when Kat steadfastly refused to move out of her way so she could pass between the couch and the coffee table. Dev reached into her pocket and pulled out the house key, which she held out to Kat. She didn't speak until Kat, obviously confused, took it from her.

"This," she said in the calmest voice she could muster, "is Rick's key. Grace is upstairs taking a nap in your room, because when I asked her where she wanted to sleep, that was where she took me." Dev forced her way past Kat, but after taking a few steps toward the front door, she turned and faced her again. Kat was still facing the other way, so Dev spoke to her back. "Tell your brother that the next time he has an emergency and needs a babysitter, to find someone else's door to knock on at six o'clock in the morning."

Without waiting for Kat to respond, Dev turned and stormed out the door, slamming it behind her. Kat stood rooted to her spot for a full minute before everything Dev had said to her really sank in. *Shit, I am such an ass.* She shook her head and turned toward the door, fully intending to go after Dev, but then she remembered that her young niece was upstairs, napping in her bed. Kat cursed herself again as she went upstairs to check on her.

❖

"Jesus, Kat, you really said that to her?" Rick asked when he came to pick Grace up that afternoon.

"You could have called me to let me know." She felt like an ass, and her brother was doing nothing to make her feel any better.

"I thought that the two of you were seeing each other."

"We were—very briefly." Kat sighed. "That ended over two weeks ago."

"I saw her the other day, and she never mentioned that you weren't seeing each other," Rick said, seemingly perplexed. "She didn't mention it this morning either."

"Why would she tell you about it? That should be my job, don't you think?"

"Yeah, I do, so how about you tell me what happened?"

She shook her head and walked into the kitchen to keep him from seeing her tears.

"Kat, talk to me."

"She slept with Laura."

"Have you slept with Dev?" Rick asked.

"What the hell does that have to do with anything?" She glanced over his shoulder and saw that Grace was still enthralled by the DVD she'd put in for her. She lowered her voice anyway. "That sounds like a fucking moronic high school thing to say. If I won't put out, she'll find someone who will?"

"Kat, that's not what I meant, and you know it. Look, you haven't been with anyone since Paula died. I know it can't be easy for you, especially when you finally feel something for someone again. My point is that you just started seeing her. Was there any talk of a commitment between you? Because if there wasn't, then you really need to rethink all of this anger you have toward her."

Kat said nothing. What the hell could she say? It happened the day after they had met. The problem was that Kat wasn't even sure what she was mad about. That first night at the opening wasn't even really a date—they'd both said as much—so what right did she have to feel this way now? She'd put it behind her as far as Laura was concerned—they worked together, for God's sake. Why couldn't she do the same for Devon?

"Personally, I think you're just afraid," Rick said.

"You know what? You need to stop now before you really piss me off."

"Kat, just listen to me." Rick leaned on the counter, a move to let Kat know that he wasn't going anywhere and that she damn well wasn't going to push him around. "Your lover died—not you. You've spent the last five years alone. Now you've met someone who actually makes you *feel* again, and you'd rather stay mad at her than give her the time of day. What are you afraid of? That if you let her in you'll lose her too? What a pathetic way to live, Kat."

He didn't give her a chance to respond, but rather marched out to the living room and gathered up his daughter before walking out the front door. Kat stood in silence for a moment, letting his words sink in. She knew he was right, but what the hell was she going to do about it?

❖

Dev seriously contemplated not answering the door when the knock came at around three that afternoon. She sat stubbornly on the floor of her bedroom, leaning against the bed, her legs stretched out in front of her. She held a loudly purring Baxter in her arms.

"She probably wants to apologize," she said to the cat. Baxter just continued purring happily as he nuzzled his head snugly under Dev's chin. Dev liked the sensation of the cold wet nose on the skin of her neck. "But we don't want to hear it, do we, little man? She's avoided me for nearly two weeks now, and all I've wanted to do is apologize, so now she can just wait and see what it's like for herself."

The knocking continued, but Dev made the decision to stay put. No matter how badly her body betrayed her by wanting to answer the door, she made up her mind and sat there without moving. When the noise finally stopped for a few moments, Dev breathed out a sigh that was part relief and part disappointment. A moment later she heard Kat's voice.

"Devon, I know you're there," she called, and the pain in her voice *almost* caused Dev to give in. Thankfully, Baxter chose that very moment in time to dig his claws into her biceps, effectively bringing her back to reality. "Devon, please answer the door. Please just talk to me."

"Where the hell were you when *I* wanted to talk?" Dev said under her breath. It didn't seem to matter to her that she had never actually knocked on Kat's door—they'd never even been home at the same times. She knew that Kat had been avoiding her, so why should she be willing to talk to her now, just because *she* wanted to talk?

"Fine," Kat said through the door. "I'm making spaghetti for dinner. It will be ready around six. Please just come by. I need to talk to you."

Dev listened carefully, and this time she heard Kat's footsteps retreating down the stairs. She leaned her head back against the mattress, staring blankly at the ceiling.

"Maybe I should call Leigh," she said while Baxter tried to wriggle free of her arms. "She's never failed to give me good advice."

❖

A few of the women in the bar acknowledged her as she made her way through. Dev managed not to get sucked into any conversations and took a seat at the bar. After a few minutes of doing her best to look like someone who had no desire to be bothered, Dev was happy to see Leigh make her way over and place a napkin in front of her.

"Give me a beer, please," Dev said as she reached into her pocket for some money.

"You need to talk?" Leigh put the draft down in front of Dev and absently wiped down the bar next to her.

"What would make you think that I need to talk?" Dev asked curiously, wondering how her old friend had always been able to read her.

"Honey, I've known you for way too many years," Leigh said. "You were never the type to come in just to relax and grab a beer. You were either in the bar to pick someone up for the night, or because you needed to talk. I can't imagine that's changed much, and since you were very adept at sidestepping the women in here tonight, I'd say that you've got a problem. I'm here if you need to talk, all right?"

Dev gave a barely perceptible nod and watched as Leigh made her way to the other end of the bar to get drinks for another customer. She'd known Leigh longer than anyone, other than Rhonda and Sheila, and Leigh probably knew her better than anyone else. She *had* come here to talk to her, after all. Perhaps Leigh's distance from Dev's life lately could add a new perspective to this current dilemma with Kat.

"You're right, Leigh, I do have a problem I need to talk about," Dev said after waiting a few minutes for her to return to her end of the bar. Fearing that if she didn't push ahead she would simply chicken out, she continued without waiting for Leigh to respond. "I think I've met someone that I want to spend more than one night with. The problem is, I think I may have fucked it all up before it had a chance to really develop into something meaningful."

"Katherine Hunter?" Leigh asked with a knowing grin. Dev shook her head in amazement. Leigh simply shrugged. "It's a gift, what can I say?" She topped off Dev's mug of beer and set it in front of her again. "Actually, Rhonda had a little chat with me the other night after the two of you left—separately. She's worried about you."

"No, she's more worried about Kat," Dev said with more sarcasm than she'd intended. "She's warned me twice now to be careful with Kat, and told me in no uncertain terms that she isn't my type."

"I get so tired of people pigeonholing people," Leigh said with a shake of her head. "How the hell does anyone know what someone else's type is? It's a bunch of crock, if you ask me. Personally, I don't think Chris is Rhonda's type, but I'd never tell her that because it's not my place. Rhonda actually told me once that she didn't think Jo was your type. We both know how wrong that was, don't we?"

"With Kat she was just trying to tell me that she wasn't into one-night stands," Dev said as she raised her mug to take a drink of her beer.

"Isn't that something Kat should make a decision about, and not Rhonda?" Leigh asked, holding Devon's gaze. "The last time I looked, Kat was a grown-up. How exactly did you fuck things up, Dev?"

Dev told her the condensed version of the story, and by the time she was done, she had finished her beer and had a full mug in front of her again.

"So you're telling me that you've never spent more than one night with anyone since Jo?" Leigh asked when she was finished with the tale.

"A few hours, really," Dev said. "I haven't wanted any more than that."

"And now you do?"

"Shit, I don't know what I want, Leigh," she said as she

raked her hand through her hair and leaned her elbows on the bar. "A part of me feels like I would be cheating on Jo if I let anyone get close to me. How the hell do I know when it's finally time to let go?"

"It may never be time to let go," Leigh said with a sympathetic shake of her head. "Look, I've never gone through anything like you did, Devon, and I would never dream of insulting you by pretending that I know what you're going through now. That being said, I have known more than a few women who've lost their lovers, and one thing I can tell you is that the grieving process is different for everyone. Some women—they're back out there in a matter of days, or weeks. For others, it can take years. No one can tell you when the time is right for you, Dev. You're the only one who can make that decision."

"Hey, Leigh," called a woman from the other end of the bar. "How about a little service down here?"

"I'll be right back," Leigh told Dev as she turned and walked away.

Rhonda didn't think Jo was my type? That revelation startled Dev, and she came to the realization that she didn't even know what her type was. It was never something she paid attention to. All she knew was that for the past four weeks, the only thing she could think about was Katherine Hunter. Kat had found a way into Dev's heart, and it was pretty evident that she wasn't going to vacate it any time soon.

"Listen," Leigh said when she came back a few minutes later. "Maybe you don't really want an opinion from an old bartender, but if you care about her, you need to tell her. Don't assume that she's a mind reader. And if she finds it in her heart to forgive you for your past indiscretions, then don't you dare do anything to fuck it up again. Go home and talk to her. What's the worst that could happen?"

"She could tell me to go to hell," Dev answered with a chuckle.

"And you wouldn't be any worse off than you are right now, would you?" Leigh reached for the empty mug, but Dev shook her head and passed a twenty across the bar. "I'll get your change."

"Keep it." She stood and pulled her jacket on before reaching across the bar and taking hold of Leigh's hand. "Thank you. I don't think I've ever told you how much I appreciate your friendship, Leigh."

"You just did." Leigh squeezed Dev's hand gently before pulling away. "Now get the hell out of here and go tell her how you feel about her."

Chapter Fourteen

It was just a few minutes past six when Dev finally worked up the nerve to knock on Kat's door.

When Kat finally did open the door, Dev looked up and words failed her. She could feel her mouth trying to form words, but there was no sound coming out. Kat was wearing skintight black slacks with a white silk blouse that enticingly displayed Kat's ample cleavage. It was unbuttoned just a little too far to be considered decent in public. Dev knew she was staring, and there wasn't a damn thing she could do about it.

"Hi," Kat said quietly. She stepped aside to allow Dev entry. When Dev didn't move, she couldn't help the laugh that escaped her as she reached out and grabbed her forearm to pull her inside. "I'd rather not give the neighbors a show."

Dev finally managed to tear her eyes away from Kat's chest and wet her lips as she looked at Kat's face. It became obvious to Dev that this evening was meant to be a seduction, but they really needed to talk. Dev had to get her libido under control, or else she would just drag Kat upstairs to bed. She put her hands between them, but when Kat leaned forward, Dev came to her senses. Instead of covering those enticing breasts with her palms, she shifted slightly so her fingers pulled the blouse closed, and she fastened a couple more of the buttons.

"What are you doing?" Kat asked in bewilderment.

"We need to talk," Dev said resolutely. "And you certainly aren't making it very easy to concentrate."

"We can talk later," Kat said, trying to push Dev's hands away from the buttons, but they weren't budging.

"That night that I went home with Laura..." Dev began as she reached for Kat's hand and tried to pull her toward the couch.

"I really don't want to hear about this," Kat said, pulling her hand away.

"That's too bad, then, because I do want to talk about it." This time Kat acquiesced and allowed Dev to guide her to the couch. "Which means you're going to hear about it, whether you want to or not."

"Fine." Kat folded her arms across her chest and looked straight ahead, the muscle in her jaw bunching spasmodically as she waited for Devon to get it over with. It irked her that the evening was not going the way she had planned. If it had, they'd already be on their way up the stairs.

"I spent that entire day confused as hell about what was going on between us," Dev said, and she finally managed to relax a bit when she saw some of the tension leave Kat's rigid body. "I rode around for hours on my damned bike, thinking about all of the reasons why I'm not good enough for you."

"Devon..." Kat tried to interrupt, but Dev shook her head to stop her.

"I finally came to the conclusion that no matter how many reasons I might be able to come up with, the only thing that really mattered was that I enjoyed spending time with you," Dev said. "I pulled into the driveway, fully intending to come over here and talk to you, but when I got off the bike, you walked outside with a woman who was leaving your house. It looked to me like the two of you were very close."

"That was Laura," Kat said, suddenly realizing the conclusion that Dev must have come to. "Devon, I..."

"No, please just let me finish," Dev said. She shifted so that she was facing Kat, tentatively reaching out and taking her hand. When Kat didn't pull away, Dev gripped it a little tighter and rubbed her thumb along the back of it. "I wasn't in a place where I could see what she looked like. Not long after that, another car pulled into the driveway, and a very pregnant woman went to your door. Again, the two of you seemed to be very close. Honestly, Kat, I didn't know what to think. I had to assume that at least one of them was your girlfriend."

Kat waited patiently, but felt powerless to stop herself as she reached out with her free hand and lightly caressed Dev's cheek.

"My objective that night was to drink myself stupid, and to do my best to forget about you," Dev said quietly. She looked at the hand she still held firmly in her own. "It wasn't working, though. I told you I never saw Laura's face when she left here that night, so when she approached me in the bar, I really didn't know who she was."

"You thought that I had a girlfriend, so you went home with a stranger?" Kat asked.

"I hadn't gone in there intending that," Dev said with a quick shake of her head. She looked up and met Kat's stare, but was surprised at the concern she saw there. She touched the tips of her fingers to Kat's cheekbone. "It was you I wanted to be with, Kat. But I knew if I came back home, I would spend the whole night lying in bed just thinking about you. Laura offered me a distraction, and I took it. It's a horrible excuse, I know, but I can't give you any better." Her voice was barely a whisper as she stared at their hands, cringing at what Kat must think of her.

"You're beautiful when you're flustered, do you know that?" Kat asked with a gentle smile. She brought Dev's hand up and pressed her lips to the palm, lingering for a moment. "Can I ask a few personal questions?"

"Anything."

"How long have you been back in Easton?"

"A little over a month," Dev said, wondering where this was going.

"And how many women have you been with during that time?"

"Two," Dev said without hesitation. She didn't want to lie to Kat—ever. *Christ, I think I'm falling in love with her.* The notion was a bit of a shock, but the rush of warmth that infused her body at the thought was oddly comforting.

"Marie?" Kat asked, remembering the first night they had met. Dev nodded. "Why? I mean, you told me why with Laura, but why Marie? If it hadn't been her, would it have been someone else that night?"

"Probably," Dev said with a feeble shrug. She fought the smile that tugged at her lips. "I told you why most of those women were there. I tried to get you to dance with me."

"It irked you that I turned you down, didn't it?"

"A little," Dev said honestly. "I thought about you that night."

"While you were with her? Really?" Kat asked.

"I'd had a nightmare that afternoon about the night that Jo died," Dev said quietly. "That night I did go out with the intention of finding someone to help me forget. When you and I met, I wanted that someone to be you."

"Laura told me that you never let her touch you," Kat said. "Is that true?"

"Yes, because it was you that filled my thoughts while I was with her." It seemed important that Kat know that she didn't sleep around a lot. "Look…I have been with two women in the past month. I would rather that you'd asked me how many I've been with since Jo died."

"How many?" Kat asked, dreading the answer she was going to get.

"I could count them all on one hand," Dev said. She wanted so badly to admit to the mistake with Chris, but she had promised

Sheila that she would never tell anyone. "In the beginning, it felt like infidelity to me. As time went on, I found that I just needed a connection once in a while. I needed to feel more than just the pain."

"Are you hungry?" Kat finally asked after a moment. The smile Dev gave her sent a chill through her.

"Starving," she said softly, her meaning clear. It wasn't food she was thinking about.

Kat stood and began to walk toward the kitchen, but Dev got to her feet as well. She grabbed Kat's hand, turning her so they were facing one another. Kat trembled when Dev's hands rested gently on her hips. Dev's expression was searching, questioning. She was obviously looking for some sign that her touch wasn't welcome. Kat had no intention of giving her that sign.

"I can't stop thinking about you," Dev said. Her pulse quickened when Kat's hands went through her hair, and Kat pulled her closer for a kiss. It was a kiss meant to convey the desire she felt, and Dev understood it perfectly. She bit Kat's lower lip gently, successfully eliciting a moan. Dev pulled away. "What are you doing tomorrow?"

"I'm going to Nessa's for dinner," she said, amazed she could remember anything with Dev's smoldering gaze on her.

"I meant a bit earlier in the day." Dev ran her hands slowly up Kat's back. "Like first thing in the morning, And maybe the afternoon."

"Nothing at all." The raw need she saw in Dev's eyes excited her more than she would have thought possible.

"Good, because I want to sleep in," Dev whispered, her lips pressed to Kat's soft neck. "And I want to wake up next to you. Only this time, I don't want us to be clothed."

"Oh God, Devon," Kat said breathlessly. She grabbed Dev's hand and moved it between her legs, knowing Dev would be able to feel the wetness through her slacks. "Can you feel what you do to me?"

"Jesus," Dev murmured as she pressed her palm more firmly against Kat's sex. She knew she was just as wet as Kat was, and she really didn't think she could wait much longer. "Please, Katherine, take me to your bed now."

Kat didn't hesitate and firmly took Dev by the hand to lead her up the stairs to her bedroom. She had never liked being called by her full given name, but from Dev's lips it was unbelievably exciting. Dev waited patiently by the bed while Kat went to turn on the light in the bathroom, leaving the door slightly ajar to allow a sliver of light into the room. Kat had thought this moment would make her nervous, but she found that she wasn't. That fact startled her just a bit.

"Is that light all right?" she asked. She walked to her and slowly pulled Dev's shirt from her pants.

"Whatever you want," Dev whispered as she allowed Kat to lift her shirt over her head. Her mind was determined to let Kat set the pace for the night, but her body was getting a bit ahead of her. Before her shirt even hit the floor, she was reaching for the buttons on Kat's blouse, and she noted with surprise that her fingers were trembling slightly. She slowly eased the garment off Kat's shoulders, letting it fall to the floor even as she reached behind her to unhook Kat's bra. When that barrier was gone, she covered a breast with her palm. Kat pressed against her hand, and Dev leaned down to take a nipple into her mouth.

"Oh God," Kat murmured as she held tightly to Dev's shoulders. After a moment she unsuccessfully fumbled with Dev's bra, and quickly gave up. "Please take this off. I need to feel you, Devon."

Dev reluctantly took a step backward and reached behind her to unclasp it with one hand. She quickly removed it and threw it down on top of the sweatshirt at her feet. She stared at Kat as they both quickly removed their pants, and then, completely naked, their bodies finally met again as they both moaned at the first contact of flesh on flesh.

"You are so fucking beautiful," Dev whispered, her lips

against Kat's ear. They were both breathing rapidly, and Dev could feel Kat's heart hammering against her chest.

"Why are you trembling?" Kat asked tenderly as she wrapped her arms around Dev.

"It's just a bit overwhelming that this is the first time you've done this in five years." She pressed her lips to the hollow at the base of Kat's throat. She nipped at the skin there gently, and when Kat leaned her head back, Dev slowly ran her tongue up to the tip of her chin. "But don't worry about me—I'll be fine. How are you with all of this?"

"I want this," Kat said firmly. She framed Dev's face with both hands and kissed her hungrily. "I want this more than you can possibly know."

Dev watched as Kat lay down on the bed, then she stretched out beside her, her hand moving slowly up the inside of Kat's thigh. When her fingers found the moisture between Kat's legs, she groaned as Kat's hips lifted in anticipation. Dev closed her eyes and murmured incoherently while her fingers slid through the wet silky folds.

"I think I can tell how much you want this," Dev whispered into Kat's ear, squeezing Kat's rigid clitoris gently between her thumb and forefinger. With her free hand, she found Kat's hand and moved it down between her own legs. "I want it just as much."

"You are so wet," Kat whispered. She loved knowing that it was her touch that had made Dev so ready for her. She slowly slid her fingers along either side of Dev's clit, and trembled as she felt Dev's hips move against her. She didn't resist when Dev forced her onto her back and straddled her, leaving the evidence of her desire on Kat's abdomen. Kat's hands were on Dev's shoulders as Dev moved her hips lower and leaned down to run her tongue in slow circles around a firm nipple. She bit the hardening peak gently, causing Kat to arch her back. "That feels so incredibly good, Devon."

Kat's hands moved slowly up Dev's sides until they reached

her breasts. Dev rose to her knees to give Kat better access, and when Kat's hands cupped her breasts, her fingers gently tugging at the nipples, Dev pressed harder into the touch. She moved one leg between Kat's and then lowered herself onto Kat.

"I want you to come for me," Dev said into her ear. She lifted her weight up again with her left arm, moving her free hand between their bodies, sliding easily through the slick folds. She held Kat's heavy-lidded gaze with her own. "Keep your eyes open. I want you to see me when you come."

"I need to feel you inside me," Kat whispered as she grasped Dev's shoulders. Her hips rose up to meet the fingers that slid easily inside her. She groaned loudly when Dev's thumb brushed against her clit, making her so hard it actually ached. "Oh, Dev, please don't stop what you're doing. I'm so close."

"Look at me," Dev pleaded when Kat's eyes began to slide closed. Her thrusts matched the rhythm that Kat set, and she said nothing when Kat's fingers dug into her shoulders hard enough to bruise. Nothing in the world mattered more to Dev at that moment than Kat's satisfaction. "You are so beautiful, Kat."

Kat pulled Dev down and buried her face in Dev's neck as the orgasm ripped through her body. Dev gasped in wonder at the sensation of Kat's inner muscles contracting tightly around the fingers that continued to stroke every last spasm out of her. Kat finally fell back onto the bed exhausted, her muscles still twitching occasionally as her body recovered.

"Jesus," Kat breathed as she released her hold on Dev and ran her fingers through her own hair, which was wet with sweat. She placed a hand tenderly on Dev's cheek as she tried unsuccessfully to calm her breathing and her rapidly beating heart. She gasped when Dev slowly withdrew her fingers and ran her hand up Kat's side. "That was incredible."

"You're incredible," Dev said with a smile as she kissed her under the chin. She rolled off her onto her side and rested her hand on Kat's abdomen, propping herself up with a hand on the side of her head. Both of them were still breathing heavily. "Thirsty?"

"I want to try and make you feel as good as I do right now," Kat said, turning her head to look at Dev.

"We have all night." Dev stood and walked to the door. "I'm not going anywhere other than to the kitchen for some water. Don't *you* go anywhere."

"God, no." Kat sighed with a feeling of contentment that she never thought she would experience again. "I'll be right here."

When Dev returned, she handed Kat a bottle of water before lying next to her on the bed once more. Kat took a long swallow before giving the bottle to Dev so she could do the same. She turned onto her side and ran a finger slowly down the center of Dev's chest. Dev struggled to set the bottle onto the nightstand without looking, then she put an arm around Kat's shoulder and pulled her on top of her body.

"What if I've forgotten how to do this?" Kat murmured, her mouth against Dev's ear. It was something that had worried her, but she had never put voice to the concern before now—there had never been a reason to. She felt herself melt in Dev's arms when she held her even closer.

"I'm pretty sure it's kind of like riding a bicycle," Dev said, stroking Kat's back slowly. "But to tell you the truth, I almost came when you did, so I really don't think it's going to take much."

"That's okay for the first time." Kat gazed at Dev's beautiful face. "But I do want to make love to you slowly sometime."

"Like I said, we have all night."

Dev moaned in pleasure when she felt Kat's fingers enter her, and every fiber of her being became focused on the exquisite pleasure caused by Kat's gentle but insistent thrusts and her thumb stroking her clitoris. It took only a moment for the fire to explode within her, and Kat held on to her as she rode the wave of ecstasy.

"I don't think I've ever seen anything quite as stunning as the way you look when you come," Kat said in obvious wonder when Dev's body finally relaxed.

"Thank you," Dev said as she dissolved into Kat's embrace. "We should probably eat something. I intend to have my way with you all night."

"Mmm." Kat smiled and rested her head on Dev's shoulder. "I never did make that spaghetti I said I was going to have for dinner."

"Why is that?"

"I had every intention of having you instead."

"And have you had enough?" Dev asked, finding the curve of Kat's ass and squeezing gently.

"Not even close."

"Lie on your back," Dev said softly. Kat did as she was instructed, and Dev moved so she was above Kat, one thigh firmly against her center. She leaned down to run her tongue along the rim of her ear and whispered, "I need to taste you, Kat. Is that all right?"

"Yes." She hissed as she pressed herself hard against Dev's thigh. The sensation it spawned made her feel as though she might pass out. "Please, Devon."

Dev kissed her hungrily, and as their tongues met, she felt a new rush of arousal. She moved her mouth down and ran her tongue lightly along Kat's neck and then to her perfect breasts, stopping to take a rigid nipple between her lips. She sucked and nibbled while she took satisfaction in the fact that Kat's nipple appeared to be directly wired to her clit. Kat moved beneath her, increasing the pressure on Dev's thigh and groaning in pleasure as her fingernails scraped up Dev's back.

Dev continued her journey down Kat's torso, dipping her tongue quickly into Kat's belly button before moving farther down to settle between her legs. Kat's swift intake of breath was clearly audible as Dev's tongue began to explore. Kat spread her legs to give Dev more room, and she cried out when Dev's tongue entered her at the same time her fingers gently squeezed a nipple.

The heady scent and taste of Kat was intoxicating, and Dev felt as though she couldn't get enough. She slid her tongue in and out a couple of times before pressing her tongue flat and bringing it up the length of her sex to the bundle of nerves straining for attention. Dev sucked the clit into her mouth, and Kat cried out, both hands going into Dev's hair as her upper body lifted off the bed.

"God...Devon," Kat said, moaning when she felt Dev's fingers slip easily inside her. She felt Dev's fingers curl upward, and then the pressure on her g-spot along with the gentle sucking of her clit caused the orgasm to sneak up on her. She cried out as the climax overtook her, causing her to convulse in pleasure. She tried to squeeze her legs together, to make Dev stop, but before she knew what was happening, she was coming all over again. The ecstasy she felt was too much, and she finally managed to get Dev to crawl back up and lie beside her.

Her lips sought out Dev's in the semidarkness of the room, and she could taste her own passion on Dev's mouth, which caused a primal groan to rip from her throat as she remembered her orgasms. Kat was out of breath, and she held tightly to Dev, whose arms around her felt so right. They kissed gently while Kat recovered from the pleasure Dev had given her.

"You are so freaking amazing," Kat managed to say after a few moments. She laughed softly before turning her head to look at Dev's face. "I've never felt this good before. I want you to feel what I'm feeling right now."

"You don't have to," Dev said as she kissed her forehead and then gently ran her fingers through Kat's hair. Her body was screaming a much different answer, however.

"I know I don't have to," Kat said before forcing Dev onto her back. "I want to. I *need* to, Devon. I need to taste you, and to feel your body move beneath my tongue when you come."

Dev moaned as Kat lowered her weight on top of her, and

Kat kissed her neck. Dev's hands were all over Kat's back as Kat took a nipple into her mouth, gently sucking and moving her tongue delicately around the hard peak. As Kat moved down, Dev's hands fell to her sides and she gripped the sheet tightly, clenching it in her fists.

Kat's tongue found her clit at exactly the same moment that Dev felt her fingers enter her, and she arched her back in response, her legs falling open even farther. She tried desperately to make the feeling last, but her body definitely had another agenda. When the orgasm exploded through her body, Dev jerked upright, calling out Kat's name. After a moment, Dev grabbed her by her upper arms and pulled her closer, kissing her passionately as she pulled Kat down on top of her once again.

Kat realized suddenly that she was crying, and it didn't take long for Dev to recognize it as well. She held Kat close, cradling her head on her breast and stroking her hair gently.

"What's wrong, Kat?" Although she whispered the question, her genuine concern was clear. She kissed the top of Kat's head, and her arms tightened instinctively around her. "Baby, what's the matter?"

"I'm sorry," Kat managed to say between quiet sobs. "I really didn't know it would affect me this way."

"God, please don't be sorry." Dev ran her fingers absently up and down Kat's spine.

"I'm not sorry that we did this," Kat said as she tightened her hold on Dev in an attempt to reassure her.

"Good. Neither am I."

"It's just that it's been so long," Kat whispered. Dev held her closer as Kat pushed her thigh between Dev's legs. She couldn't believe she was crying. What surprised her even more though, was that it wasn't embarrassing. It felt perfectly natural to be lying in Dev's arms with the last remnants of her climax fading away, and crying. She knew it probably shouldn't, but it did. "So damn long since I've come that hard, since anyone's touched me like that. And so damn long since I've even wanted to touch anyone."

"Just lie here with me and go to sleep," Dev said softly. She held Kat's head to her breast and leaned in to kiss her temple. "I'll hold you all night, if you want me to."

After a few moments, Kat was drifting, but she tried to fight it. When Dev's breathing became even, Kat wrapped an arm tightly around Dev's waist and finally allowed sleep to claim her as well.

CHAPTER FIFTEEN

Devon awoke the next morning to the weight of Kat's head still on her shoulder and Kat's hand resting lightly on her breast. Dev leaned her cheek against the top of Kat's head and tightened the arm she had around her shoulders. The contentment she felt was inexplicable, but she came to the conclusion that she didn't really want to explain it. *Maybe it's finally time to stop trying to analyze everything, and to just let it be.*

"Are you awake?" Kat asked quietly, her hand tightening slightly around Dev's breast.

"Yes," she said, running her hand down Kat's bare arm. "Good morning."

"Mmm, yes it is," Kat said. She lifted her head to look at Dev. "It's really nice to wake up with you."

"I agree." Dev kissed her forehead before reclaiming her arm and stretching her body. "Although I must admit that I like waking up naked much better than finding you next to me still fully clothed."

"So do I," Kat said, glancing at the bedside clock. "Don't you have to work today?"

"We're open late on Tuesdays, and I work until close. I don't have to be there until noon."

"Lucky me." Kat grinned as she leaned forward to take a nipple into her mouth.

"Jesus. How the hell can we have done what we did last night—all night, I might add—and yet I still want you so badly the next morning?"

"I'm irresistible, and you're insatiable."

"I thought I was irresistible," Dev said. She couldn't stop the gasp that escaped her when Kat's hand moved down her abdomen.

"You definitely are that." Kat pulled her hand away with obvious regret as she repositioned herself so that she was sitting up, her back against the headboard. She watched as Dev turned onto her side facing her, propping her head up on her hand. "I'm curious about something."

"What would that be?"

"Why?" Kat asked, and said nothing more as she waited for Dev to look at her. She reached over and ran a finger slowly along Dev's jaw. "You said you wanted to wait. What was it that changed your mind?"

Dev took a deep breath and focused her attention on her own hand, which she slid up Kat's thigh until it came to rest on her lower abdomen, just above the triangle of hair between her legs.

"You can't tell me that dressing the way you did last night wasn't indicative of your plans for me," she said.

"I know what I wanted," Kat said. "But you wanted to wait. I'm just wondering what happened to change that."

Dev knew she was just stalling, because what she had to say wasn't going to be easy. It would no doubt bring up memories that neither of them wanted to have. Kat waited patiently, her hand covering Dev's on her abdomen. Dev put her free hand on Kat's and took a deep breath.

"You and I both know that life can be taken from us in a heartbeat," she said quietly. She felt the tears threatening, but did nothing to hide them from Kat. "We both know that nothing in life can be taken for granted. I just came to the realization last night that I could very well wake up one morning and you could be gone. I would have never known what it could feel like to hold you in my arms after making love with you. I made the decision that I didn't want to let that happen."

Kat watched her intently, and she reached out to brush away a tear that had just begun to roll down Dev's cheek. She barely took note that her own tears were on the verge of spilling over as well. Kat thought that she had never heard anything so sweet—or so heartfelt—in her life.

"You are truly amazing, Devon Conway," she said quietly.

"You know, if you keep telling me things like that, I'm going to start believing it one day."

"It's true. You are so strong, but you're also so incredibly sensitive. And vulnerable. And romantic. Not to mention unbelievably sexy."

"Oh God." Dev groaned as she rolled onto her back. "You can't tell anyone those things. Sensitive and vulnerable? If those things get out, my reputation will be irrevocably ruined."

"Your secrets are safe with me," Kat said with a laugh. She decided to ask the question that had been on her mind since they had gotten into the bed the night before. "Tell me something, Dev. Is this all there is for us? Just one night?"

Dev turned onto her side again and looked into Kat's eyes as she contemplated how to best answer that question. She knew what *she* wanted, but what if it wasn't what Kat wanted? Dev was about to put her heart out there for Kat to either take or throw it back at her. For the first time since Jo died, Dev found herself actually caring about what another woman felt. She'd honestly never thought that would happen again.

"I hope not," she said. She took Kat's hand and lifted it briefly to her lips. "But if that's what you want, I would understand."

"Oh, Dev, that's not want I want," Kat said, shaking her head emphatically. She struggled with the knowledge that she could very well scare Dev off, but there were some things she felt she needed to say. "Paula died five years ago, but she spent most of the last year in the hospital. It's really been over six years since I've been intimate with anyone. If I'm being honest,

I really don't think I'm cut out for casual sex. As I said before, I've had opportunity, but no desire, until I met you. I care about you, Devon, and I would love to see what there might be for us in the future."

"Me too," Dev said. Suddenly, it felt as though a huge weight had been lifted from her heart. "But see, I was right. We aren't here alone. Paula and Jo are right here with us."

"Maybe they always will be, but that might not be a bad thing." Kat shrugged and felt a degree of comfort with that thought. She'd never been very spiritual, but perhaps Paula and Jo had wanted them to find each other. She got the distinct impression that Paula would have approved of Dev. "Tell me something. If Jo could have spent one second in your head, what would she have learned that would have surprised her?"

"Wow." She thought for a moment, and then as she rolled onto her back again, she spoke. "Jo would have been surprised at how deeply I loved her. I know I said the words all the time, but I don't think I always showed it in the little ways that I could have. If I could have another chance, I would be more attentive to her needs and desires."

"That's nice," Kat said.

"Fair is fair," Dev said, turning her head to look up at Kat. "What about you?"

"Paula would have been surprised that at the end, I wished that she would die," Kat said quietly, looking straight ahead and avoiding Dev's questioning gaze. "I could see how much she was suffering, and I didn't want her to be in pain any longer. That's pretty selfish, isn't it?"

"Not at all. Here's selfish for you—there have been times that I wished Jo would have been dead before they got her to the hospital. Then I wouldn't have had to make the decision to let her die. I've felt guilty about that many times."

"You shouldn't," Kat said, sliding down so that they were lying face-to-face. She touched Dev's cheek tenderly. "I'm sure she would understand that. No one should be forced to make those kinds of decisions, Devon."

"I think this conversation is too intense for pillow talk," Dev said. She rolled onto her back and pulled Kat on top of her. She raked her fingernails slowly down Kat's back, and reveled in the reaction she got from it. Their lips were a breath apart when Dev heard her cell phone ring. Kat started to move off her, but Dev held her in place. "I have no intention of answering it."

"You should, though," Kat said seriously. "Trust me when I say that I will not forget where we left off."

Dev sighed audibly as she reluctantly let her go, and then she stood quickly to find her pants at the end of the bed. She reached into her pocket for the phone, and saw by the readout that it was Rhonda.

"Hello, Rhonda," she said as she sat down again on the edge of the bed. Kat moved so she was behind her, and pulled Dev back between her spread legs.

"Where the hell are you?" Rhonda asked, sounding more concerned than angry.

"Good morning to you too." She tensed slightly when she felt Kat's arms go around her waist, and she leaned her head back against her when Kat's fingers began to play with her nipples. She was smiling, but Kat's touch was making it rather difficult to concentrate on what Rhonda was saying.

"Where are you?" Rhonda asked again.

"In bed," she said, closing her eyes and losing herself in Kat's touch.

"And would that be your own," Rhonda asked, "or someone else's?"

"I don't think that's really any of your business, Rhonda." She realized she was incredibly close to dropping the phone and giving herself completely to Kat, but at that moment, she really didn't care.

"Well, I'm at your apartment door, and you aren't answering,"

Rhonda said by way of explanation. "Yet your bike is parked in the driveway and your SUV is in the garage. So where the hell are you? My mother said that you were supposed to pick her up this morning to take her grocery shopping for Thanksgiving dinner. She's a little worried about you, Devon."

"Fuck." Dev leaned forward quickly, running her fingers through her unruly hair. "I'll be right there."

"Something wrong?" Kat asked with concern.

"I was supposed to pick Sheila up forty-five minutes ago." Dev snapped the phone shut and jumped out of bed to get dressed. She leaned over and kissed Kat fully on the lips, smiling with genuine regret. "I'm so sorry. I completely forgot that I was supposed to take her shopping for Thanksgiving. I don't know why she insists on waiting until the day before to do her shopping. God, I really wanted to spend the entire day with you."

"There will be other days, Devon, and I'll still be here when you get back. Just see to it that *you* don't forget where we left off."

"Not a chance," Dev said as she slipped her shoes on without tying them. She tried her best to ignore the intense thud of arousal that made its presence known between her legs. She sucked in a breath and shook her head slowly when Kat took her hand and guided it to her bare breast. "Trust me. Not a chance in hell."

❖

"Were you at Kat's?" Rhonda asked in amazement when Dev began the ascent to her apartment door where Rhonda stood waiting. "You're not wearing a bra."

Dev knew that from where Rhonda was standing she couldn't see Kat's front door. She reached into her pocket and pulled out her keys before looking at Rhonda.

"I'm not wearing underwear or socks either, but I didn't realize you were the undergarment police." Dev slipped her key into the lock. She stepped aside to allow Rhonda entry first. "You don't need to wait. I'll call Sheila and tell her I'm on my way as soon as I shower."

"Please tell me you weren't with Katherine."

"If I didn't know better, I'd think you didn't like her, Rhonda." Dev walked to the kitchen and set her keys on the counter.

"I do like her, Dev. That's why I don't want to see her get hurt."

Dev stared at her in disbelief for a moment, wondering if Rhonda had meant that the way it had sounded.

"All right then, if I didn't know better, I'd think you didn't like me."

"Jesus, Dev, you know I love you," Rhonda said as she took a seat on the couch and tried her best to sound apologetic. "It's just that ever since Jo died, you've been a wreck."

"I did what I needed to do for *me*, Rhonda," Devon said defensively. She leaned forward with her elbows on the counter. "I had a lot to deal with when she died, and I needed to get away from here. *Everything* reminded me of her. I'll be the first to admit that I probably could have handled things a bit differently, but I guess that's why they say that hindsight is twenty-twenty."

"Why are you back here, Dev?"

"My family is here. You and Sheila. I grew up here. I wanted to come back. What I don't want is this interrogation as to what my motives were."

"Did Chris have anything to do with your decision to come back?"

"No," Dev said incredulously. "Until the day I came to your gallery, I hadn't seen or spoken to her since the funeral. Why in the world would you think she had anything to do with my coming back?"

"I don't know." Rhonda shook her head and looked at the floor. Even though she knew Chris had always been attracted to Dev, Rhonda knew Dev had absolutely no interest in Chris. She chalked it up to the insecurities of being involved with someone so much younger than she was. "I just worry sometimes that Chris might leave me."

"Has she cheated on you?" Dev asked. She felt like a hypocrite acting as if this thought shocked her, but she had taken Chris at her word when she'd told Dev she'd been faithful to Rhonda since that night.

"How did this turn into a discussion about me and Chris?" Rhonda asked with a tremulous laugh, clearly trying her best to dodge the question.

"Fine. I'm smart enough to know a roadblock when I see one, but I swear to God—if she ever hurts you, I'll take care of her myself," Dev said as she straightened up again.

"So, are you sleeping with Kat?" Rhonda asked after a moment, successfully ignoring Dev's comment and changing the subject.

"I spent the night with her, yes. But I don't intend to hurt her, and I think that you need to realize that she's a grown-up, and is quite capable of making her own decisions. We've spent quite a bit of time together talking, and last night was the first time anything sexual happened between us."

"You know that she has a daughter?" Rhonda asked carefully.

"Yes, I've met Vanessa. So, I guess the answer to your next question is yes, I know Kat is going to be a grandmother in another couple of months. I also know her lover died five years ago, and she hasn't been intimate with anyone since. And for your information, it was Kat who was more than willing to have a one-night stand with me, but that wasn't what I wanted. We've made the decision to see where this goes between us, and I'm going to ask her to come to dinner at Sheila's for Thanksgiving. Do you have any problems with this so far?"

"No." Rhonda stood and walked toward Dev. Dev took a wary step backward, but the kitchen wasn't that big, and before she knew it, Rhonda was holding her in a fierce hug. Dev had no choice but to hug her back. "I'm happy for both of you, Devon, and I hope everything works out. All I've ever wanted is for you to be happy, and I'm glad you've finally decided to move on."

"Moving on, yes, but I will never forget Joanne," Dev said as she pulled away from Rhonda. "Just as I would suspect that Kat will never forget Paula, nor would I want her to. And I don't want anyone walking on eggshells around me. You can talk about Jo, all right?"

"Okay," Rhonda said with a sincere smile. She reached into her pocket for her cell phone and motioned Dev toward the bathroom. "I'll call Mom and let her know you're on your way. Unless you'd rather I take her shopping, and then you can just go back to your little love nest."

"I definitely would rather that, but I promised Sheila that I'd take her, and I intend to do it," Dev said before turning to make her way to the bedroom. She was glad that Sheila had talked her out of telling Rhonda about what had happened between her and Chris. There was no way that easing her own guilt would be worth the pain that confession would cause.

Chapter Sixteen

S he's coming over for dinner tonight?" Nessa asked.
"Yes, honey," Kat said, holding the phone between her ear and her shoulder. She was finally done with the preparation, and it was time to put the lasagna in the oven to cook. She glanced at the clock and saw that Devon would be there in about thirty minutes.

"Mother, I told you I wanted details," Nessa said, causing Kat to chuckle quietly. "You're being awfully close-mouthed about this whole thing. Why is that, exactly?"

"Because there wasn't anything to tell." She poured herself a glass of wine and went to take a seat on the couch. She waited a few moments to give Nessa time to catch on to the nuance of her statement.

"There *wasn't*? Meaning there is now?" Nessa sounded positively ecstatic, which caused Kat to laugh out loud. "What happened, Mom?"

"She spent the night here last night," Kat said after a moment of contemplating whether she really wanted to discuss her sex life with her daughter.

"On the couch?"

"God, you aren't going to make this easy for me, are you?"

"No, I'm not. You canceled our dinner tonight for her, I presume. So you might as well get used to it."

"She slept with me, in my bed, and before you humiliate me further, yes, we had sex."

"It's about freaking time, Mother," Nessa said with a satisfied sigh. "So…how was it? Was it worth the wait?"

"Yes, definitely," Kat said as she remembered the tender way that Dev had touched her. She'd been nervous as hell about being intimate again after so long, but the moment Dev had touched her, all of her anxieties disappeared. It had been everything she'd thought it would be, and so much more. For so long, she hadn't thought she'd be capable of making love with anyone ever again, but Dev's urgency and passion had brought out things that she hadn't even realized were still buried deep inside her.

"You sound content, Mother," Nessa said. "Is this something you want to continue?"

"Yes, it is." She took a sip of her wine and set the glass on the coffee table.

"And does she?"

"Yes." Kat closed her eyes and leaned her head back as she finally allowed herself to put words to the thoughts that had been going through her mind all day. "I honestly don't know if this is something that will become serious or not, but I really like her. I know that *I'm* hoping it will."

"I'm really happy for you, Mom," Nessa said. "I hope you know that."

"I do know that. And you really have no idea how much that means to me, honey."

"Maybe you should bring her over for dinner this weekend," Nessa said. "I'd like to get to know her better, especially if this might turn into something serious."

"I'll think about it," Kat said, glancing at her watch. "She's going to be here soon, and I still need to walk Buddy." At the mention of that magical word, Buddy jumped up from his spot on the end of the couch and watched her intently, his head cocked to one side and his tail moving tentatively back and forth.

"I can take a hint. Have fun tonight, but not *too* much fun."

"And what exactly constitutes too much fun?"

"Just don't stay up all night. People your age need their rest, Grandma."

"Very funny." Kat grabbed Buddy's leash. He jumped down from the couch and waited rather impatiently at the door, his tail wagging frantically as he stared unwaveringly up at the knob. "Tell Josh I said hi, and I'll see you both soon."

❖

Kat checked her hair for the umpteenth time as she glanced at her watch once again. Dev had called earlier in the afternoon and let her know she would be home around eight, and Kat had suggested that she come over for dinner. Kat had been a bit surprised when Dev had invited her to Thanksgiving dinner at Sheila's, but she hadn't hesitated in accepting. She'd been planning on spending the day alone because Nessa and Josh would be with his parents, and her brother and his family would be with Kat's parents. Even if one of those options held any appeal for her, she knew that she wasn't welcome in either home. Josh's parents hated her because she was a lesbian, and they held the opinion that Nessa wasn't good enough for their son. If it wasn't so obvious that Josh was devoted to Nessa, Kat would have insisted that they stop seeing each other long ago.

Kat couldn't believe how nervous she was. It felt almost like waiting for her prom date to show up—at least how it *should* have felt had she really been looking forward to her prom. She let out a deep breath before heading back down to the kitchen. When she was halfway down the stairs, the doorbell rang, and her heart doubled its pace in her chest.

"Hi," Dev said with a grin when Kat opened the door. She held out a bottle of red wine as Kat motioned for her to come in.

"Your timing is perfect," Kat said with a nervous smile of

her own. After shutting the door, she went to the kitchen and set the wine bottle on the counter. "I just got back from taking Buddy for his walk."

"You told me you were making lasagna, but I didn't know if I should bring anything," Dev said, suddenly feeling inexplicably nervous. *Jesus—after last night, there shouldn't be any nervousness or shyness left between us, should there?* "I thought wine should be a safe bet."

"It's great, but you really didn't need to bring anything." Kat placed her hands tentatively on Dev's hips. As much as they had shared the previous night, Kat had to admit she wasn't completely sure how to act now. When Dev leaned into her for a kiss, she loosened up a bit, and she felt Dev's body relax as well. "God, I've thought about doing that ever since you left my bed this morning."

"I can't tell you how sorry I am about that," Dev murmured. "If you want me to stay tonight, I promise it won't happen again tomorrow. We don't have to be at Sheila's until three."

"Do you really have to ask?" She gasped when she felt Dev's thigh insinuate itself between her legs. "Christ, I'm seriously considering skipping dinner altogether now."

"Mmm." Dev pressed her lips to the hollow at the base of Kat's throat before pulling back slightly. "As tempting as that sounds, we did that last night, and I haven't eaten anything all day. Maybe we could hold off on dessert until after dinner this time."

"Okay." Kat pulled away from her reluctantly. "Wine?"

"Please." She took a seat on the couch, and despite her declaration of not being a dog person—or perhaps because of it—Buddy jumped up and made himself comfortable next to her. When Kat returned with their wine, Dev pushed Buddy off the couch to make room for Kat, who sat close to Dev, one hand resting on her thigh.

"Nessa wanted me to invite you to dinner at her place this

weekend," Kat said quietly. She knew it was possible Dev might not be ready for "family" get-togethers, but she reminded herself it had been Dev who invited her to share Thanksgiving with her family. Kat saw it as a low-risk venture on her part. She knew that if she really wanted things to become serious between the two of them, she wouldn't be able to sit back and wait for Dev to make all the moves. "You don't have to say yes—I'm sure they would understand."

"I think I might like that," Dev said quietly. She'd never met any of Jo's family, other than Chris—mostly because their parents hadn't wanted anything to do with either of their daughters once they had come out of the closet. Family was important to Dev, and she knew it was probably based at least somewhat in the fact she'd never really had a true family of her own. It seemed important now for her to be involved with Kat's family. "Unless *you'd* rather do something else, of course."

"No." Kat took Dev's hand in hers. Their fingers entwined as Kat lifted them up to place a kiss on the back of Dev's hand. "I would love to have you meet Josh. He really is a great guy."

"Just let me know what time." It amazed Dev that everything felt so *right*. It was comfortable, and as much as some aspects of that revelation scared the hell out of her, it also made her feel incredibly content. "What made you come back to Easton after Paula died?"

"What do you mean?" Kat asked, wondering at the sudden change in the subject.

"Well, you said you were living in California when she died," Dev said with a shrug. She brought their hands onto her lap and rested them on her thigh, her thumb softly rubbing the back of Kat's as she spoke. "You told me there's no love lost between you and your parents, so I just wondered why you decided to come back here."

"It was Vanessa, actually," Kat said with a smile as she leaned her head on Dev's shoulder. "She was sixteen, and she knew she wanted to go to Lafayette College. Rick had been bugging me to come back here too, so I just made the logical choice."

"I just want to go on record as saying I'm happy you made that choice," Dev said, resting her chin on top of Kat's head.

"Me too. I'm also incredibly happy you made the decision to come back here."

"So am I." Dev tried not to think too much about the desire that swelled within her. The scent of Kat's shampoo mingled with the light touch of cologne was bringing back visions of the previous night. She felt her pulse quicken, and fought to keep her breathing even.

"You're trembling, Devon." Kat sat up and looked at her with concern. "What's the matter?"

"You think dinner could wait for an hour or so? All I can seem to think about is finishing what we started this morning."

"What happened to waiting for dessert?" Kat asked, her voice thick with desire. The look Dev gave her was smoldering, and she felt a rush of liquid fire through her center.

"I seem to be losing my self-control when it comes to you. All I want is to have you naked in my arms."

"Dinner will be ready in a minute," Kat managed to say. No sooner did she get the words out of her mouth than the timer went off. She smiled ruefully as she forced herself to stand on legs that seemed far too weak to support her. "I think it might do you some good to wait until after dinner anyway."

"You're trying to torture me, aren't you?" Dev leaned her head back against the couch and squeezed her legs together to stop the pulsing. As soon as Kat had gotten up, Buddy jumped into Dev's lap. She began to absently scratch behind his ears, and he rolled over onto his back in an obvious attempt to get a belly rub out of her.

"I'm glad you seem to think you're the only one suffering here," Kat called from the kitchen. "Come eat dinner so we can move on to dessert that much quicker."

"Sounds good to me," Dev said to Buddy, who simply wagged his tail happily in response.

❖

Dev somehow managed to finish her meal, and she didn't even complain when Kat insisted that they do the dishes before indulging in dessert. But as soon as Kat closed the dishwasher, Dev couldn't stand it any longer. She moved in behind Kat and threaded her arms around her waist, then immediately moved her hands up and under the front of Kat's sweater. She was rewarded with a throaty moan from Kat, and when Dev's hands cupped her breasts, Kat arched her body into the touch and leaned her head back against Dev's shoulder.

"I need your hands on me," Kat said as she turned in Dev's arms. Their lips met in a frantic kiss, and Dev felt herself get even wetter as Kat's tongue moved along her lower lip possessively. She felt Kat's hands at the front of her jeans trying desperately to remove them, and Dev reached down to stop her.

"Please, Devon, I need to feel you."

Without a word, Dev reached down and put an arm behind Kat's knees, then swiftly picked her up. They kissed hungrily as Kat's arms went around her neck, and Dev carried her up the steps to the bedroom.

"Close the door, or else Buddy will be up on the bed with us," Kat said breathlessly, and Dev complied by pushing the door shut with her foot. She put Kat down so they stood facing each other, and again Kat's hands went immediately to Dev's jeans, working quickly to try and remove them.

Dev was mesmerized by the pulse pounding erratically in Kat's neck as she pulled the sweater up and over Kat's head. She let the garment drop to the floor before staring openly, slowly, at every curve and swell of Kat's body. She never looked away as she kicked out of the jeans that were now down around her ankles. Kat removed her own pants while Dev stripped the rest of her clothes off, and then Kat lay down on the bed, waiting for Dev.

Dev eased onto the bed and lowered her body on top of Kat's. She moaned in pleasure when Kat's legs went immediately around her thighs, successfully pulling Dev hard against the spot where Kat obviously needed her touch the most.

"I don't think this is exactly where we left off this morning," Dev murmured before running her tongue lightly along the outer rim of Kat's ear.

"No?" Kat asked, pressing herself even harder against Dev's pelvis, thoroughly enjoying the exquisite pleasure that shot through her. "Why don't you remind me, then?"

Dev quickly rolled onto her back, pulling Kat with her so Kat was on top, straddling her. Dev's hands went to Kat's butt and held her tightly for a moment before bringing her fingernails slowly up Kat's back, causing Kat to rock back hard against her pelvis.

"I think this is where we were," Dev informed her with a feral grin.

"Oh Christ, Dev," Kat murmured as she rocked back and forth against Dev, the friction bringing her closer to orgasm. "I'm so close now. I need to come so badly."

"Not yet, baby." Dev moved her hands to Kat's hips and urged her upward until Kat hovered above her, firmly gripping the top of the headboard. Dev reached one hand up to cup Kat's breast, her thumb and forefinger applying just enough pressure to the taut nipple to cause Kat to lower her hips involuntarily. Dev put her other arm around Kat's waist and pulled her closer as she claimed her with her mouth. The scent and taste of her caused a flood of memories from the previous evening, and Dev had to fight the urge to reach down and touch herself.

"Oh, yeah, Dev," Kat moaned loudly when she felt Dev pull her clitoris between her lips. Kat moved against her rhythmically as Dev sucked her, occasionally biting gently. "So fucking good… please…don't…stop."

I never want to stop. I want this moment to last forever. Dev hesitated for just a split second before grasping the fact that she really meant it. She hadn't realized just how much she had ached for this—not just a quick fuck with someone she'd never see again, but something real. Not until that first kiss she'd shared with Kat.

She tightened her grip around Kat's waist and held on to her as she worked her closer to orgasm. When she felt Kat's body stiffen and then buck against her, Dev held on even tighter and continued to manipulate her clitoris with her tongue until Kat finally collapsed and moved to lie next to Dev on the bed.

"You are so incredibly sexy," Dev said. She turned onto her side and ran a hand slowly up Kat's torso.

"So, is that what you were planning this morning?" Kat ran her thumb along Dev's cheekbone.

"More or less." Dev moved her hand to the small of Kat's back and pulled her closer before kissing her possessively. *"And it was the only thing I could think about all damn day."*

"I think I could kiss you forever," Kat said, resting her forehead against Dev's and moving her hand slowly up Dev's side to cup a breast. She grinned when Dev squirmed under her touch. "But right now, I want very much to make you come."

"Yes, please," Dev said, allowing herself to be pushed onto her back. Kat insinuated her thigh between Dev's legs and leaned down to take a nipple into her mouth. Dev arched up to meet her, and Kat moved slowly down her torso, torturing Dev with light kisses along the way. Dev jerked when Kat's fingers slid into the wetness between her legs. "Oh yes, Kat. So good."

When Dev felt Kat's fingers slide inside her, she couldn't stop her hands as they moved up to touch her own breasts. She squeezed her nipples as she surged up to meet Kat's insistent thrusts. As soon as Kat took Dev into her mouth, the orgasm exploded through her, and Dev allowed it to take over all of her senses. When she couldn't stand the sensations any longer, she grabbed Kat by the shoulders and pulled her up to lie on top of her.

"Wow," she said breathlessly. "I really don't think I'll be good for much else the rest of the night after that. Good thing you insisted we eat dinner first."

"One and done?" Kat joked before kissing Dev's exposed neck.

"Jesus, I can't answer that right now." Dev chuckled and shook her head. "You seem to drive all coherent thought from my mind whenever you touch me. Ask me that question again in a few minutes."

Kat moved so that she was lying next to Dev, perfectly content with Dev's arm around her shoulders and her own arm draped across Dev's torso. She felt safe for the first time in years. She didn't want the moment ever to end.

"I'm a little embarrassed," Dev said after a few moments.

"Why?"

"I can honestly say that no one has ever made me come as quickly as you seem to be able to. I thought the first time last night was a one-time thing, but you seem to awaken every nerve in my body, and I have absolutely no control over my reactions."

"So what is there to be embarrassed about?" Kat asked. She looked up and ran a finger from Dev's chin to her collarbone. "Personally, I think it's sexy as hell. You do things to me that no one else ever has too."

"Like what?" Intrigued, Dev shifted so that she was lying on her side. She propped herself up on one elbow to look down at Kat.

"All you have to do is look at me and I get wet," Kat said, feeling her cheeks flush at the frank admission.

"Mmm." Dev ran her hand down Kat's belly and then between her legs. When she met no resistance, she slid her fingers easily through the silky folds. "That's some pretty useful information to have."

"Oh, Jesus," Kat whispered as she pressed her forehead against Dev's shoulder and let her legs fall open. "I guess you aren't one and done?"

"No, not tonight," Dev said, her lips close to Kat's ear. "Maybe not ever, given the way you make me feel."

CHAPTER SEVENTEEN

D̲o they know about us?" Kat asked, feeling uncharacteristically nervous. She had only met Sheila a few times, when she brought food to Rhonda at the gallery, but she liked her. Rhonda had been a good friend to her ever since they'd met, and Chris—well, quite frankly, Kat didn't give a rat's ass what Chris thought of her.

"That we're sleeping together?" Dev asked with a grin as she pulled the Durango into Sheila's driveway. While she didn't mind riding the Harley as long as there was no snow or ice, she didn't want to subject Kat to the near-freezing temperatures.

Kat glanced away from her. "You have to stop looking at me like that," she said, reaching for Dev's hand. They had a lot of time to make up for, and the past two nights hadn't been nearly enough. If she had her way, they would just skip Thanksgiving altogether. "I can't be responsible for my actions."

"You're too beautiful not to look at," Dev said. When Kat turned her head to look at her, Dev leaned over and kissed her tenderly. "So please don't ask me not to look at you."

"Fuck. How is it that I can still be so aroused? God knows I should be sated after last night and this morning."

"Well, I'm glad to know I'm not the only one who may have trouble making it through the rest of the day."

"You never answered my question," Kat pointed out, trying her best to ignore her racing pulse. "Do they know about us?"

"Rhonda does, so my best guess would be that everyone does." Dev smiled and shrugged apologetically. "What was I going to do? She knew the truth when I came home that morning with no bra on. Do you mind that they know?"

"I don't care who knows," Kat said. She framed Dev's face with her hands and kissed her thoroughly, not stopping until she elicited a moan from her. "Just something to think about until we can be alone again later."

"Thanks a lot," Dev muttered, raking her fingers through her hair. She glanced into the back of the SUV. As if reading her mind, Kat shook her head vehemently and laughed as she reached for her door handle.

"As much as I want you right now, I am not going to make love with you in the car. At least, not in Sheila's driveway while there's a turkey dinner waiting inside."

❖

"Thank you so much for inviting me, Sheila," Kat said as they followed her into the living room and sat on the couch.

"You're always welcome here, Katherine." Sheila shot a glance and a wink toward Devon. "There's beer, wine, and soda in the kitchen, Devon. Why don't you get something for the two of you?"

"You want anything?" she asked Sheila as she stood.

"No, I'm fine."

"Are we early?" Dev asked when she returned with a couple of beers. She handed one to Kat as she took a seat next to her once again.

"You know Rhonda and Chris." Sheila shook her head ruefully. "They can't make it out the door without fighting. Rhonda called a few minutes ago to tell me they would be late."

"Just let me know when you want me to start on the potatoes."
Dev took a drink from her bottle.

"You cook?" Kat asked in surprise.

"Are you forgetting that I made meat loaf for you?"

"Dev, I've had Sheila's meat loaf before. I know that you
didn't cook it."

"She's a smart one, Dev," Sheila said, smiling at them both.
"If you have any brains in that head of yours, you won't let this
one get away."

I don't intend to. She somehow managed to tear her gaze
away from Kat and looked pointedly at Sheila.

"And what exactly does that mean?" she asked with a smile
she couldn't suppress.

"Did you really think that Rhonda wouldn't tell me?" When
neither of them answered, Sheila laughed. "I love you, Devon,
and I truly want you to be happy again. I can honestly say that
you look happier today than you did when you first came back
here. If Katherine had anything to do with putting that gleam in
your eye again, then that's all that really matters."

Dev watched in silence as her godmother stood and walked
to the kitchen. After a moment, she turned her head to look into
Kat's questioning gaze.

"*Are* you happy?" Kat asked her quietly. She reached over
and took Dev's hand, entwining their fingers and squeezing
gently.

"Yes," Dev said without hesitation. It had been so damn long
since she'd been happy, she almost didn't recognize the feeling.
She nodded to emphasize her point as she lifted Kat's hand to her
lips. "Yes, I believe I am. Thanks to you."

"So am I." She set her bottle on the coffee table and cupped
Dev's cheek with her free hand. "You make me feel so many
things I thought I would never feel again. Happiness is just one
of them."

"Want to go upstairs and see my old room?" Dev asked with

a devilish smile. Kat laughed, and Dev felt her pulse quicken yet again. *How is it that she can affect me this way?*

"You are so bad, Devon Conway," she said before kissing her again.

"It's all your fault. I think I need to go take a cold shower."

"No. I want you hot and ready when we leave here later this evening."

"I don't think that would be a problem even if I took twenty cold showers between now and then." Dev pulled her hand from Kat's and stood to walk a few feet away from her. "But I do need to stop touching you, or I just might be forced to have my way with you right here on the floor."

Kat watched Dev disappear into the kitchen. She took a sip of beer and relaxed into the couch, reveling in the knowledge that she had the ability to make Dev happy. It gave her a warm feeling inside to know she could cause that. This complete and utter contentment wasn't something she'd thought she would ever feel again, especially in conjunction with a woman she'd known for just about a month. A noise startled her, and she looked toward the foyer when she heard the front door open. Chris walked in looking surly, and Rhonda was right behind her, appearing equally irritable.

"Kat." Chris nodded in her direction before disappearing into the kitchen.

"Hi, Rhonda," Kat said after Chris had left. Apparently the party had been moved into the kitchen, and no one had notified her. "Happy Thanksgiving."

"I suppose it is for some people," Chris said, emerging once again with a single bottle of beer in her hand. Kat noticed that she glanced at Rhonda, who was pointedly ignoring her.

"Thank you for helping with that last opening, Kat," Rhonda said with a forced smile as she took a seat in the chair opposite the couch. "You'll never know how much I appreciate it."

"You know I love to help out at the gallery. Did you sell anything?"

"Three pieces," Chris said gruffly. She took a big swig of beer before looking at Rhonda again. "I guess I'll have to give that money to Devon too."

"You don't have to give me anything." Dev reclaimed her seat next to Kat. She reached for Kat's hand without thinking, and she noticed that Chris was staring at their contact. "I'll even give you back the damn money you already gave if it'll make you happy."

"I don't want the damn money," Chris said before storming out of the room again. Rhonda simply forced a smile and a shrug when Kat and Dev looked at her.

"We had a bit of a disagreement before we left the house," she said. "I guess she's still a little pissed off."

"A little?" Dev asked with a humorless laugh. She released Kat's hand and leaned forward.

"What the hell are you two fighting about now?" Sheila asked as she took a seat in the other recliner next to her daughter.

"Infidelity," Rhonda said without looking at any of them.

"Hers, or yours?" Sheila asked carefully.

"Like I would ever cheat on anyone," Rhonda snapped.

"Did she cheat on you?" Dev asked. She shared an uneasy glance with Sheila. *I am such a fucking hypocrite.* Dev panicked a bit when Rhonda looked at her for a long moment before looking at Kat. *Shit, she told her!*

"I'm so sorry," Rhonda said to Kat.

Dev saw the alarm in Sheila's posture, and they shared another covert glance before they both quickly looked away.

"For what?" Kat asked, clearly confused.

"I guess she felt the need to purge herself of her past indiscretions," Rhonda said quietly. Dev braced herself for what she was sure was coming next. "She said she propositioned you a couple of months ago."

"Oh," Kat said quietly, not really knowing what to say. She glanced at Dev, who seemed to be totally confused. She cleared her throat and looked back to Rhonda. "I'm sorry I never told you. I turned her down, and she never approached me again, so I just thought it was better to not even mention it."

"I don't blame you, Kat," Rhonda said. "I blame Chris and her uncontrollable hormones." She turned her attention to Devon. "So, tell me about the two of you. I'm sure that you're in that 'can't keep your hands off each other' phase, right?"

"Yeah," Dev said, hoping that her initial fear didn't show on her face. She had the distinct feeling that she'd dodged a bullet, and Sheila looked incredibly relieved too. She knew that once this all had time to sink in, she would be pissed at Chris, but all she felt at the moment was relief.

"Excuse me." Sheila stood.

"Mom, please don't do anything stupid," Rhonda said quickly. "We worked through it, and she just needs to be alone for a few minutes."

Sheila simply nodded and waved as she made her way down the hall to the bedroom where Chris had sequestered herself. Rhonda took a deep breath before turning her attention back to Devon and Kat.

"Why, Rhonda?" Dev asked quietly. It was a question she had asked many times before, and she knew Jo had asked it of Rhonda more than once. Even Jo had realized that her twin was a loose cannon. "Why are you still with her?"

"I love her, Dev." She shrugged, just as she had always done when asked that question. "Sometimes I wish to God that I didn't, but I can't just change the way I feel about her, can I?"

"So no matter how much she hurts you, you'll stay with her?"

"Please just let it go, all right? We were talking about the two of you, weren't we?"

Dev sighed loudly as she went to get each of them a fresh beer. She glanced down the hallway when she heard Sheila and Chris yelling at each other, but made no move to try and intervene. She saw that Rhonda was trying her best not to listen to the fracas. Not that any of them could hear actual words anyway.

"Please talk to me," Rhonda said to Kat when they were alone. "How are things really going for the two of you?"

"So far so good." It bothered her that Dev hadn't even remarked about Chris having made a pass at her. It was as though Dev was suddenly preoccupied with something else. There was an uncomfortable silence as she and Rhonda tried to ignore the voices coming from down the hallway, but even though they couldn't make out any of what was being said, it was distracting. After a few moments, Rhonda stood and disappeared down the hall.

"I'm sorry about all of this," Dev said when she returned with a new beer for Kat. She sat down and put her arm around her, pulling her close so that Kat's head was on her shoulder.

"Are all of your family get-togethers this explosive?" Kat asked in an attempt at levity.

"Pretty much. Sheila never liked Chris, and it's been a sticky situation ever since the two of them started living together."

"I'm sorry I didn't tell you that Chris came on to me," Kat said. She didn't know why she felt the need to apologize, but for some reason it seemed important that Dev not hold it against her.

"Don't be sorry," Dev said quietly. She closed her eyes as the guilt washed over her. Even though it had absolutely nothing to do with what was happening between the two of them, she had the overwhelming desire to admit her transgression. "You told me there were women who made it clear to you what they wanted. I just never thought one of those women would have been Chris."

"I'm still sorry, Dev," she said. "I never should have kept it from Rhonda, or from you. I didn't know that Chris was like that all the time."

"Katherine, I need to tell you something," Dev said.

The seriousness of Dev's tone coupled with the use of her full name caused Kat to tense with apprehension, but Dev didn't get a chance to say any more. They sat up straight when they heard the bedroom door flung open, and Rhonda stormed out into the living room.

Rhonda stared at Dev for a moment, looking as if she were going to cry, and then she just shook her head before snatching up her coat and walking out the front door, slamming it hard behind her. Dev shrugged when Kat looked at her, but she saw something in Dev's expression that worried her. She didn't have the opportunity to voice her concern because Sheila and Chris followed closely on Rhonda's heels.

"Let her go," Sheila said.

"I have to go after her," Chris was saying as she picked up her jacket. "Just let me take your car, Sheila."

"*You* need to stay the hell away from her," Sheila said as she spun around to face her. The motion caused Chris to jump back a step. Sheila might have been in her late sixties, but she still had the ability to instill fear when she wanted to. "Besides that, you know as well as I do that she won't want to talk to you right now."

"What's going on?" Dev asked cautiously.

"She knows, Devon," Sheila said, turning to look at her. Dev felt her heart sink. This was definitely not going to be pretty.

"Thanks to you, you meddling bitch," Chris said to Sheila with a vehemence that startled all of them. She turned her attention to Devon and took a few steps toward her. "Why the hell did you have to tell Sheila about what happened? Why couldn't you have just kept your damn mouth shut about it?"

"Get out of my face, Chris," Dev said as she stood to face her. Dev glanced at Kat out of the corner of her eye and could tell that she was totally mystified as to what was happening.

"Did you tell her too?" Chris asked, catching the look and motioning toward Kat. "Jesus, Devon, you're probably more of a slut than I've ever been. Have you told your newest conquest about all the women who shared your bed before her?"

"Don't do this, Chris." Dev clenched her fists at her sides and willed herself to not strike out. It would be so easy—she'd wanted to slug Chris so many times throughout the years. She forced her hands to relax and then shoved them in her pockets.

"Fuck, it's not a secret anymore, Devon." Chris waved her hand in a grand gesture. "We *all* know about it. Hell, I'm sure the entire neighborhood knows about it. Why not tell Kat what happened too?"

"I'm going to go find Rhonda," Dev said before taking a couple of steps toward the front door. Sheila reached out and grasped her forearm in a deceptively strong hold. "Let me go, Sheila. I need to try and explain this to her."

"She won't want to talk to you right now, Devon," Sheila said, putting words to what Dev had already known but didn't want to think about. "Hell, I'm sure she won't want to talk to any of us for quite a while."

"I'll go," Kat said. She had no clue what they were talking about, but she had the feeling she wasn't going to like it. Someone should go after Rhonda though, to make sure she was okay, if for no other reason. "She'll talk to me."

"Oh, that's priceless." Chris snorted laughter. "But you're right—she'll listen to you because you're fucking *Saint* Devon, who we all know can do absolutely no wrong in Rhonda's eyes."

Dev couldn't help herself. She wasn't thinking clearly anymore. In one fluid motion she yanked her arm free of Sheila's grasp, pivoted on the balls of her feet, and cocked her fist back. She was aware somewhere in the far reaches of her consciousness that Kat yelled for her to stop, but there was something more powerful driving Dev's actions in that moment. The next thing Dev knew, Chris was lying flat on the floor, and Dev dropped to her knees with a blinding pain shooting up her arm.

"You fucking bitch!" Chris yelled through clenched teeth, her hand covering her jaw where Dev's fist had made contact. She tried to get up, but Kat placed a foot firmly in the center of her stomach to hold her in place. Chris struggled, but to no avail. "Let me up, damn it!"

"Here," Sheila said, emerging from the kitchen with a towel she filled with ice from the freezer. Dev took it and held it to her rapidly swelling knuckles as she winced in pain. "Do you think it's broken?"

"I don't know." Sheila helped her get to her feet. Dev risked a glance at Kat and was struck by the anger she saw brewing. "I'm so sorry about this."

"Shouldn't you be apologizing to me?" Chris asked incredulously from her position on the floor, Kat's foot still planted squarely in the middle of her torso. "I think my jaw is broken. Do any of you cunts give a damn?"

Not really, Kat thought as she moved her foot.

"I'll go talk to Rhonda." Kat still wasn't entirely sure what the hell was going on, but she had a pretty good idea. It wasn't something she even wanted to think about. She went to Dev and grabbed her uninjured arm a bit rougher than she had intended. "But you're coming with me, because I want to know what the hell just happened here, and why exactly Rhonda won't want to talk to any of you. And you should probably get that hand x-rayed."

"I'll get Chris to the hospital," Sheila said in resignation. "One of you call me later and let me know what happens."

Chapter Eighteen

Kat reached into Dev's pocket and extracted the keys to the Durango before silently helping her into the passenger seat. *How in God's name can a seemingly perfect day turn into such a complete disaster so quickly?* Neither of them said a word until they were about a mile away from Sheila's house.

"She probably went home," Dev said, knowing that was where Kat was headed anyway. Dev sat with her head leaning against the window. She hated the uncomfortable silence that had engulfed them, and felt that she needed to say something. She gingerly shifted the ice-filled towel on her hand and grimaced again. "Fuck, this thing hurts."

"Are you going to tell me what the hell happened back there?" Kat wasn't sure she even wanted to know. Not knowing seemed to be easier.

"Chris and I slept together." Dev was disgusted by her own words and could only imagine what Kat was thinking. A glance in her direction gave Dev no clue to that mystery, and Kat kept her eyes glued to the road before her, giving no indication that she even heard her.

"You already told me about that," Kat said after a rather lengthy moment of silence. Her temper was rising, and she didn't care what Dev thought of her. "But I find it hard to believe that Rhonda wasn't aware of what happened between the two of you before you met Jo."

"She did know about that."

"You told me you'd been with two women since you got back." Kat refused to look at her. "Was that a lie?"

"No."

"You cheated on Jo?" Kat was incredulous. She wanted to pull the truck over and shake some damn sense into her. It had never occurred to Kat that Dev would have cheated. Everything she'd told Kat led her to believe that she'd been hopelessly in love with Jo.

"I've never cheated." Dev so badly wanted Kat to believe her. She stared out at the passing houses because she didn't trust herself to look at Kat while giving this confession. "I loved Jo with all my heart, Katherine. She was everything to me. The night she died, I called Rhonda after I got the call from the hospital. She wasn't home because she and Chris had had a fight. She was staying at Sheila's, and Chris met me at the hospital. I was in no condition to drive home after Jo *and* our baby died, so Chris offered to drive me home. She ended up staying with me because she thought that I might do something stupid. I can admit now that if she hadn't stayed, I honestly might have done something. I couldn't seem to wrap my head around the reality of having to live my life without Jo. I don't know how long it took me to finally fall asleep, but I do know that it had been light outside for quite some time. Chris was sleeping on the couch."

Dev tried to fight back the tears that always accompanied thoughts of that horrible night, and memories began to flood back in torrential waves. When she was certain she had her emotions under control once again, she took a deep breath and went on, grateful that Kat was waiting patiently and not prodding her to go on before she was ready.

"When I woke up and realized that someone was in the bed with me, I actually wondered for a moment if it had all been nothing more than a nightmare." Dev finally turned her head so she could watch Kat's reaction to this, but there was none. If Dev didn't know better, she might think Kat wasn't even listening to her. But then she saw her reach up and wipe away a tear. Dev quickly redirected her gaze out the windshield. "When she woke up and started touching me, I allowed myself to imagine that it was Jo. I can't even begin to tell you how much I *wanted* it to be Jo. She sure as hell looked the part. I knew deep down that it wasn't her, but that didn't stop me. I hadn't gotten a chance to say good-bye because she never regained consciousness. I fooled myself into thinking this was the way I could say good-bye to her. I know it's not a good reason, Kat, but I was in so much pain that I couldn't think straight. I don't know if I can even begin to make you understand the things that were going through my mind when I woke up that morning."

"So that's why you decided to leave town after the funeral?" Kat pulled into Rhonda's driveway and turned off the ignition. "It wasn't just because you couldn't go on without her?"

"Jesus, Katherine, it was everything," Dev said in frustration. "If that hadn't happened, I might not have left—I really can't say for certain. I know I wouldn't have left without a word to anyone. I was a coward. I knew I could never face Rhonda day after day with that kind of secret between us. It was hard enough when she was helping me with the funeral arrangements."

"You were going to tell me something before all hell broke loose with Chris earlier," Kat said. She turned in her seat to face Dev. "What was it?"

"Everything I just said."

"Really? And why is that? Because you knew what they were yelling about?"

"God, no. I had no idea what was being said, I swear." She left the ice on her right hand as she reached for Kat with her left. An incredible feeling of relief washed over her when Kat didn't pull away from her touch. "I wanted to tell you because you were so upset about Chris having made a pass at you. I decided that I didn't want this thing to come between us. I thought you deserved to know the truth."

"Thank you for that." She looked down at their joined hands.

"I really should have taken you to the hospital first to get that taken care of."

"I'll be all right. Just go in and talk to Rhonda. I'll wait right here because I have a feeling she wouldn't let me in anyway."

"Let me see your hand." Kat gently palpated the flesh around Dev's knuckles and watched her face for any signs of added distress. "I think you did break something, Devon. I don't think it's terribly bad, but we're going to the hospital as soon as we leave here."

"I'm not going to argue with you." Dev let out a choked laugh before resting her good hand gently on Kat's cheek. "Maybe you could ask Rhonda for some aspirin or something for the pain?"

"I'll try to convince her to let you come in." Kat leaned over to place a kiss on Dev's cheek.

For a moment, Dev allowed herself to believe that everything would work out.

❖

Dev closed her eyes, but it was only a few minutes before Kat came back out to get her.

"She's going to let me in the house?" Dev's disbelief was obvious.

"She's actually tickled pink that you punched Chris." Kat tried, but failed, in her attempt to suppress a chuckle. "In fact, I think she intends to congratulate you. Besides that, you need more ice for this hand. What you've got here is pretty much melted."

Rhonda was waiting at the front door for them, a freezer bag full of ice in her hand. She exchanged it for the towel that was now soaking wet.

"That looks pretty nasty." Rhonda grimaced while they all took seats around the dining room table.

"You should see the other guy," Dev said, trying to lighten the somber mood. Rhonda just smiled wanly and shook her head. "I think I broke her jaw."

"Good for you." Rhonda nodded to emphasize her point. Dev could tell by Rhonda's body language that she was still incredibly pissed, but at least they were talking. "You really should have gone to the hospital, though, Dev. It looks like you broke your hand."

"I needed to try and explain things to you."

Kat handed her the aspirin that Rhonda had provided, and she swallowed them with the glass of water that was set in front of her. She sat back in her chair looking intently at Rhonda.

"What's to explain? You slept with my lover. That's pretty self-explanatory, don't you think, Devon?"

Dev repeated everything she had told Kat on the ride from Sheila's. Rhonda listened without interrupting. At some point, Kat had brought her good hand into her lap and was holding it tightly. When Dev was finished, Rhonda continued to sit in silence, and Kat made the decision to inject her own thoughts on the matter, whether they were wanted or not.

"I'm not trying to excuse either of them for what happened, Rhonda, but I can certainly see how it *could* have happened," she said quietly as she tightened her grip on Dev's hand. "I know that if Paula had a twin sister, and she offered me solace a few hours after she died, I doubt that I would have been strong enough to say no. At least I had time to prepare for Paula's death. I can't even begin to imagine the state of mind that Devon must have been in that day."

"It's not the first time that Chris has done something like this. I honestly don't know if I have it in me to forgive her again. I don't want to live the rest of my life wondering if she's screwing around on me. Devon, I know how much you were hurting when Jo died, and I don't blame you for what happened."

"Chris was hurting too, Rhonda." Dev wondered why in the world she was attempting to defend Chris, but the comment about *Saint Devon* doing no wrong still rubbed her the wrong way.

"I know that, Devon." Rhonda sounded tired. Not just emotionally, but physically as well. "But you can't convince me that she didn't make a conscious decision to get into that bed with you. The fact that she has always been attracted to you just leads me to believe she knew exactly what she was doing, and she wasn't just seeking comfort in a time of distress."

"She said you'd forgive Devon." There was a part of Kat that wanted to feel sorry for Chris. That wanted to believe Chris had been in just as much pain as Dev had been. But she knew it was Chris's own doing that made Rhonda so quick to absolve Dev and to hold Chris responsible for everything that had taken place between them.

"I don't even care anymore. I know I'm a good person and I deserve better than her. I just need to keep telling myself that, and hopefully someday I'll actually believe it."

"God knows I loved her sister with all my heart, and I hate to talk about Chris like this, but she is absolutely nothing like Jo." Dev glanced at Kat before looking back at Rhonda. She pulled her good hand away from Kat and reached over to take Rhonda's. "You really do deserve so much better than her. There are a lot of women out there who would be more than happy to be involved with you. You just need to dump Chris and get yourself out there to find someone."

"Yeah, right." Rhonda snorted. "Are you going to help me with that?"

"I introduced you to Chris, remember?" Dev laughed and removed the ice from her hand. Her knuckles were a beautiful shade of bluish purple. "I really don't think you want my help in the relationship department."

"Tell me something, Dev," Rhonda said quietly. "Why is it that you seem to do so well for yourself in that area? Why didn't *you* get stuck with the evil twin?"

"Just lucky, I guess." She looked at Kat's fingers softly caressing the bruises on her knuckles. "I should really get my hand taken care of. Are we okay?"

"We're fine," Rhonda said as they all stood. She hugged Kat

and then held Dev in a tight embrace. "I'm so glad you decided to come home. And thank you so much for slugging Chris. Maybe you finally knocked some sense into her."

"It's nice to dream, but I wouldn't bank on that. Call Sheila, all right? She's worried about you, and none of this was her fault. I asked her not to tell you, and she didn't because we both knew it would only hurt you."

"I'll let her know that I'm all right, but I won't promise any further conversation—at least not this evening." Rhonda walked them to the door and held it open for them. "Call me if you need anything."

❖

It was close to eleven when they finally pulled into Kat's driveway. Dev had drifted off during the short ride home from the hospital, but she opened her eyes when she heard Kat shut off the engine.

"Sorry," she said groggily as she sat up and rubbed her left hand over her face. "I guess I dozed off for a minute."

"Don't be sorry. You've had one hell of a day. And I'm sure the pain medication they gave you isn't helping you stay awake."

Dev looked down at her hand, which was in a splint. She tried to flex her fingers, but nothing seemed to be working correctly.

"I thought for sure I was going to be coming home with a cast."

"You fared much better than Chris." Kat grinned, and Dev couldn't help the soft chuckle that escaped. They had run into Sheila in the emergency room and learned of Chris's broken jaw. Luckily, Dev had been taken back to be x-rayed before Chris was released. It wouldn't have done either of them any good to see the other that soon after their confrontation. "Just remember that you do have a couple of small fractures, and the doctor doesn't want you doing anything with your hands for a few days. If you make it any worse, they *will* put a cast on it, and I know you'll hate that."

"Yes, Dr. Hunter," Dev said with a defeated grin. She'd been dreading this moment all evening. Kat seemed to be okay with everything that had come to light, but they hadn't really had a chance to talk too much about it. About what it might mean for their possibilities of building a relationship. Dev had decided while she was in the hospital that she would give Kat an out by not just assuming they were going to be spending the night together. "Can I see you tomorrow?"

"Tomorrow?" Kat was obviously surprised by the question. "Why not tonight?"

"I just thought that maybe you'd want to cool things off a little bit, given the events of the day." Dev winced at the pitiful way her statement came out, but she could only hope Kat wanted to be with her as much as she wanted to be with Kat.

"Then my suggestion is that you stop trying to think so much." Kat reached out and stroked Dev's cheek tenderly. "I allowed my insecurities to dictate how I reacted when I found out about Laura. What happened between you and Chris is three years in the past, and believe me, I have no doubts concerning the way you feel about her now. I don't want to stop seeing you— unless that's what you want."

"No. It's almost as if the more time I spend with you, the more time I *want* to spend with you. I'm not entirely sure how you've managed it, but I seem to think about you all the time. It scares me to realize that the only other person I've ever felt this strongly about was Jo."

"What do you think that means?" Kat was suddenly scared to death that Devon was about to tell her she loved her. Kat knew that what she was feeling was indeed love, but she wasn't entirely certain she herself could say those words. Rick had been right about her fears. Everyone in her life she'd ever said that to was gone—other than him and Vanessa. Gone either by death or abandonment. Kat honestly didn't think she could deal with either of those happening with Dev. It was a silly superstition, she knew, but it was definitely something she thought about.

"I'm not sure I'm ready to think about what it might mean," Dev said, even though she knew in her heart *exactly* what it meant. *But it's too soon to say those three little words, isn't it?* With Jo, she hadn't said it for a month or more, even though she had known it without a doubt by their third date.

"Then we won't think about it yet." Kat hoped the relief she felt wasn't evident in her voice. "There will be plenty of time to think about it all later. Right now, I just need to feel your skin against mine."

"That sounds incredibly nice." Dev held up her injured hand. "But I'm not sure how useful I'll be with this."

"We don't have to do anything but sleep, Devon." Kat leaned in and kissed her on the lips.

"Your place or mine?"

"Yours. I just have to run in and let Buddy out for a few minutes. You go on up, and I'll be there before you know it."

CHAPTER NINETEEN

Because of Dev's hand injury, Kat informed Nessa they wouldn't be able to make it to dinner that weekend, but they made plans for the following Wednesday. Kat knew Dev was going crazy not being able to use her hand at work, but it meant a lot to her that Dev had every intention of keeping her word about taking it easy.

Dev had bought two new toothbrushes—one to take to Kat's and one for Kat to use at her apartment. They had begun to alternate where they spent their nights, with one night in Kat's house, and the next at Dev's apartment.

Dev had also decided to invest in a second motorcycle helmet for Kat. It had been difficult to maneuver the bike the first few days after the hand injury, but it was getting easier every time she rode it. She had to admit though that it was about time to put the bike away for the winter season. No doubt the snow and ice would be arriving soon. She knew she would miss the freedom she felt when riding the Harley, which was why she insisted on riding it while the weather was still halfway decent.

"Hey, Devon!" her office manager shouted.

"Yeah!" she called back without looking up. She glanced at her watch and saw that it was almost two. *Damn, I missed lunch again.* "What is it?"

"There's someone here to see you!"

Dev grabbed a cloth and wiped her hands, being careful of her still-tender knuckles. *I don't have time for this.* She tossed the rag at Larry—her lead mechanic—before stalking across the floor to the office area.

"This better be good, Rita."

"Oh trust me, it is." Rita walked back to her desk. "She's in your office, Dev. I wouldn't keep that one waiting too long, if I were you."

Dev ran her hand absently through her hair as she made her way into her office, but she stopped in her tracks when she saw Kat sitting on the edge of her desk waiting for her. She kicked the door shut behind her. Kat stood and kissed her on the lips.

"I thought you were working today," Dev said with a smile as Kat slipped her arms around her neck.

"Are you complaining?"

"Not at all. I would never complain about you dropping in to see me. To what do I owe the pleasure of this visit?"

"I figured you hadn't eaten lunch, so I decided to come by and take you out." Kat pulled her closer and kissed her in what was supposed to be a quick brush of lips, but when Dev's hands moved to her ass and pulled her closer, it turned into much more than she had intended.

"We could just skip lunch and lock the door," Dev murmured as she pulled away.

"Do they all know that you're a lesbian?"

"I told them when I offered them their jobs." Dev let go of Kat to allow her to resume her seat on the desk. "I didn't want there to be any problems because of it somewhere down the road. They all seem to be pretty cool about it."

"I'm not sure they'd be so cool with us having sex in your office." Kat laughed.

"Are you kidding me?" Dev walked around her desk to take a seat. "There are two men out in the garage right now—do you honestly think it would bother them if two women were in here having sex? My guess is that they'd like to watch."

"I'm not interested in having an audience." Kat shook her head and gave Dev a mischievous grin. "I want you alone, and for much longer than a lunch break."

"Be careful, or we might not make it to Nessa's for dinner." The way Dev's eyes darkened caused a stirring between Kat's legs.

"I'm sure she'd understand." Kat decided that a change in subject was definitely in order. Otherwise, she would no doubt end up tearing Dev's clothes off her and throwing her down on the desk. *Audience be damned.* "You haven't been using your hand, have you?"

"I've been good. Although I am learning rather quickly that I'm not ambidextrous. It's not easy turning a wrench with my left hand."

"Poor baby," Kat teased, reaching out and cupping Dev's cheek. "Maybe you'll think twice before hitting someone next time. Even though she did deserve it."

"There won't be a next time." Dev glanced at her watch before standing. "I'm sorry, Kat, but if I want to get out of here at five, then I have to skip lunch. I'll be fine until dinner."

"I can see that I'm going to have to start packing you a lunch, aren't I? It's probably the only way you'll eat every day." Kat stood and waited for Dev to come to the front of the desk to meet her. "I'm on my way home now."

"I had a call from Rhonda this morning," Dev said as she put her arms around Kat. "Chris finally got the last of her things out of the house."

"Where's Chris going to live?"

"I don't know, and honestly, I don't care. They still have to figure out what they're going to do about the gallery, though. I'm just glad that Rhonda finally kicked her ass out."

"Me too." Kat pulled away reluctantly. Being this close to Dev was distracting. "I need to go now. You'll be at my place and ready to go to Nessa's after you're showered?"

"Absolutely." Dev kissed her before reluctantly releasing

her. The smile was still plastered on her face when Rita walked in a moment after Kat had gone.

"Girlfriend?" she asked with a knowing smile. When Dev didn't answer, Rita merely shook her head and chuckled quietly. "She's a looker, that one. You could certainly do worse."

Dev was more than a little surprised at the comment. She didn't know Rita all that well, but she had assumed she was as straight as they came. She tilted her head in acknowledgment but didn't say anything. As she headed back out to the garage, she thought about Rita's question.

Was Kat her girlfriend? On the surface it certainly seemed that way, but they hadn't really discussed what was happening between them since they had agreed to see where it was headed. There was no question that Dev wanted things to move forward, and she was pretty sure Kat did too, but the word *love* still hadn't been spoken between them. Dev decided tonight would be the night that she would take that step. It scared the hell out of her to think Kat might not feel the same way.

❖

"Mom, could you please help me in the kitchen?" Nessa asked not long after Dev and Kat had arrived. Kat followed her, leaving Dev and Josh to get better acquainted.

"So, Devon, Kat tells us you're an auto mechanic," he said when they were alone.

"Yes." Dev nodded, feeling uncharacteristically nervous. This felt an awful lot like being invited to the parents' house for dinner. She took a sip of her wine and tried to relax a bit.

"How did you ever get interested in that?" Josh asked, and Dev noticed for the first time that he really was a good-looking young man. His blond hair and blue eyes gave him a boy-next-door kind of look.

"My brother took me for a ride on his motorcycle when I was about eight years old, and I've been fascinated by anything that has an engine ever since." Dev shrugged, feeling herself loosen up. It helped to be on the subject of something she was passionate about. "I've always been obsessed with figuring out how things work, and I was lucky enough to be able to make a career out of it. Of course, if I had turned my attentions to electronics instead, I'd probably have enough money to retire by now. Who knew computers would end up being so essential to everyday life?"

Dev smiled wryly at the realization that Josh had probably never known a time when there weren't computers. *God, I feel so old.*

❖

"You two have been spending an awful lot of time together, haven't you?" Nessa asked as she watched Kat tossing the salad.

"I thought that I was summoned in here to help. I didn't realize I was going to be interrogated."

"You are helping me." Nessa shrugged and motioned for her to continue what she was doing. "You're helping me to understand what's going on in your life. Have you told her that you love her?"

Kat faltered in her actions as she looked at Nessa, but she said nothing in response to the question. How could she possibly make her understand why she feared those words so much?

"Okay," Nessa said slowly when the silence lengthened. "Has Dev said it to you?"

"No."

"She does though—you know that, right?" Nessa said this as though it was common knowledge. "It's so obvious when she looks at you. It's the same way you look at her. It's the same way you looked at Paula, Mom."

"I am not going to discuss this with you, Vanessa Louise," Kat said firmly as she put the utensils down on the counter.

"Calling me that isn't going to shut me up, Mom, and not saying the words isn't going to change the way you feel." When

Kat turned to walk out of the kitchen, Nessa quickly placed a hand on her arm. "If you love her, you should tell her. I don't want you to be alone, Mom. You deserve to be happy. You deserve to be loved."

"I can't tell her." Kat shook her head and fought the tears she felt threatening. She met her daughter's steady gaze for a moment before admitting defeat. Kat walked to the kitchen table and took a seat, knowing that she would need to explain her apprehension. She waited for Nessa to sit down across from her before going on. "I really don't expect for you to understand, Nessa, but everyone I've ever said those words to are gone from my life. My parents disowned me, and Paula died. I can't bring myself to say it to Devon because I honestly don't think I could stand it if something were to happen to her too."

"But if it did, Mom, would it hurt any less because you hadn't said the words out loud?" Nessa searched her face for a moment before Kat finally shook her head. "I'm still here, and so are Uncle Rick and Aunt Barb, and little Grace. This isn't some jinx that you somehow put on people, you know."

Kat just stared in silence, wondering in amazement just when her daughter had grown up. It didn't seem so very long ago that *she* was the one giving this type of advice to Nessa. She reached out to take Nessa's hand gently in her own.

"I know you're right, honey," she finally managed to say after a moment. "But this is a hurdle that I need to get over on my own. I do love Dev, very much. We just haven't talked yet about where this might be headed between us. I'm not even entirely sure *she's* ready for anything more at this point. I promise I'll tell her when I'm ready to, all right?"

"Just don't wait too long, Mom. God forbid, if something were to happen to her before you told her how you feel, you'd never forgive yourself."

❖

Kat was uncharacteristically quiet on the drive home, and Dev finally gave up trying to engage her in conversation. When she pulled the Durango into the driveway and turned off the engine, she shifted slightly in her seat to face Kat.

"What's wrong?" she asked quietly. Kat shook her head, but Dev spoke again before she could open her mouth. "Please don't tell me it's nothing. I can see that something is bothering you. Have I done something wrong?"

"God no," Kat answered quickly as she reached out and grasped Dev's hand.

"Is something wrong with Nessa?" A horrible thought occurred to her. "Is the baby all right?"

"They're fine." Kat glanced down at their hands for a moment, incredibly touched that Dev would be concerned about Nessa and the baby. She looked back to Dev's face with a forced smile. "It's really nothing, okay? I'll be fine. I just get a little worried sometimes when I think how fast she's grown up. And God, I'm going to be a grandmother soon. I'd always hoped that wouldn't happen until I was at least fifty. It all just gets a little overwhelming at times."

"Are you sure that's all it is?" Dev wasn't sure she believed it, but she didn't really have a good reason not to.

"Yes." Kat leaned over and kissed Dev softly on the lips, lingering for a moment to take in the scent of her. "Let's get inside and go to bed."

"Are you sure you don't want to be alone?"

"I'm quite sure." She brought Dev's hand to her lips and kissed her knuckles, never breaking their eye contact. "I want to be with you. I *need* to be with you, Devon. Don't you know that?"

"Honestly, no." She really didn't know anything for certain, but it was definitely nice to hear. "But I do now."

"Then I guess maybe I should let you know that a little more often, because I really do."

Dev followed her inside the house, and Kat took Buddy out

for his walk. On her way up the stairs, Dev looked into the living room and stopped short. Hanging above Kat's fireplace was the painting Jo had done of her. She sank down on the stairs, staring. She looked at every line, every shadow, and wasn't sure if she was okay with it or not. It was so intimate. So, well, Jo. Was it okay to have it here, in the place where she was falling in love with someone new? She let out the breath she was holding and pulled herself back to her feet. She made her way up the stairs and got ready for bed.

Kat came into the room and saw Dev sitting up in the bed, the sheet pooled around her hips.

"Tired?" Kat slowly began to remove her own clothes, thoroughly enjoying the hunger she saw in Dev's eyes.

"Not in the least," Dev answered with a slow smile. She patted the mattress next to her.

Kat slid under the sheet and nestled against Dev's warm flesh, her head on Dev's shoulder. She sighed contentedly.

"Are you tired?"

"No, I'm not," Kat said, her fingers moving lazily across Dev's abdomen. She immensely enjoyed the way Dev's muscles twitched under her touch. "You are so incredibly sexy, Devon."

Dev moaned when she felt Kat's mouth close around her nipple, her tongue making the peak harden almost instantly. She spread her legs in anticipation when she felt Kat's hand slowly move down her leg and then back up the inside of her thigh. She arched her back slightly when she felt a finger brush against her clit, and moaned in pleasure when she felt Kat slowly enter her.

"So sexy." It was a whisper, spoken close to Dev's ear. Kat pushed the sheet aside before moving down her body, trailing kisses along the way. As she settled between Dev's legs, she glanced up. "I want you to come for me, baby."

"Trust me when I say that won't be a problem." Dev leaned her head back against the pillow that was propped up behind her. She threaded her fingers through Kat's hair when she felt her mouth close around her and begin sucking lightly. Within moments, she was calling out Kat's name and coming so hard she thought her heart would burst out of her chest. She grabbed Kat by the arms and pulled her up to kiss her hungrily, then she pressed her forehead against Kat's, gasping for breath. "Jesus, that was incredible."

"I want you to fuck me," Kat whispered. "I need to feel you inside me, Devon."

She swung a leg over Dev's body to straddle her. Dev was still sitting up in the bed with Kat on her lap, and she moved her hand between them to slide her fingers through the wetness that awaited her touch. Dev took a nipple in her mouth as Kat shifted slightly to take her inside.

"Fuck me hard, Dev," she said, her head thrown back. "It feels so good, baby. Please make me come."

Dev ignored the pain in her injured knuckles and thrust into Kat while her thumb glided back and forth against her clit, pushing Kat closer and closer to the edge. Her free hand moved to the small of Kat's back, pulling her closer while she gently bit and sucked her nipple. When Kat stiffened and cried out her pleasure, Dev slowed her thrusts but didn't stop completely until Kat collapsed against her. Dev slowly pulled her fingers out.

"I didn't hurt you, did I?" Kat moved so they were facing each other, and she brought Dev's right hand up to her lips and kissed the still-bruised knuckles.

"No, I'm fine. It hurts a little, but I'll be okay."

"I'm so sorry."

Dev shook her head as she put her hand on Kat's cheek, slowly moving her thumb across the cheekbone.

"I love you, Katherine," Dev said quietly. There it was. She had thought she would never put her heart on the line again, had in fact convinced herself that she wouldn't. Dev got the feeling that her admission had scared Kat, who tensed and looked away. Suddenly she wished she hadn't been the first one to say those words. "I'm sorry."

"No, Devon," Kat said, looking as if she might cry. "God,

please don't ever be sorry for telling me how you feel. I'm just not sure I'm ready to say those words back to you yet. And *I* am truly sorry for that."

"It's okay." Dev's chest tightened with disappointment. "I can see how you feel by the way you look at me. And I saw the painting in the living room. I can't believe you bought it. So don't apologize for not being ready for it. Trust me—I know it's not easy to let yourself love again. I just need you to know that I didn't say it in the heat of the moment. I've been thinking about it for a while now."

"I know, and so have I." Kat finally looked away from her as she rolled onto her back, staring up at the ceiling, almost as though she expected the answers to all of her questions to be written there. "I hope you really do know how I feel about you, Devon. I'm trying so hard to overcome my irrational fears, but it's proving to be much more difficult than I ever imagined it would be. I hope that you can be patient with me and just give me a little more time. I bought the painting because Jo really captured your beauty, and I think anyone who comes over should see that beauty. The same beauty I love to see next to me every morning. You don't mind, do you? I was hoping it would be a good surprise."

"Of course I don't mind. And I'm touched that you did it. I admit, it was a little weird seeing it here at first, but I know Jo would approve. Thank you. And I'm not going anywhere." Dev put her arm across Kat's torso and allowed Kat's arm around her shoulders as she lay her head on Kat's chest. "I'll be right here as long as you'll let me be here."

Kat willed her tears not to fall. She was so scared that she would lose Dev if she opened her heart and truly let her inside. Kat didn't think she could survive if that were to happen again. But she was beginning to believe that Nessa had been right. Not saying the words certainly didn't change the way she felt.

Chapter Twenty

H ello?" Kat said into the receiver as she hastily picked up the phone after the second ring. She hoped it wasn't Dev calling to tell her she was going to be late. It was almost six, and Sheila and Rhonda were due for dinner in less than an hour.

"Kat?" She heard a male voice, and it was obviously strained.

"Josh?" All of Kat's senses were suddenly on alert. He sounded as though he had been crying. "Where's Vanessa? What's happened?"

"There was an accident," he said through sobs.

Jesus Christ, this cannot be happening. I cannot deal with any more loss in my life.

"Are you all right?" What she really wanted to know was if her daughter was all right. When Josh didn't answer right away, she felt her heart clutch in her chest. "Josh, I really need for you to tell me what happened. Where's Vanessa?"

"Hospital. God, Kat, there's a problem with the baby."

"What about Vanessa?" She wanted desperately to scream, but she somehow managed to keep her voice calm so she didn't freak out Josh.

"I don't know. They won't let me see her."

"Where are you?" Kat turned off the oven and grabbed her car keys from the kitchen table.

"I'm in the ER at Easton Hospital."

"I'll be there in a few minutes," Kat said before hanging up the phone. After making sure that the door was locked behind her, she pulled out her cell phone to call the garage, praying that Dev was still there. When someone answered, she began to speak without preamble. "I need to speak with Devon Conway. This is Katherine Hunter—it's an emergency."

Kat slammed her car door shut and started the engine before Dev finally picked up. To Kat, it seemed as though hours had passed while she waited to hear her voice.

"Kat, what's wrong? Are you all right?"

Kat took a moment to catch her breath. She closed her eyes and let herself be soothed by the sound of her lover's voice. Just knowing Dev was there made her feel like everything was going to be okay. The knot of panic in her chest eased a bit and she realized she had been silent for too long.

"Kat?" There was an edge of panic in Dev's voice.

"I'm okay." Kat turned on the windshield wipers. *Why didn't I notice it was snowing when I came out here?* "It's Vanessa. Josh called and told me that she was in an accident. I'm on my way to the hospital right now. I'm sorry, but I won't be able to finish cooking dinner for Sheila and Rhonda."

"Is Nessa all right?"

"I don't know." She put a hand over her mouth to stifle a sob. "There's a problem with the baby, Dev. I need to be there with her."

"Of course you do. I'll call Sheila and let her know that we'll need to reschedule. I'm sure she'll understand."

"No, you can finish dinner," Kat said, not wanting Dev to put her life on hold and rush to the hospital where she wouldn't be able to do anything anyway. "Just turn the oven on, and it should take about forty-five minutes. Hopefully I'll be home before you even finish eating."

"I'll be at the hospital, Kat. I'm leaving here in a few minutes."

"Please be careful, Devon. The weather's getting nasty out here."

"I will be. You be careful too, all right? I'll see you soon."

Kat closed the phone and put it in her pocket as she tried to steady her breathing. She gripped the steering wheel tightly in an attempt to stop her hands from trembling before starting the car. It wouldn't do anyone any good if she got into an accident on the way to the hospital.

❖

Kat was surprised to see Josh standing outside waiting for her when she parked the car and headed for the emergency room entrance. She walked quickly toward him, trying her best to push from her mind the awful thoughts of all the horrible things that *could* have happened.

"Have you heard anything?" she asked as she strode past him without so much as a glance in his direction. "What happened, Josh?"

"They haven't been out to see me yet." He managed to match her hurried strides and they walked back into the building together.

"Why won't they let you see her?"

"She isn't stable," he said.

She turned on her heel to face him, and he almost stumbled in his attempt to stop his forward motion. That was when she saw the gash that was stitched up on his forehead and noticed that his arm was wrapped in a bandage. All the anger went out of her system when she saw the streaks on his cheeks from his tears. Kat took him in her arms without a word and held him tightly.

"She'll be all right." Kat wondered how she would be able to convince him of that when she wasn't entirely confident of it herself. His body jerked in her arms as he tried to quiet his sobs. Kat held him tighter and finally allowed her own tears to come. "She has to be all right, Josh. I honestly don't think I could survive it if she isn't."

"Excuse me, Mr. Lewis?" a female voice asked from behind Kat. Josh pulled away from Kat and straightened up as he vigorously wiped away his tears and looked at the doctor expectantly.

"You're here with Vanessa Hunter?"

"How is she?" Kat asked.

"I'm sorry, who are you?" the doctor asked as she turned her attention to Kat.

"I'm Vanessa's mother. Katherine Hunter."

"I'm Dr. Larson. I'm the ER doctor this evening." She held out a hand in greeting. Kat just stared at it for a moment, thinking it was nuts to stand on formality while she was dying inside. As though driven by some automatic response system, Kat gripped her hand briefly.

"Will you both please come with me?"

The fact that the doctor hadn't answered her question did not escape Kat's notice. She tried desperately not to think about what it might mean. They were about to be led back into the ER when Kat suddenly remembered that Dev was on her way.

"Excuse me, Dr. Larson." She grabbed the doctor's forearm, causing her to stop and face her. "My lover is on her way here. Could we leave word with someone so that she doesn't worry when she arrives and I'm not out there?"

"Of course," the doctor said with a warm smile. If Kat's admission that she was a lesbian had surprised her, it certainly didn't show in her expression. "What's her name?"

"Devon Conway."

"I'll be right back." She went to speak with the triage nurse briefly. When she returned, they followed her through a door that was marked *Authorized Personnel Only* and waited while the doctor talked to another nurse who was manning the central island. When she was done, she beckoned to them to follow her and escorted them down a short hall to a curtained cubicle. Before entering, she stopped again and turned to face them.

"Where's Vanessa's obstetrician?" Kat asked.

"She's out of town for the weekend. I've put a call in for her to let her know what's happening, but I haven't heard back from her yet. The obstetrician on call has examined her, and I assure you that we're doing everything we can to help your daughter and her baby."

"I'm sorry, I didn't mean to imply otherwise." Kat suddenly felt like a pompous ass.

"Vanessa is awake, and she is somewhat stable at this point. She's suffered what's called a placental abruption, and we're worried about the baby at the moment. Vanessa is hooked up to a fetal monitor, and at the first sign of distress to the baby, we'll have to induce labor and deliver immediately. Hopefully, we won't be faced with that option."

"What is a placental abruption?" Josh asked quietly. Kat looked at him sadly, thinking that he looked and sounded every bit the concerned husband and father.

"The placenta provides oxygen and nourishment to the baby while it's in the womb." The doctor was speaking directly to him, but she glanced at Kat occasionally to make sure that they both understood everything she was telling them. "When an abruption occurs, the placenta tears away from the uterus, and in severe cases it can cause significant danger to both the baby and the mother. However, I believe that what we're dealing with is a mild abruption, and my hope is that she won't need to be induced. At this point, I don't believe that Vanessa herself is in danger. She hasn't suffered any vaginal bleeding, but she is complaining of contractions, and at this point she is experiencing some minor pain in the abdominal region."

"The baby is in danger?" Josh asked with a horrified look on his face. Kat reached out and took his hand in hers. He squeezed her hand gratefully, but didn't look at her.

"We are monitoring the baby's vital signs, and we will induce labor if things change. If everything remains as it is now, we'll probably keep her here for observation for a few days, and she'll be able to carry the baby to term, but she would be on strict bed rest until the delivery. Things do look good right now, but I need you both to know what we're facing before you go in to see her."

"Does she know about all of this?" Kat was numb. At some point during the doctor's explanation of the situation, her mind had switched to auto pilot.

"Yes, I spoke with her before I came out to get you." Dr. Larson nodded to them before opening the curtain and allowing them to enter.

"Hi, Mom," Nessa said with a tremulous smile. Kat quickly went to her and smoothed her hair back from her forehead. Nessa looked at Josh and held out her hand, which he took as he stood on the opposite side of the bed. Kat saw the unshed tears about to fall from her daughter's eyes. "I don't want to lose this baby," she whispered.

"You won't, honey," Kat said, trying not to let Nessa see her fear. She leaned down to press her lips to Nessa's forehead. "Everybody here is going to make sure of that. You're strong, and I know that baby is too. Neither of you are going to give up without a fight."

"No, we won't." Nessa gave a broken laugh and then turned serious again. "I know you had dinner plans this evening with Devon and her family. I'm so sorry I screwed that up."

"Oh, sweetie, don't worry about that. The only thing you should be concerned with is getting well. Maybe you should try and sleep for a bit, all right?"

"Will you be here when I wake up?"

"I'm not going anywhere." Kat hoped her smile was more reassuring than she felt. She turned to see Dr. Larson still standing by the curtain. "Will she be moved to a room soon?"

The doctor nodded. "Probably in about an hour or so." She gestured to Kat. "You can go back to the waiting room and I'll come let you know when we move her."

"Thank you." Kat looked back to see Josh leaning over Nessa and kissing her cheek softly. It broke Kat's heart to see how much this was shaking him.

"I'll be with your mother, all right?" he asked tenderly as he traced her cheekbone with his index finger. "As soon as they move you to a room, we'll be up to see you again."

"Is Devon here, Mom?" Nessa asked when Josh straightened up again.

"She's on her way, honey. She'll be here long before you get moved."

"Can she come see me too?" All three of them looked at the doctor, who simply nodded. "Thank you."

❖

Devon cursed herself for not replacing the battery in the Durango. It was snowing pretty hard, and she was still having trouble keeping her emotions under control in order to concentrate on the road conditions. Conditions that were rather treacherous for motorcycle riding to begin with.

She tried desperately not to let the overwhelming fear she had felt when Rita had informed her that Kat was on the phone, and that it was an emergency, take over her senses again. It brought every fear and feeling of desperation to the forefront, just as it had the night she had gotten the call about Jo. That was definitely something Dev did not want to go through again in this lifetime.

She was only a couple of blocks from the hospital and waiting at a red light to make a left turn when she took her helmet off and tried to wipe the moisture off her visor. Muttering under her breath, she put it back on and tightened the strap just before the light turned green. As she accelerated, she almost didn't see the truck that ran the light. She was barely able to swerve out of his way, but she lost control of the bike, and it skidded out from under her.

She was vaguely aware of people standing around her, of someone on a cell phone calling for an ambulance. As she tried to sit up, she cried out in excruciating pain at the burning in her right side, and then everything around her went black.

❖

"Tell me what happened, Josh," Kat said when he returned with coffee for them.

"We were going out to dinner," he said, and Kat could tell he was still in shock. "I was driving. We were on Route Thirty-Three. Some idiot was going too fast for the conditions, and he tried to move into our lane to pass the car in front of him. He clipped the front of our car, and we went off the road. It all happened so fast, Kat. There wasn't anything I could do."

"It's okay, Josh. It wasn't your fault. What did the doctors say about your injuries?"

"There's just this cut." He touched the stitches on his forehead and winced slightly at the pain. "And a sprained wrist. They did a CT scan, but said I didn't have a concussion."

"That's good." Kat leaned her head back against the wall. She glanced over at the clock hanging on the wall and saw that it was just after seven. *Dev should be here by now.* Maybe she'd decided to stay home to have dinner with Sheila and Rhonda after all. Kat decided to just rest for a moment, then call her. It had been a little over two weeks since Devon had said she loved her, and Christmas was in less than a week. She suddenly regretted that she still hadn't uttered those words in return. Sitting there, waiting for her daughter, she knew that Nessa was right. Life was precious, and there was no reason to wait any longer. She would tell Devon she loved her the first moment they had together.

❖

"Kat."

Josh shook her gently, and she awoke to see the doctor walking toward them. She sat up and looked at the clock again. Over an hour had passed. She looked at Josh and saw that he appeared just as worried as she felt.

"Is Devon here?"

"No, I haven't seen her." He shook his head, but never took his eyes from the doctor.

"Ms. Hunter?" Dr. Larson had a serious look on her face, and Kat felt her heart rate speed up again.

"Is it Vanessa?" The doctor took a seat next to her, and Kat felt herself go into complete panic mode. "Jesus, what's happened?"

"Devon Conway was brought into the ER a few minutes ago."

Kat felt as though an iron fist had suddenly grabbed her heart. She stared at the doctor but was wholly unable to form coherent thoughts. She felt Josh's hand on her shoulder, but it was only on the outer edges of her awareness. *Jesus, no. How much more of this can I possibly be expected to deal with?*

"She's in x-ray right now, but the attending physician is pretty sure she has a few broken ribs, and they're preparing her for surgery to fix her shoulder, which was pretty banged up. She is awake, and there aren't any immediate signs of a concussion. She's lucky the accident only happened a couple of blocks from here and that our emergency personnel were able to get to her as fast as they did. Also, her quick reflexes more than likely saved her life."

"Is she going to be all right?" Josh asked softly, posing the question that Kat couldn't bring herself to ask.

"I can't deal with any more of this," Kat murmured. She felt Josh's hand on her arm. She looked over at him with tears coursing down her face. The doctor was completely forgotten for the moment.

"Yes, you can," he said with conviction as he squeezed her arm. "You can because you have to, Kat. Vanessa *and* Devon both need you to be able to deal with it. So do I. We all need you right now."

Kat stared at him, trying desperately to make sense of everything he had said. She knew he was right, and she forced herself to take a deep breath and square her shoulders as she turned back to face the doctor.

"Is she going to be all right?"

"She's in good hands here," Dr. Larson said. "There's absolutely no reason to think that she won't make a full recovery, but you do need to understand that there are risks involved with any type of surgery."

"Can I see her?"

"I'll check with the attending physician and try to find out when she'll be back from radiology. She's probably going to be sedated, but I'll make sure that you can see her tonight."

"Thank you." When the doctor left, she felt Josh's arm go instantly around her shoulders, and she succumbed to the comfort he was offering.

"Devon will be okay," he said quietly. "All three of them will."

CHAPTER TWENTY-ONE

"Rhonda and Sheila are on their way." Josh put his cell phone back in its holder at his hip.

"Thank you for calling them." Kat forced a smile as he took his seat next to her again. Rhonda and Sheila needed to know what was happening with Dev, but she'd known she would never be able to make that call. She was grateful for Josh's presence. "I can't believe this is happening."

"Should I call your parents?" he asked hesitantly. Kat heard him, but she only stared at a spot on the floor near her feet without speaking. "Vanessa told me that you don't get along with them, but wouldn't they want to know what's going on with her and the baby?"

"Honestly?" Kat shook her head slowly and finally turned her head to look at him. "I don't know if they would care. They haven't taken an interest in her life before. But I suppose it would just be one more thing for them to hold over my head if they didn't know about it. I'll call my brother, and maybe he'll see fit to tell them. Have you called your parents yet?"

"They're on their way here," he said, and she felt sorry for him when she saw the pained look on his face. He really was a good young man, and it killed him that his parents disliked Kat.

"As well they should be." Kat nodded once and placed her hand on his knee, squeezing gently. It wasn't his fault his parents were assholes. "This is their grandchild too, after all. I'm going to go outside and call Rick. You come get me the minute you hear anything about Vanessa *or* Devon."

Rick wasn't home, so she left a message on the machine telling him what was going on. She was about to call Laura to let her know she wouldn't be at the clinic in the morning when she saw Josh's parents making their way from the parking garage. Kat snapped the phone shut and shoved it in her pocket before going back inside.

"No news yet?" She resumed her seat next to Josh. He shook his head but said nothing, and she leaned in closer to him. "Your parents are here, honey. I think I'll go wait on the other side of the room."

"No." Josh shook his head adamantly. His eyes were pleading, and the sight made her heart break. "Please stay, Katherine. You might think I only said it to make you feel better, but I really do need you right now. Please don't let them chase you away."

What could she say to that? She nodded her agreement just as they came through the doors and hurried over to them.

"Joshua, what happened?" Carol Lewis asked as he stood to embrace her. Her hand went right to the sutures on his forehead when they parted. "Are you all right?"

"I'm fine," he said. Kat cringed when he made it a point to look back at her.

"Oh, hello, Katherine," Carol said before returning her attention to Josh. "You should sit down, Joshua. This cut looks nasty."

He did as he was told. "I'm fine, Mom. We're waiting for them to give us an update on Nessa's condition."

It didn't escape Kat's notice that his parents didn't seem the least bit concerned about Nessa—who also happened to be the mother of their grandchild. To Carol, all that mattered was that her little boy was injured. Bill, Josh's father, stood next to her, silent as usual. Kat wouldn't be surprised if Carol had to give him permission to speak. The anger Kat felt was boiling to the surface, but she wanted to remain calm for Josh. It wouldn't do anyone any good for her to lose her temper over something she'd never be able to change.

Kat simply looked away and gripped Josh's hand when he reached out for hers.

"Maybe you should go home and rest, honey," Carol said.

"I'm staying here, Mom."

"But there isn't anything you can do."

"He can be here for Vanessa," Kat said without bothering to even look at her. "*That's* what she needs right now. Do you even care that she might lose the baby?"

Carol looked as if she was going to say something in response, but her husband took hold of her arm and led her quickly outside.

Kat sighed. "I'm sorry, Josh."

"There's no need to be. I was about to ask her the same question."

"Kat!" Sheila called the second they entered the waiting room. Kat stood and allowed herself to be held by Sheila. "How is Vanessa?"

Kat cried at the simple question. How was it that Sheila was asking about her daughter before she asked about Devon, when Josh's mother seemed as if she couldn't care less? She held tighter to Sheila when she felt Rhonda embrace them both. After a moment, Kat managed to take a step back and compose herself.

"They're monitoring the baby, and they may have to deliver by c-section if her condition worsens," she said.

"What about Dev?" It was obvious to Kat that Rhonda was dreading the answer to that question.

"I haven't been able to see her yet. She was in x-ray the last I heard. The doctor said they would let me know when I could go back and see her."

"Ms. Hunter?" a voice from behind her asked, almost as if on cue.

Kat turned quickly to see the ER doctor approaching. "Yes?"

Kat's impatience was obvious. *I really can't handle any more bad news. Please just let this be something good.*

"We've moved your daughter upstairs to a private room. Things are going fine so far, but we're still monitoring both her and the baby's vital signs. If we can make it through the night without any complications, then my guess is that she'll be able to carry the baby to term."

"Oh, thank God." She hugged Josh, who had come to stand by her side when the doctor arrived.

"Also, Ms. Conway is back from radiology, and I've arranged with her doctor for you to be able to see her. I can take you back there now, if you'd like."

Kat turned her attention to Sheila, who was obviously worried about Dev. Sheila shook her head in response to Kat's unasked question.

"You're what she needs right now, sweetheart," Sheila said quietly. "Go and talk to her. We'll be waiting right here for an update."

"Thank you," Kat said, but somehow those words didn't seem adequate to her. She hugged her before turning her attention to Josh. "You go on up to Nessa's room, and I'll be there as soon as I can, all right?"

He nodded. Just then, his parents returned to the waiting room. Hopefully Bill had been able to talk some sense into his wife, but Kat didn't hold out much hope for that. She turned and allowed the doctor to lead her to Dev.

"I want to thank you for this," Kat said as they walked. "It seems as though you've been doing a lot for me tonight that you didn't really have to do."

"Believe me, I know how difficult it can be for someone to get in to see their partner if they aren't legally married." Dr. Larson said softly as they walked. "Thankfully, it's never been much of a problem at this hospital, but it's easier for everyone this way. You won't be able to stay with her long because they need to get her into surgery to repair her shoulder. She is sedated, so she may not be aware that you're even there with her."

"Thank you again," Kat said when the doctor left her alone with Devon.

She wiped a tear off her cheek as she stood there and stared at Dev, who was lying in the bed looking incredibly helpless and vulnerable. After a moment, she walked to the side of the bed and took Dev's limp hand between both of hers. It was so cold. Kat wanted nothing more at that moment than to take Devon in her arms and hold her there forever. "Devon, can you hear me, baby?"

Dev's hand twitched slightly, but her eyes remained closed. Kat tried not to think about all of the tubes and monitors that Dev was hooked up to. If she gave in to that, she knew that she would break down completely. The memories of Paula's final days threatened to invade her mind, but she steadfastly refused to let those thoughts take hold.

"Devon, I really need you to get well, baby," Kat whispered through the tears. She raised the unresponsive hand to her lips momentarily. "I love you, Devon. I am so sorry I didn't tell you that before, but I do love you. I can't lose you, sweetheart."

Dev's voice was so quiet that Kat almost didn't hear her. She probably wouldn't have heard it if Dev hadn't weakly squeezed her fingers at the same time. Kat stared in anticipation as Dev's eyes slowly opened for just a moment.

"What did you say, baby?" Kat leaned closer so she could hear her better.

"Don't...make me...do this again...just to hear you...say that," Dev managed in a strained whisper. The words made Kat laugh out loud through her tears, and she reached out to touch Dev's face.

"I promise that I will tell you so often that you'll get sick of hearing it, just as long as you get better."

Dev grinned weakly. "I'll never get tired of it. I might not remember you said it when I get out of here, though. I think they have me on too many drugs."

"I'll remind you, baby." It was obvious that Dev was trying to hide the pain she was in, and that knowledge induced a new bout of tears from Kat. "I'll make sure that you never again have to question how I feel about you."

"I love you," Dev said.

"I love you too," Kat said with a tremulous smile. She watched in silence as Dev succumbed once again to the drugs they had given her. She brushed Dev's hair from her forehead while she listened to the constant beeping, and the steady sound of her breathing. It had been a source of comfort with Paula—to know that she was still breathing. She thought back to what Dev had said to her when they had the conversation about Paula's death.

At least with Jo it happened fast. I was in too much emotional pain to be able to realize it at the time, but I truly think it was a blessing. She didn't have time to suffer. With the cancer, you both had to suffer through it for those two years.

Kat shook her head as she reached over and stroked Dev's cheek. Faced with the situation now, she honestly didn't think that either scenario was better than the other. They had been planning dinner with family just a few hours ago, and now Dev was lying here looking so fragile, about to be taken in for surgery. How could anyone think this would be easier than knowing that death was coming?

"Excuse me," a nurse said as she came to stand by the other side of Dev's gurney. Kat looked up at the nurse with tears coursing down her cheeks. "We need to get her up to surgery now. Are you going to be all right, ma'am?"

Kat just nodded as she stepped away from the bed. *Jesus, I really need to get a hold of my emotions. I can't let Nessa see me this way.*

"Will you be in the waiting room?" By this time there were a number of people in the relatively small space, waiting to transport Devon to the OR. "I can make sure someone notifies you when she comes out of surgery."

"I'll be in my daughter's room. Her name is Vanessa Hunter. I really need to know when Devon gets out of surgery. I would really appreciate it. Please."

"Don't worry about it." The nurse nodded. "I'll find you."

Kat turned away from her when they began to wheel Dev from the room, but she stopped them by reaching for Dev's hand. She squeezed it gently as she leaned down to kiss her on the lips.

"Please be okay, baby. I really need for you to be okay."

The nurse was silent as she watched this exchange, and when Kat finally let go of Dev's hand, she took Kat by the arm and led her back toward the waiting room.

"My name is Katherine Hunter," she told the nurse when she saw Sheila and Rhonda stand and walk toward them. "My daughter is Vanessa Hunter. I cannot stress how important it is that I know as soon as Devon Conway is out of surgery."

"I'll find you," the nurse said once again before disappearing back into the emergency room.

Kat took the time to update Sheila and Rhonda on Dev's condition, and then they insisted that she go up to Nessa's room. She kissed them both on the cheek before walking toward the elevator, trying all the way to let go of the image of Dev looking so fragile.

CHAPTER TWENTY-TWO

I'm not leaving," Kat told the nurse who entered Nessa's room around ten o'clock to inform everyone—yet again—that visiting hours had ended an hour before. "I'll sleep right here in this chair, but I am not leaving my daughter."

Kat had made sure that every nurse on the floor knew she was also waiting for word on Devon and knew which room she would be in while she waited for that word. Furthermore, she was pretty certain they all understood that she would have someone's head if they failed to alert her the very moment Dev was out of surgery.

"Come on, Joshua," Carol said as she stood and looked down at him expectantly. "Your father and I will take you home with us for tonight."

"I'm not leaving either," he said without getting up. He shook his head adamantly as he looked from his father to his mother. "I won't leave Vanessa when she needs me the most."

"Bill," Carol said, shooting a glance at her husband, who had remained almost completely silent the entire evening. Kat had to stifle a laugh at the thought that maybe he was intimidated by being in the same room as not one, but *two* lesbians, since she had asked Rhonda and Sheila to come up and wait with them. *God, I really am on the verge of losing my mind.*

"Let him stay," Bill said, his exasperation clear. Rhonda caught Kat's eye, but all Kat could do was shrug in surprise. "He needs to be here with her right now, can't you understand that?"

"I don't want to leave him here with *those* women," Carol said, clearly thinking she'd spoken low enough that no one could hear them, but Kat did. And Kat could tell that Rhonda and Sheila had heard it as well.

"Yes, Bill, you really should be careful," Kat said in a theatrical whisper. "If you leave him here with us, we might just turn him into a lesbian. How in the world would you explain *that* to all of your friends?"

"Mom!" Nessa said in an attempt to admonish, but it was obvious that she was trying her best not to laugh.

Carol Lewis took her husband's arm firmly and led him out of the room without another word, and Kat finally relaxed with an audible sigh.

"Don't you dare apologize for that," Josh said with a chuckle when Kat looked at him. "They both deserved that and more, if you want my honest opinion."

"Trust me, Josh, the look on your mother's face was more than worth it," Kat said with a little giggle of her own.

Kat was inordinately pleased to see the smirk on the nurse's face as she checked Nessa's vitals. "Now that we've all had our fun," the nurse said, "I really do need you all to leave. There's nothing else that any of you can do tonight, and she needs her rest. If there are any changes, the doctor will call immediately."

"I'm not leaving," Kat said again as Rhonda and Sheila stood to leave.

"Me either," Josh chimed in, holding on to the arms of his chair as if he intended to never let go. The poor boy looked as if he would break out in tears at any moment, and it broke Kat's heart to see him so distraught.

"I'll go speak with the doctor," the nurse said with an exasperated sigh as she headed out the door and toward the nurse's station.

"Don't go," Kat told Sheila as she stood to face them. "I can't tell you how much it's meant to me to have you both here."

"We'll just be down in the waiting room," Rhonda said. "Please call my cell phone the minute you hear anything about Devon."

"I will, and you do the same if they happen to find you first," Kat said before hugging them both and watching them leave. She walked over to stand next to Nessa's bed, smiling down at her.

"Mom, you really don't need to stay here all night."

"Yes, I do." Kat reached out to brush a stray lock of hair from her cheek as she spoke. "You're my little girl, and I need to be here with you."

"I'm okay."

"I know," Kat said, even though she knew no such thing. Nessa needed to make it through the night before they could be certain everything would be all right. Kat made no attempt to point that out to her though. "I also need to be here for Devon when she finally wakes up."

"Did you tell her how you feel about her yet?"

Kat nodded as she fought tears. "I finally said it to her tonight, just before she went into surgery. I just hope it wasn't too late."

"Don't think like that." Nessa glanced past Kat's arm and motioned for Josh to come closer. When he did, she took his hand and squeezed it gently. "Could you go get her some coffee or something? Food would probably be good too, because if I know my mother, I'm sure she hasn't eaten anything in hours."

"I'll be right back." Josh leaned over and kissed Nessa on the cheek.

"Is something wrong? Something you don't want Josh to know?" Kat asked.

"No, Mom. I want to talk about you," Nessa said, but she raised a hand to stop Kat's question. "And he gets a little uncomfortable when you and I talk about personal things. He isn't close to his parents like I am with you, and he just doesn't think that parents and children should talk so openly about sex."

"He's adorable, Vanessa," Kat said as she sat on the edge of the bed, being careful not to disrupt any of the medical equipment Nessa was hooked up to. "I'm so glad that the two of you found each other."

"So am I." Nessa grinned. "You aren't going to get out of this by changing the subject, though."

"Get out of what?"

"I pushed you to tell Devon that you love her." Nessa refused to give her an opportunity to protest. "Yes, I did, and I didn't even stop to think of what you might be going through. I know the reason you told me for not wanting to tell her, but is there more to it than that?"

"Honey, I don't know what you're talking about."

"You haven't been with anyone since Paula." Nessa seemed to be struggling with her words, and Kat waited patiently for her to continue. "You never dated or anything, Mom. You don't feel guilty, do you? Like maybe you're cheating on her?"

"No, sweetie." Kat stared at Nessa in disbelief. That had been *exactly* the reason that she hadn't dated in the first couple of years. To her it was as though she would have been trivializing what Paula had meant to her by going out with someone else. But Dev was different. It was as though Dev understood everything that she was thinking and feeling. Dev knew what she had gone through, and she felt as though she could be herself around her. This wasn't something she had ever discussed with Nessa, and she found herself wondering once again when Nessa had grown up so much. "I don't feel guilty about loving Devon. The reason I didn't date is because it never seemed to feel right. With Dev it does."

"But you feel guilty about something, Mom. You can't hide your feelings from me, and you know that. So what's wrong?"

Kat thought about the only thing that really made her feel guilty about Paula dying. Nessa really didn't need to hear it right now, and Kat really didn't want to cause her any more stress than she was already dealing with. But Kat knew that she would tell her anyway, because she never had been able to deny Nessa anything.

"Mom, please talk to me."

"Toward the end, when things were really bad for Paula, I think that I might have wished for it be over."

"Jesus, is that all?"

"It isn't enough?" Kat was dubious. "My God, Nessa, I wished for her to die. What kind of a monster does that make me?"

"Mom, I never told you this because you had so much to deal with, and I didn't need to add my guilt to everything else." Nessa placed a hand gently on Kat's knee. "But I made that same wish. I could see that what she was going through wasn't just causing her pain, but it was slowly killing you as well. I felt so guilty about making a wish like that. I had actually convinced myself that I killed her."

"Oh, baby, it wasn't your fault." Kat shook her head as tears rolled down her cheeks.

"I know that now, Mom, and it wasn't your fault either. I've come to the realization over the past few years that it's probably a normal reaction when someone is suffering through a terminal illness. You shouldn't feel guilty for wishing that her misery would end."

"Ms. Hunter?" Dr. Larson stepped into the room.

"Yes?"

"You seem to have been successful in ruffling the feathers of every single nurse assigned to this floor," she said with a slight grin. "Did you actually threaten bodily harm if you weren't notified immediately when Ms. Conway came out of surgery?"

"Not exactly," Kat said defiantly, refusing to back down.

"You'll have to excuse her—she's in love." Kat didn't need to look at Nessa to know she was smiling.

"Yes, I can see that. Ms. Conway is very lucky."

"I'm the one who's lucky," Kat said. She stood up a little straighter in spite of the flush she felt rise to her cheeks. "I've lost one lover to death, and I don't intend to lose another."

"I'm sure that the staff here will agree with you." Dr. Larson picked up Nessa's chart as she spoke. "I've arranged for you and Mr. Lewis to be able to stay the night here with your daughter. And I will give you my personal guarantee that you will be notified, if not the very moment Ms. Conway is out of surgery, then at least the moment she is out of recovery. Good enough?"

"Yes." Kat said gratefully. "Thank you very much."

❖

"Excuse me, Ms. Hunter?" a voice asked from what seemed to be a million miles away. There was a hand on her shoulder, shaking gently. "Ms. Hunter, are you awake?"

"What?" Kat frantically searched the room, trying to figure out where she was. She looked at Dr. Larson as she sat up and tried to stifle a yawn as her heart pounded so hard against her chest that it hurt.

"Ms. Conway is in recovery now. Everything went well, and she woke up asking for you."

Kat felt a little of the stress she had been dealing with melt away. She glanced at Nessa, who seemed to be sleeping peacefully. Josh was sitting in a chair next to the bed, his head resting on the mattress next to Nessa's hip and her hand resting on the back of his neck. She swallowed around the lump of emotion in her throat before looking back at Dr. Larson.

"Can I see her?"

"She'll be moved to a room soon, and I'll speak with the nurses. Someone will come up and get you when you can see her. I'm sorry I had to wake you up, but you insisted."

"Thank you again—for everything." Kat knew those words were woefully inadequate for all the doctor had done for her and her family. Kat watched her as she left the room, then looked back at Nessa and Josh. For the first time since receiving the phone call from him eight hours earlier, she allowed herself to hope that everything really would be all right.

CHAPTER TWENTY-THREE

Devon awoke to the feel of fingers gently caressing her cheek. When her eyes fluttered open and she saw Kat next to her, she squeezed the hand holding hers.

"Hey, baby," Kat said. "You really scared the hell out of me, Dev."

"That wasn't my intention." Her throat was scratchy, and she motioned for a glass of water, which Kat promptly poured and handed to her.

"Take it easy. The nurses say that your stomach may still be a little queasy from the anesthetic. I'm going to go out on a limb and guess that throwing up wouldn't be good for you right now."

"How is Nessa?" Dev asked as she handed the cup back to her. "And the baby?"

"So far, so good." Kat held up her crossed fingers. "She's sleeping right now, and Josh is with her. She might have to spend the rest of her pregnancy in bed, but I think that would be preferable to an emergency c-section."

"What's *my* damage?" Dev finally dared to ask the question that she was dreading the answer to.

"They didn't tell you?"

"From what I understand, I haven't really been too coherent since they brought me in here. If they did tell me, I don't remember."

"Then you don't remember seeing me before you went into surgery?" Kat grinned at her.

"No…that I remember." Dev laced her fingers with Kat's and smiled at the blush that touched her lover's cheeks. She raised Kat's hands to her lips and met her gaze. "You want to tell me what you said again, just in case I'm remembering it wrong?"

"I love you," Kat said without hesitation. She took a deep breath. "I honestly didn't think I would ever fall in love again, but there is definitely something irresistible about you, Devon Conway. I'm not sure what you did to me, but I'm afraid I've fallen pretty hard."

Dev laughed, which apparently was a mistake given the wince of pain that followed. Kat stroked Dev's cheek with the hand that wasn't still being held tightly.

"And here I thought that I was the one who fell under *your* spell. God, Kat, you are so beautiful."

"Ha!" Kat snorted laughter. "I'm a mess right now. I've been up for damn near twenty-four hours now. I don't know why everyone had to end up in the emergency room on the same night."

"You're still beautiful," Dev insisted. She patted the bed next to her. "Get in here with me."

"I think it's going to be quite a while before you're ready for that kind of activity, honey," Kat said, laughing for the first time in what felt like ages. "You just got out of surgery to repair a badly damaged shoulder. You've got a broken collarbone and two broken ribs, and you're just damn lucky that you don't have a more serious concussion. Thank God you've got a hard head."

"I knew it would come in handy someday."

"Ms. Hunter?" a man's voice said from behind her.

Kat turned without a word to face the surgeon who had taken care of Dev. He was dressed in clean blue scrubs, but the growth of beard on his face indicated that he hadn't shaved in quite some time.

"I just received a phone call from Dr. Larson," he said, and suddenly all of her senses were on high alert. "Your daughter is being prepped for an emergency c-section."

"Fuck," Kat whispered. She turned to look at Devon when she squeezed her fingers.

"You need to be with her. I'm pretty sure I'm not going anywhere any time soon."

"I'll be back as soon as I can." Kat leaned down and pressed her lips to Dev's forehead. "I love you so much, baby."

"I love you too." Dev let go of her hand. "If you get to see her before they take her in for delivery, tell her I'm thinking about her."

Kat nodded before she hurried out of the room. Dev took as deep a breath as she could before leaning her head back and closing her eyes.

"How are you feeling?" the doctor asked when they were alone.

"Other than having the sensation of a two-hundred pound weight on my chest? Just peachy." She opened her eyes when she heard the doctor snort.

"That's normal after this type of rib injury, but you are breathing on your own, which is a very good sign," he said.

"When can I go home?"

"Ask me again in a couple of days, and I may have an answer for you." He replaced the chart on the foot of her bed. "What you need right now is plenty of rest. I'll be back around to see you in the morning."

Great. I'll probably be stuck in here for Christmas. Dev sighed again, trying not to think about how very much she hated hospitals.

❖

"Kat." Josh shook her shoulder to wake her, and when she looked at him, he tilted his chin to indicate that the doctor was headed their way. They both stood quickly and went to meet her.

Kat was immeasurably relieved to see the smile on the doctor's face.

"Everything went fine," she said before either of them could question her. She placed a hand on Kat's forearm. "You have a very beautiful granddaughter. The baby is in the nursery, and will have to remain there for a week or two, but she seems to be very healthy considering everything she's been through in the past few hours. Your daughter will be ready to receive visitors in a little while. Would you like to see the baby in the meantime?"

"Yes." Kat felt as if she were in a daze. She knew that the goofy smile she saw plastered on Josh's face was mirrored in her own expression, and she pulled him into a tight embrace with a relieved laugh. "Congratulations, Daddy."

"Thanks," he said, hugging her back just as tightly. "Let's go see the baby, Grandma."

"We may just have to find a different name for her to call me." Kat laughed again as she wiped a tear from her cheek. "I'm not sure I feel old enough to be a grandma quite yet."

❖

Kat sat staring at Nessa as she slept. The baby was indeed beautiful, and she couldn't wait for Nessa to wake up so she could tell her all about the little bundle of joy. She'd gone back to see Dev, but she had been asleep too. Rather than waking her, Kat had decided she would sit with Nessa for a little while and let Dev rest.

Just when she started to think she would have to wake Nessa up, she slowly opened her eyes and looked around the room, her gaze finally settling on Kat. Kat could feel that smile still plastered to her face.

"Hi, sweetie." Kat reached out and took her hand.

"Is everything all right?"

"You have a baby girl. I left Josh down in the nursery because

I don't think he can bear to be pulled away quite yet. I think he's fallen in love."

Kat saw by the set of her daughter's shoulders that she had finally relaxed—no doubt for the first time since the entire ordeal began.

"How's Devon?"

"She's doing as well as can be expected. She wanted me to tell you that she's thinking about you. You're all going to be fine, honey."

"Good. Maybe you can finally get some sleep now. When are you guys going to move in together?"

"Whoa...slow down a minute." Kat couldn't help but laugh. "I'm not sure either of us is ready for a commitment like that."

"Yeah—that's why you spend every night with her and you share all of your meals with her, right? Christ, Mom, you guys practically live together as it is. The only thing keeping it from being official is that she's still paying you rent for the apartment."

"Nevertheless, I think that's something she and I will decide on—without your input, thank you very much." Kat felt as though her heart would burst. She hadn't experienced this much happiness in a very long time.

❖

When Kat walked into Dev's room on Monday morning, she laughed when a full house greeted her. Sheila gave her a quick hug and then ushered her to Dev's side, unceremoniously pushing people aside. Kat shrugged helplessly at Rhonda, Leigh, and Rick, who had stopped by to say hello and check on Dev. Dev's office manager was seated next to Dev's bed, gently admonishing Dev for taking time off work.

"Hey," Dev said with a big smile as she took Kat's hand. "Did you happen to talk with the doctor yet?"

"He says that you can go home on Wednesday, *if* there are no problems between now and then," Kat said. It warmed her heart to see how happy Dev looked, even bandaged up. "I'm really hoping that you'll be home for Christmas. How are you feeling today?"

"Better. How is Nessa?"

"She's going home tomorrow. The baby will have to stay for a little longer, but she should be home in a week or two also."

"Good. When do I get to see the baby, Grandma?" She squeezed Kat's hand a bit tighter, and she chuckled when she saw Kat blush at the sound of laughter coming from everyone in the room.

"I'm never going to get used to that. Maybe you can see her on Wednesday before you go home. She can't leave the nursery, and you aren't really in any condition to travel."

"Did they name her yet?"

"Catherine Paula Lewis."

"That's nice," Dev said with a genuine smile. "Are you okay with it?"

"I think Paula would have been proud." She had cried when Nessa and Josh had told her the baby's name, and she really didn't want to do it again now in front of all these people. It was enough to be holding Dev and feeling something so deep she felt she would burst.

She leaned over and kissed Devon on the lips before whispering, "I love you, Devon."

About the Author

PJ Trebelhorn was born and raised in the greater metropolitan area of Portland, Oregon. Her love of sports—mainly baseball and ice hockey—was fueled in part by her father's interests. She likes to brag about the fact that her uncle managed the Milwaukee Brewers for five years and the Chicago Cubs for one year.

PJ now resides in eastern Pennsylvania with Cheryl, her partner of many years, and their menagerie of pets—six cats and one very neurotic dog. When not writing or reading, PJ spends her time rooting for the Flyers, Phillies, and Eagles, or watching movies.

Visit her at her Web site at www.lesbianfic.com/SMF/ or on Facebook: pjtrebelhorn.

Books Available From Bold Strokes Books

Witch Wolf by Winter Pennington. In a world where vampires have charmed their way into modern society, where werewolves walk the streets with their beasts disguised by human skin, Investigator Kassandra Lyall has a secret of her own to protect. She's one of them. (978-1-60282-177-4)

Do Not Disturb by Carsen Taite. Ainsley Faraday, a high-powered executive, and rock music celebrity Greer Davis couldn't be less well suited for one another, and yet they soon discover passion has a way of designing its own future. (978-1-60282-153-8)

From This Moment On by PJ Trebelhorn. Devon Conway and Katherine Hunter both lost love and neither believes they will ever find it again—until the moment they meet and everything changes. (978-1-60282-154-5)

Vapor by Larkin Rose. When erotic romance writer Ashley Vaughn decides to take her research into the bedroom for a night of passion with Victoria Hadley, she discovers that fact is hotter than fiction. (978-1-60282-155-2)

Wind and Bones by Kristin Marra. Jill O'Hara, award-winning journalist, just wants to settle her deceased father's affairs and leave Prairie View, Montana, far, far behind—but an old girlfriend, a sexy sheriff, and a dangerous secret keep her down on the ranch. (978-1-60282-150-7)

Nightshade by Shea Godfrey. The story of a princess, betrothed as a political pawn, who falls for her intended husband's soldier sister, is a modern-day fairy tale to capture the heart. (978-1-60282-151-4)

Vieux Carré Voodoo by Greg Herren. Popular New Orleans detective Scotty Bradley just can't stay out of trouble—especially when an old flame turns up asking for help. (978-1-60282-152-1)

The Pleasure Set by Lisa Girolami. Laney DeGraff, a successful president of a family-owned bank on Rodeo Drive, finds her comfortable life taking a turn toward danger when Theresa Aguilar, a sleek, sexy lawyer, invites her to join an exclusive, secret group of powerful, alluring women. (978-1-60282-144-6)

A Perfect Match by Erin Dutton. The exciting world of pro golf forms the backdrop for a fast-paced, sexy romance. (978-1-60282-145-3)

Father Knows Best by Lynda Sandoval. High school juniors and best friends Lila Moreno, Meryl Morganstern, and Caressa Thibodoux plan to make the most of the summer before senior year. What they discover that amazing summer about girl power, growing up, and trusting friends and family more than prepares them to tackle that all-important senior year! (978-1-60282-147-7)

The Midnight Hunt by L.L. Raand. Medic Drake McKennan takes a chance and loses, and her life will never be the same—because when she wakes up after surviving a life-threatening illness, she is no longer human. (978-1-60282-140-8)

Long Shot by D. Jackson Leigh. Love isn't safe, which is exactly why equine veterinarian Tory Greyson wants no part of it—until Leah Montgomery and a horse that won't give up convince her otherwise. (978-1-60282-141-5)

In Medias Res by Yolanda Wallace. Sydney has forgotten her entire life, and the one woman who holds the key to her memory, and her heart, doesn't want to be found. (978-1-60282-142-2)

Awakening to Sunlight by Lindsey Stone. Neither Judith or Lizzy is looking for companionship, and certainly not love—but when their lives become entangled, they discover both. (978-1-60282-143-9)

Fever by VK Powell. Hired gun Zakaria Chambers is hired to provide a simple escort service to philanthropist Sara Ambrosini, but nothing is as simple as it seems, especially love. (978-1-60282-135-4)

Truths by Rebecca S. Buck. Two women separated by two hundred years are connected by fate and love. (978-1-60282-146-0)

High Risk by JLee Meyer. Can actress Kate Hoffman really risk all she's worked for to take a chance on love? Or is it already too late? (978-1-60282-136-1)

Missing Lynx by Kim Baldwin and Xenia Alexiou. On the trail of a notorious serial killer, Elite Operative Lynx's growing attraction to a mysterious mercenary could be her path to love—or to death. (978-1-60282-137-8)

Spanking New by Clifford Henderson. A poignant, hilarious, unforgettable look at life, love, gender, and the essence of what makes us who we are. (978-1-60282-138-5)

Magic of the Heart by C.J. Harte. CEO Susan Hettinger and wild, impulsive rock star M.J. Carson couldn't be more different if they tried—but opposites attract in ways neither woman can resist. (978-1-60282-131-6)

Ambereye by Gill McKnight. Jolie Garoul is falling in love with her assistant. The big problem is, Jolie is a werewolf. (978-1-60282-132-3)

Collision Course by C.P. Rowlands. Tragedy leaves Brie O'Malley and Jordan Carter fearful and alone. Can they find the courage to take a second chance on love? (978-1-60282-133-0)

Mephisto Aria by Justine Saracen. Opera singer Katherina Marov's destiny may be to repeat the mistakes of her father when she becomes involved in a dangerous love affair. (978-1-60282-134-7)

Battle Scars by Meghan O'Brien. Returning Iraq war veteran Ray McKenna struggles with the battle scars that can only be healed by love. (978-1-60282-129-3)

Chaps by Jove Belle. Eden Metcalf wants nothing more than to flee from her troubled past and travel the open road—until she runs into rancher Brandi Cornwell. (978-1-60282-127-9)

Lightbearer by John Caruso. Lucifer dares to question the premise of creation itself and reveals that sin may be all that stands between us and living hell. (978-1-60282-130-9)